THE
EXTINCTION
EVENT

THE
EXTINCTION
EVENT

David Black

A Tom Doherty Associates Book
New York

Geography has been rearranged in some cases:
The Mycenae in this book is not the city in Onondaga County, but one in Columbia County, on the Hudson River.

THE EXTINCTION EVENT

Copyright © 2010 by David Black

A Forge Book
Published by Tom Doherty Associates, LLC
175 Fifth Avenue
New York, NY 10010

www.tor-forge.com

Forge® is a registered trademark of Tom Doherty Associates, LLC.

ISBN 978-0-7653-2261-6

First Edition: May 2010

Printed in the United States of America

0 9 8 7 6 5 4 3 2 1

For Barbara, Susannah, and Toby

and Alec, Chris, Richard

and Elaine Kaufman

ACKNOWLEDGMENTS

To my agent and friend, Mel Berger, who told me I should write the book; my publisher, Tom Doherty, who believed in the project; my editor, the extraordinary Bob Gleason, who kept me honest; and his assistant, Ashley Cardiff, who did work above and beyond the call of duty.

They, hand in hand, with wand'ring steps and slow,
Through Eden took their solitary way.

Milton, *Paradise Lost*

·

The Hudson Valley Electric Company pylons stalked like *War of the Worlds* tripods down the hillside, across the field, and through the Rip Van Winkle Trailer Park five miles outside Mycenae, New York.

Inside a double-wide trailer with gardenia-filled window boxes, eight-year-old Kim Janette lay in bed, gazing out her louvered window at the clouds scudding across the moon, low to the horizon, huge, yam orange. Stars were coming out, bright points on the darkening sky as if the heavens were a photograph being developed.

Craning her neck, she made out one of the Dippers she'd learned about in school. Big Dipper? Small Dipper? No, *Little* Dipper . . . Big, Little—she wasn't sure. But the constellation, which seemed to hang close to the Earth, too close to the Earth, made her feel claustrophobic.

The wind was rising, scratching a branch across the trailer roof. In the distance, on a far-off farm, bulls—she thought they were bulls— made a sound like a bureau being scraped across a floor. She shivered. Probably, she told herself, frightened, from her fever. One hundred and two point four when her mother took it before dinner. Low. For her.

She tried to remember back before she was sick. All she could conjure up was a memory of sitting with her mother somewhere, picking wild strawberries, small as her fingernails, sweet. Her mother's mouth dripped with juice. Even her teeth were stained red.

The branch—was it a branch?—scratched the trailer roof again. Again, she shivered. Her eyes were hot. They'd probably take her back to the hospital. Soon. She hated the Emergency Room waiting area with its cracked orange and yellow plastic chairs and the daytime TV program

with the sound turned so low you couldn't hear what people were saying. Waiting sometimes as long as an hour, or more, to be admitted. Then,
waiting another hour while she shivered naked under the paper smock
they made her wear. Listening to her mother go over the story again
from the beginning.

Why couldn't she see the same doctor every time?

As a doctor talked, her mother clamped her mouth shut, so tight her
lips turned pale.

Kim knew the doctor's question made her mother angry. Knew why
it made her angry.

We can't afford it.

Watching the moon rise and lose its bloody glow, becoming smaller,
more silvery, Kim tried to imagine what it would be like when she got
better. First thing, she told herself, she'd ask her mother to take her back
to the wild strawberries. They could sit in the field, as they had before
she got sick, and eat the tiny berries, their lips getting red with the juice.

Maybe the image caused her hemorrhage. When she tried to call
her mother, the blood rising from her throat, filling her mouth, made her
cough, gag. She tried unsuccessfully to call again. Her mouth filled with
blood. She was ashamed: the sheets, blanket would have to be changed
again. Washed again. More money wasted.

Hopelessly, she watched the moon, now small as a quarter, and far,
far away—as far as the stars, which had also retreated. Left her behind.

She tried to swallow back the blood. But it kept coming, spilling from
her mouth even though she tried to clamp her lips shut to keep it from
messing the bedding.

Surrendering to the almost luxurious feeling of getting light-headed,
she thought, at least tonight she wouldn't hear the ghosts, who most
nights muttered to her in a language she couldn't understand.

The sky—moon, stars—were now so far away she couldn't see them.

Part One

JACK

1

"Oh, God," the man said. "Oh, God . . ."

"Sometimes to get over the fence, you need a little boost," said the hooker he was in bed with. "Hang on, honey."

The hooker, Jean Gaynor, wriggled out from under her john and on hands and knees crawled across the sagging king-sized mattress to the foot of the bed in the motel room. Mottled ass in the air, her prominent vertebrae like a ridged prehistoric backbone, she leaned over and fumbled for a tumbler, which she examined. The glass was dirty, streaked with a little cloudy water on the bottom.

"Hang on, Chief," Jean said.

She stumbled out of bed and lurched into the bathroom. The man, Frank Milhet, who was almost three times Jean's age, rolled over onto his back and gazed at the stained ceiling with unfocused eyes. The stain resolved itself into a cow, a continent, a face . . . Like Jean, Milhet was naked. Unlike Jean, who had been partying for three days with other marks and had a gray pallor, Milhet was flushed pink. An unhealthy pink. The pink from a Saturday-morning cartoon.

Earlier that night, Milhet had met Jean in the bar attached to the office of the Dutch Village Motel, a one-story, pale-blue-shingled hot-sheet dump on County Route 9, a few miles north of Niverville, New York. Across the road was a cornfield. The shoulder-high stalks clattered in the August heat. Even at ten o'clock at night, the air was still, stifling, oppressive. It carried a whiff of damp ashes. Somewhere, far off, someone tried to start a lawn mower. Over and over. Unsuccessfully. Maybe someone who couldn't sleep. Or someone who just got home from a swing shift. Or someone soon to leave home for the lobster shift. Moonlight made everything shine like new tin.

Squatting on top of the far right end of the motel office building was a fake windmill. Each vane was made of two rows of nine-inch squares that, without sailcloth, looked like empty window frames. The vanes were bolted in place. A high wind would shatter them before they ever turned. The neon sign arched between the bottom two vanes advertised *Color TV, in-house channels* and displayed, outlined in the neon tubes, a reclining figure in thigh-high boots that was supposed to represent Rip Van Winkle, sleeping soundly, presumably undistracted by the motel's *in-house channels*, which carried one old VCR loop of *Rear Action Babes*. Spaced in a neat row in front of the individual cabins were five early-sixties concave circular chairs, like an array of miniature radio-telescopes.

When Milhet spotted Jean in the bar, about six-thirty that evening, she was sitting in one of the cracked, burgundy-leather banquettes, nursing an Irish whiskey, a pencil-mustache of whipped cream on her upper lip, eyes prowling the nearly empty room for a mark, for someone who could slip her a quick thirty for a gram of coke—more cut, mannitol baby laxative than coke—which the bartender kept behind the bar in the Yellow Pages, filed humorously, he thought, under *fishing, supplies*.

Over the front door, ill-fit in a rectangle that looked recently cut, wooden bristles along the saw-lines, new curdled-cream-colored foam tucked around the machine, an ancient, rust-speckled air conditioner rhythmically groaned, loud-soft, loud-soft, like a man suffering from the heat.

The bar had a funk of stale tobacco, cats, sour beer, and a cloying antiseptic stink wafting in from the candy floss–colored deodorizing pucks in the men's room urinals.

Through the opening door—as Milhet entered—came the sound of the distant lawn mower engine catching, a roar as it started up diminishing to a purr as it continued. The closing door cut off the sound.

Jean sat facing the bar, her back reflected in a mirror on the opposite wall. The spiderweb of black cracks in the cloudy glass gave the impression of an old-fashioned photographic plate of the Milky Way, and through that cosmic-looking tangle you could see the black roots at the back of Jean's blond head. It also reflected Milhet, facing the mirror, sliding, back to the bar, onto a high stool, his eyes, like Jean's, predatory.

Jean smiled. Milhet smiled.

She hadn't expected him to be there. He knew she was always there. Within half an hour, they were in the motel room, laying out lines on the scarred bureau top. A broken drawer angled out of the bureau front. A single straight-backed wooden chair lay on its side on the floor, knocked over when they entered the room and Milhet reached around Jean and grabbed her ass, which she professionally twitched.

A cracked lamp with a bare red bulb cast a bloody light. The TV, which was on when they entered the room, broadcast news about a hurricane, baptized Ruby. A satellite photo of the Gulf Coast from Tallahassee to Mobile filled the TV screen with the hurricane's whorl, which looked like a giant thumb print.

"A westward moving tropical wave is producing high winds and an advisory . . . ," the TV newscaster was saying. "Global warming may increase the frequency and intensity of . . ." Milhet was having trouble focusing. "Moving northeast liable to make landfall sometime tomorrow morning at . . ."

Through the open bathroom door, Milhet gazed with zombie eyes at Jean, who rinsed the glass, filled it two-thirds with fresh water, and, unfolding an origami-like paper bindle, spilled in a gram of coke. She lit a small butane torch and heated the solution, constantly swirling it, waiting for the drug, spiraling like an insignificant galaxy, to start crystallizing into a rock of crack.

"The trouble with immediate gratification," Jean said, "is it takes so long."

She dropped a pinch of baking powder into the glass, which cracked from the heat, spilling the solution.

"Damn!" she said.

Jean backed out of the bathroom to avoid cutting her bare feet on the broken glass on the floor.

Reaching over, Milhet snagged his pants and, from a pocket, took out another bindle of coke.

"You want me to run out to the shop," Jean asked, "get a Pyrex?"

"Don't we have another glass?" Milhet asked.

He crossed the room, picking up another tumbler, and gave her the glass and the drugs to cook up.

"Keep it more away from the flame," he said, "so it doesn't crack, okay?"

He embraced Jean from behind and moved his hands over the front of her body.

"You get *me* any hotter," Jean said dully, "I'll crack."

2

Jack Slidell's cell phone rang, two old fashioned trills, imitating a bell from a Fifties rotary telephone, a retro touch that pleased Jack. Jack fumbled in the bedsheets. The cell rang again. Jack found the phone under a pillow tossed to the foot of the bed. Answered it.

"Slidell."

Jack, a muscular sixty, had the body of a laborer and the manner of a gentleman. He got the muscles from working construction in his twenties to put himself through Columbia Law School, where he got his polish. Ever since his divorce when he was in his early fifties, women had begun telling him he reminded them of Sean Connery.

"If only they'd thought that when I was thirty," Jack used to say before he stopped taking notice.

"Who?" Jack asked the telephone. "What?"

Where? *When*? thought Jack, who had spent two years before law school as a general assignment reporter on the New York *Daily News*.

"I'll be right there," he said.

The digital clock on his Bose Wave radio blinked 12:00 red. Jack never set it.

In Jack's bedroom it was always midnight.

3

Outside the Dutch Village Motel, the neon sign fizzed. Rip Van Winkle's left hip boot flickered. Jack drove past the office, where, through the dirty window, he saw the night clerk asleep in a chair in front of a small TV, grainy blue light from the screen pockmarked his face. On the wall behind the night clerk was a calendar with a photo of a girl in a green thong standing next to a tractor tire as tall as she was. On the counter was an iron desk spike, used for paid bills, and on a fraying wire was a button that rang a buzzer in the back of the house, where the clerk often slept in front of a TV.

Jack swung his car behind the office and stopped in front of the detached cabins, which had been built in the early Fifties and hadn't been painted since. He parked in front of Cabin 4, the only unit with a light on inside. The thin drapes were streaked with soot and glowed red from the lightbulb in the room. When Jack turned off the car engine, he heard the sizzling neon sign, the whine of the cicadas in the woods behind the motel, and from across the road, the rattle of corn stalks. Far off, Jack heard a power mower. The air had a trace of the sweet smell of cut grass. The air was heavy with the threat of the storm moving up the East Coast.

Jack knocked on the door and called, "Frank!"

No answer.

He knocked again, called again, "Frank, you in there?"

No answer.

Jack tried the door, which was unlocked. Not a good sign. Jack figured it was stupid to enter, so he entered. The room reeked of something chemical. Burned rubber? Frank sprawled, obviously dead, half off the bed. An OD? In the corner of the room, Jean curled, beaten so badly her body was purple with bruises. Unconscious.

From outside, Jack heard the siren of approaching State Police cars. Their revolving red and white lights flashed through the thin motel curtains. Jack upended the wooden chair—a mistake, Jack thought, leave the scene intact—and sat in it, waiting. On TV, the weatherman stood in front of a blue-screen projection of the hurricane, which was growing. The low pressure plugged Jack's ears. The storm was coming.

The door slammed open. Two cops burst in, guns drawn. Aimed at Jack.

"Easy," the first cop said to Jack, who, hands in the air, slowly stood, saying, "You know what they say: *Walk careful among the dead, and don't trust the living. . . .*"

CHAPTER TWO

1

Milhet & Alverez—a law firm in Mycenae, New York, which catered to the Hamptons' refugees who had begun moving into Columbia County—was in an uproar. Secretaries and clerks stood in groups of threes and fours, gossiping and glancing sideways through Jack's office door at Jack, who, rumpled and unshaven after the previous night's misadventures, was cleaning out his desk, packing everything in a brown cardboard banker's box.

Earlier, while the police were questioning Jack, Frank's partner, Tony Alverez, ten years younger than Jack, arrived at the station house on the corner of South Third and Division Street. At five o'clock in the morning, when the cops released Jack, Alverez was waiting, impeccably shaved, wearing his blue shirt with its high white collar, and red suspenders like bloody vertical stripes under his seersucker jacket.

"This is the fourth time in the past two years, I've gotten a late-night call from the police about you," Alverez told Jack. "Maybe you should take some time off."

Outside Jack's window, two stories down, on Howard Street, a small crowd milled, faces tilted up, eyes squinting in the sun, hands to foreheads like military salutes, as if they were looking at an eclipse, locals who had heard rumors. The breeze blew one woman's long hair out behind her like living snakes.

"Jack doesn't look so good," one of the clerks said.

"You don't get a lot of beauty sleep in jail," another clerk said.

"Obstructing justice, resisting arrest—," a third clerk started.

"The boss was in trouble," the first clerk said. "Jack was trying to keep things quiet."

"Yeah, well," the second clerk said, "murder is noisy."

"We don't know Frank was murdered," the third clerk said.

"Jack should've called EMS," the first clerk said.

"Jack should've let his machine answer the phone," the third clerk said.

The second clerk nodded and said, "Someone rings you at three a.m., you know you haven't won the sweepstakes."

"Remember that time Jack was late for court," the third clerk said, "and Frank had to bail him out of—"

"Which time?" the second clerk asked. "We talking the assault? Or the disturbing the peace? Or the—"

"The time that bartender said Jack was full of piss and vinegar," the third clerk said. "And Jack tried to prove him wrong about the vinegar."

"I thought he'd be disbarred for sure," the second clerk said.

"What a knucklehead," the third clerk said.

They all smiled. They liked Jack.

"If the hooker dies," the first clerk said, lowering his voice, "they hit Jack with manslaughter three, accessory."

"Is he leaving the firm?" the first clerk asked.

"No," the second clerk said, "he's cleaning out his desk because they're giving him a free trip to the Virgin Islands."

Caroline Wonder, one of the firm's new hires, rushed past the gossiping clerks into Jack's office.

"Speaking of virgins . . . ," the second clerk said, following Caroline with his eyes.

Caroline, twenty-eight years old, was a thoroughbred, a Dutch-Knickerbocker bluestocking with a character as straight and strong as the whalebone reinforcing the corset she would have worn a hundred years ago. Even without the corset, she had a waist you could span with two hands, a face like an ivory cameo, and hair as pale as heated tungsten.

Ever since she started working at Milhet & Alverez, Jack called her Five Spot.

When she asked him why, Jack shrugged.

Caroline didn't trust Jack. She slammed Jack's door behind her.

"When God handed out brains," she said, "you thought he said *rain* and ran for cover."

"The woman on the phone," Jack explained, "said Frank was in trouble. . . ."

"And Frank asked her to call you? Jack, you know that's an old scam."

"The boss *was* in trouble."

"And now he's dead. And you're up the creek. Given your reputation. I'm surprised they didn't shoot first. . . ."

From a bottom drawer, Jack took a few files, a penknife, an antique silver letter opener, and an old wooden desk nameplate, which Caroline picked up.

"Put it down, Five Spot," Jack said.

Caroline examined it.

"Hand carved," she said.

"I said, *put it down*."

"What is it? Walnut?"

Jack made an unsuccessful grab for it.

"*Jack Slidell, Attorney at Law*," Caroline read.

Jack grabbed it.

"What's the big deal?" Caroline asked.

"I made it when I was a kid," Jack said. "Sixth grade. A gag."

Caroline studied Jack, who dropped the nameplate into the banker's box.

"From the first day I was here," Caroline said, "you never did like me."

"I like people who earn what they get."

"So do I. That's why I'm working here, not in the city, at my uncle's office."

"I heard when you passed the bar, your uncle dropped Frank a note."

"That's called a *reference*."

"That's called a free ride."

"You always believe rumors, Jack? I heard a rumor, one going around the office. Something about your saying going to bed with me would be like making love to a bicycle."

"Maybe it was *icicle*?"

"No, it was *bicycle*."

At the door, Caroline half-turned back to Jack and said, "I'm a twelve-speed. . . ."

And slammed out.

2

With its red-flocked wallpaper, greasy in spots, couches lining the walls, and crystal lamps, Saul's Grill evoked one of the brothels that populated Mycenae ever since the War of 1812, when all the other whaling ports in the Northeast were blockaded by the British. The walls were covered with pictures of notorious local madams, including a late-nineteenth-century engraving of Kate Church, an early-twentieth-century photogravure of Rae Ann Best, and the faded snapshot of Eleanor Fitzpatrick, called Fizz by everyone in town, who died at ninety-seven in 1976.

Jack sat in a banquette with a law-firm colleague—a former colleague now that Jack was no longer employed by Milhet & Alverez—Robert Flowers.

"She's been in the firm, what . . . three months?" Jack said. "I've been there five years. And *she's* telling *me* what's good, what's not good for business."

Robert wasn't paying attention to Jack. He was gazing at a beautiful woman with red hair and long legs.

"Robert," Jack reached across the table and tapped a finger in front of his friend. "Robert . . ."

"Why don't I ever date women with seams on the back of their stockings?"

"You're lucky to date women with seams on the back of their legs."

Robert, who was thirty-one, nearly half Jack's age, had the square jaw and slicked-back hair of a model in a Forties Arrow Collar ad. The old-fashioned aristocratic look of a Berkshire boy, raised over the Massachu-setts border in Great Barrington, who prepped at a third-tier school, not Choate or Andover, but Wilbraham Academy, and was educated at Am-herst; who, in Mycenae, set himself apart by emphasizing his Congrega-tional roots and, in Great Barrington where he still lived in his ancestral home, a forty-minute commute to Mycenae, played up his New York style. A kind of patroon superciliousness compared to his hometown, Indian-pudding, down-home, Minuteman Massachusetts ways.

Robert set himself apart chronologically, too, wearing old-fashioned clothes: blousy shirts that made him look as if he were one of Paul Re-vere's Sons of Liberty, large turn-of-the-century bohemian floppy bow ties, and his great-grandfather's moth-eaten frock coats. He could have been a character from one of Washington Irving's tales or, on alternate days, from a story written during Melville's Pittsfield days.

Jack was eating deep-fried scrod—today, as usual, cod—his daily lunch, which daily Robert noted by telling the old joke about the Bosto-nian in San Francisco who asked a cop where he could get scrod and the cop replied, "That's the first time anyone asked in the pluperfect tense."

But today Robert missed his cue. He was eating sausage, white *boudin*, and drinking heavily, rye and bitters.

"Jack, getting caught in a motel that charges by the hour with your boss's corpse, an unconscious hooker, and a roomful of drugs . . . Maybe Caroline's got a point."

Robert spotted a diner at the next table who was about to fork an oyster into his mouth.

"Don't eat that oyster!" Robert cried.

The diner lowered his fork. Robert leaped to his table and shook the oyster off the fork back into the shell.

"You're not from here . . . ?" Robert asked the stranger.

"I was born here," the stranger said.

"Then it's time you learn how to do this thing right," Robert said. "Mycenae's a seaport! Though," he muttered, "you'd never know it to-day." He doused the oyster with Tabasco and raised the shell. "Pepper sauce and no fork. Open your mouth."

The stranger opened his mouth, into which Robert tilted the oyster. As the stranger, gasping because of the Tabasco, reached for water, Robert sprinkled the hot sauce onto the other eleven oysters.

"You'll get used to it," Robert said to the stranger, who was gulping water. "See?"

Robert took one of the oysters from the man's plate and swallowed it, then returned to his own table, where he caught the waiter's eye and pointed at his empty whiskey glass.

"The boss sure liked the ladies," Robert said.

"Robert . . . ," Jack started.

"One night, Frank took me to Angie Carmen's house," Robert said. "We were having a cocktail, chatting to the girls—Frank was waiting for his favorite kid to come back to the line-up—and there was this sales-man there from down south, Pittsburgh, Detroit—"

"Detroit's not south," Jack said.

"—who kept asking one of the girls to do a somersault." Robert ig-nored Jack. "The girl says, *A somersault*? The guy from down south says, *You know, you put your head between your knees*. And she says, *Mister, if I could put my head between my knees, I wouldn't have gotten married four times*."

The waiter delivered the rye and bitters, which Robert slugged back.

"I assume the cops are going through Frank's files," Jack said. "For leads."

"You mean who'd want to kill a lawyer?" Robert asked. "Who wouldn't?"

"I wish you weren't leaving the firm," Jack said. "With both of us gone—" Jack shrugged. "Until I get back, Five Spot needs all the help she can get."

"If you get back," Robert said. "Why do you call Caroline Five Spot?"

Ignoring the question, Jack said, "The ink on her diploma isn't dry. She's never had a case on her own."

"You had most of the interesting work," Robert said. "Most of what I was doing were little *fix-me* cases. Someone's brother gets busted, drunken driving, someone's kid gets a speeding ticket . . ."

"You won't reconsider?"

"As my daddy says, *only the captain goes down with the ship*. Frank was the captain. He's gone. You were first mate. I'm in the lifeboat. Jack, the mess you're in, you'll be lucky if they let you into court for your own trial."

3

Caroline stood in the high double doors of her uncle's Hudson River mansion, Tabletops, her eyes closed, her face raised to the mild breeze. Up the river, the Rip Van Winkle Bridge lights looked like a leftover Christmas decoration strung across the Hudson. The lights of Mycenae, half a mile downriver, cast a sulfurous glow in the sky. Clouds were massing over the Catskills. A storm was brewing. Caroline remembered the stories about how thunder was caused by the ghosts of Hendrick Hudson's men bowling in the mountains.

Behind her, the parlor was filled with Empire furniture. In front of her, the French doors led to a colonnaded gallery with an ironwork balcony. Beyond the gallery was a formal garden. The statuary in the garden, satyrs and nymphs, voluptuous goddesses and priapic gods, was pocked and chipped. The immortals had seen better days.

Caroline said, "Hibiscus." She took one last deep breath before turning back into the room. "That smell always makes me feel sixteen years old. My first dance. Willie Jerome sent me a hibiscus corsage. A big red blossom. He was so nervous when he put it on, he stabbed me with the pin and stained the dress, that beautiful organdy dress, with blood."

Caroline's uncle, Devitt Wonder, called Dixie, was mixing a drink at a wicker bar cart. Dixie was a healthy eighty-six. Tall, thin, vigorous, although deceptively fragile looking, in his white linen suit, he had an almost ghostly appearance, a specter from the Gilded Age.

Dixie said, "The secret of a Ramos gin fizz is—"

"—*cold* egg whites," Caroline said. "Dixie, every time you whip up one of those concoctions, you say the same thing."

"And every time I say it, Sweetpea, you tell me I've said it before."

Caroline's sister, Nicole, swept in. She was a darker, more sultry version of Caroline. The folded inner canthus of her eyes gave her face an oriental cast. Her hair hung below her waist.

"Come on, you two," Nicole said, "dinner's waiting."

"Wait on us a moment, Nicole. I have to quiz your sister on something."

Nicole glanced from Caroline to Dixie.

"She's not going to quit her job and go to work for you, Uncle Dee."

"One of our ancestors must have married a witchy woman," Dixie said. "You two girls are always reading my mind."

"It doesn't take magic to guess what you're thinking, Dixie," Caroline said.

"Caroline," Dixie said, "the firm you're in, word around town is a storm's coming and no one's taped the windows."

"You're the one who taught me not to be a quitter, Dixie," Caroline said.

"I hope," Dixie said, "I also taught you not to be foolish. I can offer you a good job."

"I already have a job, Dixie," Caroline said. "And I'm going to make a go of it, even if I have to run the place alone."

CHAPTER THREE

1

Jack walked into Samaritan Hospital with a detective, Al Sciortino, a childhood friend. Even in the air-conditioned lobby, Sciortino had sweat stains under his arms and on his collar. He had a Marine haircut the color of iron filings, eyes that registered so little emotion they looked like pinpoint cameras, and fingers so stubby they seemed to be missing a joint. As usual, he smelled of cigars and Bay Rum.

"Coke laced with cyanide?" Jack asked.

"If the glass didn't crack," Sciortino said, "if they'd cooked it up into a rock, most of the poison would have precipitated out."

"And smoking it?"

"There wouldn't have been enough cyanide in the vapor to kill him."

"But Frank got impatient, huh?"

Sciortino nodded. "Snorting the coke."

"If someone wanted to kill him," Jack said, "how could he be sure Frank wouldn't wait?"

"Lucky for the girl," Sciortino said, "as far as drugs go, Frank wasn't a gentleman: *No ladies first.*"

2

In the hospital intensive care ward, Jack and Sciortino stood by Gaynor's bed, looking at her, unconscious, her face a mass of bruises the blue-black of eggplant. The fluorescent ceiling lights reflected off the tubes going into and out of her body. Monitors chirped.

The attending doctor, Peter Rodaheaver, unhooked a clipboard from the foot of the bed.

"Mr. Slidell, your boss was dead before he had a chance to say *hallelujah*!"

"He must have had time to tell the girl to call Jack," Sciortino said.

"So he knew he was in trouble," Jack said.

"You snort cyanide, I think you *know* you're in trouble," Rodaheaver said. "For a second. Before trouble don't matter anymore. You figure beaten like that the girl knew she was in trouble, too."

"If Frank took off on her," Sciortino asked, "why would she call Jack for help?"

"Frank wouldn't have hit the lady," Jack said, "let alone whale on her."

"So," Sciortino asked, "you got any idea who played her like a snare?"

"You find anything in his files?" Jack asked.

"Yeah," Sciortino said, "just like on tee-vee, we got six people looking at every single memo he ever wrote."

"You think anyone would mind—"

"If you went snooping? Aside from the department, the troopers, and the DA?"

Jack nodded at a floral arrangement, a cluster of white blossoms with fringed petals.

"The blooms for her?" Jack asked.

"They came a couple of hours ago," Rodaheaver said.

"Any note?" Sciortino asked.

Rodaheaver shook his head *no.*

"An order form?" Jack asked. "The florist's name?"

"Nothing," Rodaheaver said. "They were left at the desk."

"We'll check it out," Sciortino said.

"Is she going to make it?" Jack asked Rodaheaver.

"You better hope so," Sciortino said to Jack. "She dies, there's no one to say you didn't kill her."

3

Caroline and Nicole strolled through Mycenae's Court Square, past the cottages with their Dutch-style second-floor front doors and double front stairs. From an open window came a recording of Sidney Bichet's "Preachin' Blues." Caroline swung a wide-brimmed straw hat from its pink ribbon. Too colorful to be wearing under the gusty, lead sky.

"I can't believe you won't take Uncle Dee's job," Nicole said.

Caroline didn't answer.

"If you want to prove yourself," Nicole said, "do it in a business that's not going out of business."

Caroline still didn't answer.

"Caroline," Nicole said, "sometimes I think you're as crazy as a chameleon on plaid."

Caroline turned onto Roscoe Conkling Street, nicknamed in the late-1880s Skunk Alley by a disgruntled Democrat. Nicole gestured in the opposite direction.

"Where are you going?" Nicole asked.

"The bus stop," Caroline said.

"You know what they used to say: *Good girls don't take the bus.*"

"They also used to say: *A lady doesn't wear panties in the summer. It's bad for the hygiene.*"

"Caroline, ever since you were a girl you've made things hard for yourself."

"A guy at the office thinks I had the job handed to me. Because of Dixie."

"So you're going to ruin your career because of a guy, what a guy said?"

Caroline didn't answer.

"Who is this guy?" Nicole asked.

"No one," Caroline said. "No one special."

Nicole studied her sister. Caroline stood in the humid night, backlit by a streetlamp, her body showing through the thin fabric of her dress, as she thought of Jack.

"Yeah?" Nicole said. "He must be something to get to you that much."

"What are you talking about, Nicole?"

The bus, maroon with gold trim, designed to look like a trolley, ground up, stopped. Caroline stepped on it.

"He didn't get to me," Caroline said.

The bus moved off.

"I can see that," Nicole said to herself. "Didn't get to you at all."

CHAPTER FOUR

1

The clerk at the Dutch Village Motel stood behind the counter, a stack of paid bills in front of him. He glanced at one, then impaled it on the old-fashioned iron desk spike. Near his elbow was the button that rang a buzzer in the back of the house. When the door opened, he looked up. A man wearing cowboy boots and a cowboy hat entered, the turned-up collar of his blue nylon windbreaker muffling his voice.

"Last night," the man asked, "you were on duty?"

The clerk nodded, trying to get a look at the man's face.

"An older man with a young woman," the man asked. "He checked in?"

"Yeah," the clerk said, "then checked out. Permanent."

"Someone visited them?" the man asked.

The clerk nodded, this time wary.

"Would you recognize him," the man asked, "this other fellow?"

The clerk hesitated, looking a little too hard at the man.

"What's the matter, boy?" the man asked.

The clerk went to hit the buzzer button with his palm, but the man grabbed his wrist, stopping him.

"Who you going to call?"

"I . . . I wasn't."

"You were going to hit the button."

"No, I . . ."

"Only one other thing you could've been reaching for."

Holding the clerk's wrist, the man lifted the clerk's hand over the desk spike.

"This," the man said.

And he slammed the clerk's hand onto the spike, impaling it.

2

Jack leaned on a fence in the city's waterfront park, watching a barge move up the Hudson River. The water smelled fetid. Rotting vegetation and spilled oil. The wind rippled the water's surface, making it look like crumpled tin foil. Sciortino sauntered up and leaned on the fence next to Jack.

"The clerk at the motel, the one Frank died in last night," Sciortino said. " 'Bout an hour ago, he was murdered, stabbed half a dozen times with his desk spindle."

"If the man used an accordion file," Jack said, "maybe he'd still be alive."

"Jack," Sciortino said, heaving himself back from the fence, "we never met. I never told you any of this." He took a step away. "I couldn't have," he added. "After all, you're a suspect."

3

Jack parked his blue Mustang convertible in front of a condominium near the Marina, a renovated boarding house, which from the 1920s to the early-1960s had doubled as cat-house and which in the late 1990s was gutted and rebuilt. The vapor lights cast a sulfurous glow on the half-empty parking lot. On the Hudson, shadowy boats rode at anchor.

Jack got out of his car, the door slam sounding hollow in the dark. Across the parking lot, a torn page from *The Racing Form* chased itself in circles; the wind ruffled the cuffs of Jack's slacks. His jacket over his shoulder, Jack headed toward the door of his condominium.

From the water, mist rose in strands, like a beaded curtain, which, opened, revealed other mists, elongated ghostly figures, like alien Tall Grays, drifting onto shore.

Jack felt droplets on his face.

The spectral mists passed Jack in endless procession. Muffled footsteps seemed to be hurrying by. Warning whispers seemed to swirl out of the air. And soft, dreamy music, singing? Jack couldn't make out the words.

Jack felt a tickle on his cheek. He turned and saw a cadaverous face vanishing into the mists behind him.

"What do you want?" Jack asked.

Whoever it was laughed, and the laugh sounded like ripping canvas.

"Who are you?" Jack asked.

Whoever it was began singing again. Minor strains. Words still indistinct.

Jack shivered.

"Don't start something you can't finish," the specter whispered.

When Jack was twelve years old, on the way home from a school chorus trip to a state competition, he had shared a row in the bus with a girl two years older than he was. She was already well developed. Her nipples, the size of egg yolks, pressed against her tight white ribbed pullover. What was her name? Jack couldn't recall. In the dim blue light flickering from passing streetlamps, Jack had fumbled under her top, the first time he had ever touched a woman's breasts. Daintily, she plucked up the hem of her skirt, inviting Jack to touch her nylon-covered crotch, which Jack did, finding a surprising moistness. She moaned and told Jack, "Don't start something you can't finish."

"What do you want!" Jack hissed, grabbing a wrist. Not bony as he had expected, but massive.

Out of the mists loomed a hulking man with a face ruined by bar fights and disappointment. More from disappointment. He wore a pea-green workshirt, gray work pants held up with both a belt and suspenders, and well-worn high-top old-fashioned fawn-colored lace-up work boots. Jack's older brother.

"What are you doing here, Bix?" Jack asked.

"Looking after you, Jackie," Bix said, twisting off Jack's grip on his wrist. His voice was breathy, with a whistle from when he was punched in the throat as a kid.

"Did you just see someone?" Jack asked. "Thin guy? Hear something?"

"Heard you shouting, baby-boy," Bix said.

"I'm not the baby of the family anymore."

"Sure, you are, Jackie. And just like old times, you're in trouble again."

Jack took one last glance around. The mists seemed to stand still. Rank upon rank of ghosts.

Jack opened the door to his building. Bix followed him in.

Silently, they went up in the elevator to the top floor, where Jack unlocked his apartment door. Inside the apartment—mirrors reflecting the light of the shadowy boats outside, lots of chrome and glass—Jack tossed his jacket onto a chair, turned on a table lamp, and sank into the black leather couch.

"You get the job at the prison?" Jack asked.

"Have to change my registration," Bix said. "You know the Republicans control those jobs."

"I'd help you if I could," Jack said.

"Never asked you for help, Jackie," Bix said. "Never will."

"But you help me," Jack protested.

Bix waved his hand.

"Your boss," Bix said, "these high jinks of his, not smart, Jackie."

"Everyone knew Frank had a weakness for trade," Jack said.

Carefully, Bix lowered himself into a black leather chair.

"A man like that, a lawyer and all, what's he doing in a crib like the Dutch Village with a noseful of powder?"

"After his divorce, Frank used to say, *If I'm going to pay for love, it ain't going to be alimony*. And the drugs? Well, here's a guy worked his way up from the docks to law school—"

"One of us, yeah."

"—got the dream job, dream wife—"

"Except it was somebody else's dream."

"He's pushing retirement, never sowed his wild oats—"

"Man should know you plant in spring, not autumn. You know, Jackie, you got a lot of Frank in you."

"Because we're both poor boys who learned how to wipe our feet before entering the parlor?"

"Your boss's death. Wasn't an accident, was it, Jackie?"

"You cut the product with cyanide, you don't get repeat customers."

"Who'd want to kill him?"

"Man's been a lawyer almost forty years. Who wouldn't want to?"

"Who'd want to frame you?"

"No frame. I was the wild card. Frank keels over. The gal calls me. I show up. That wasn't in anybody's plan."

"You think?"

"Anyway maybe it was an accident."

"Maybe tomorrow morning I'll wake up rich."

Jack shrugged.

"Who beat up the young stuff?"

"Not Frank. If he did *before* he snorted the cyanide, why would she call for help. And *after* he snorted—"

"He wouldn't have been able to see her, let alone hit her. So what are we saying? Someone comes in, sees her calling you, hanging up the phone . . . ?"

"He hits her."

"Maybe harder than he meant to."

"Harder than he meant to a dozen times?"

Bix shrugged.

"Man likes his work. He got carried away."

"Leaves her for dead."

"And calls the cops knowing you'd show up."

"His lucky day. He's got a patsy to take the rap for the hooker."

"Except she doesn't die."

"If she ever wakes up," Jack said, "we find out who hit her. If she doesn't . . . ?"

Jack and Bix exchanged a look.

"I'm not going back," Jack said, "not to where I started."

"You worked hard," Bix said. "No reason why you should. But things being what they are . . . The old place . . . No one's used it since we grew up, left . . ."

Jack looked out at the shadowy boats.

"Take some time out there, Jackie, a week, two. Get out of the spot-light."

Bix stood, huge in the glass-and-chrome room.

"Thanks for stopping by, Bix," Jack said.

"You're blood," Bix said. "Family's all anyone's really got."

After Bix left, Jack pressed the replay button on his answering ma-chine and heard, "Jack, this is Judge Long. I've been trying to reach you all day. Give me a call at home. It's pretty important."

CHAPTER FIVE

1

The cleaning lady was just turning off her vacuum when Caroline let herself into the dim reception area of Milhet & Alvarez.

"What're you doing here in the middle of the night, Miss Wonder?" the cleaning lady asked.

"Couldn't sleep," Caroline said.

"Most people can't sleep drink hot milk, don't go to work."

"That's my trouble, Sue. I've spent my life trying to prove I'm not most people."

As Caroline headed toward her office, the cleaning lady said, "Mr. Slidell . . . Guess he couldn't sleep either."

2

Jack heard Caroline enter his office. Or ex-office. But didn't respond. Jack sat in his desk chair, facing away from his desk, looking out the window at the city and the Hudson River night. His jacket was off, his shirt sleeves rolled up, not to the forearms like a professional, but to his biceps like a laborer.

On his desk was a bottle of Ezra Brooks. In his hand was a half-full glass of bourbon.

"You know," Caroline said, "we don't encourage drinking in the office."

"I didn't need encouragement," Jack said.

Caroline picked up the bottle.

"There's another glass in the cupboard," Jack said.

"I wasn't planning to join you," Caroline said.

"I know."

"In anything."

"You don't know what you're missing."

"Am I supposed to play Twenty Questions to find out what you're doing here?"

Softly Jack sang "Shake, Rattle and Roll."

Wearing dresses, the sun comes shining through . . .

"You keep standing in front of the window like that," Jack said, "we could make it an oral exam."

"With you all it would be is a pop quiz," Caroline said, moving away from the window so the lights of the city no longer outlined her body.

She dropped the bottle into the wastebasket beside Jack's desk.

"I'd rather see a church burn than good liquor wasted."

"I never thought I'd hear you quoting Robert."

"I was quoting him quoting his daddy."

Caroline fought a smile. Jack noticed, said, "You hate to admit it, but I can be a charming SOB. . . ."

"Robert does quote his daddy a lot," Caroline said.

"Family's all anyone's really got."

"Another quote from Robert's daddy?"

"No," Jack said. "Someone else."

Jack took a sip of the bourbon.

"I'm moving. Down to the boat basin."

"That creepy place? It looks like a shantytown from somewhere down south. The Mississippi Delta. Someplace."

"Where I grew up," Jack said.

"Sorry," Caroline said, "I . . ."

"Just until things quiet down," Jack said. "I wrote a general memo with the address. In case anybody needs me. No phone in the place. So I'll keep my cell charged. For a while at least. You got the number. I put that in the memo, too."

"That's what you came in for?" Caroline asked, glancing at the bank of file cabinets lining the hall outside Jack's office. One drawer was not pushed in all the way. "Not to look through Frank's files?"

"In a couple of hours," Jack said, "I went through a couple of decades of paperwork, right."

"Maybe a couple of months?" Caroline said. "Ending a couple of days ago?"

Jack ignored her.

"I can run the cell off the car engine if I have to," he said.

"Find anything interesting in Frank's files?" Caroline asked. "A smoking gun? A confession? Something to flush out Frank's killer?"

"Funny," Jack said, "how we both assume he was murdered. . . ."

"I was joking, Jack," Caroline said.

"Right," Jack said. "I talked to Judge Long." He finished what was in his glass. "Looks like my license is going to be suspended."

"Oh, Jack. . . ."

"At least. Maybe something worse."

Jack swung his chair around.

"Do me a favor, Five Spot?"

Caroline nodded.

"Fish out that bottle for me."

Caroline hesitated, then retrieved the bourbon bottle, which she handed to Jack.

"And on your way out . . ."

"Don't let the door hit me in the ass?"

"Something like that."

Jack swiveled his chair back around, facing away from Caroline. She left. Jack poured himself another half glass and took a long pull.

3

Jack parked beside a small fishing cabin in a marsh on the fringe of town. A dozen other cabins, all needing repair, stretched along the Hudson.

A few skiffs lay upside down, their curved, ribbed bottoms making them look like giant beetles.

Jack climbed out of his car with a single suitcase and a new bottle of Ezra Brooks in a paper bag and walked along some half-rotted planks into his shack. Jack inhaled the familiar childhood smell of mud and rotting wood.

Inside, he put down his suitcase, tilted the glass chimney of a kerosene lantern, snapped a match on his thumbnail and lit the wick. Over the windows, the white curtains were stiff with soot. On a table beside the bed, which ran along the far wall, was a gray ceramic basin and white enameled pitcher with a chipped red enameled line decorating the pour spout. Above the basin and pitcher a small shaving mirror hung on a twopenny nail. The slate sink had an old-fashioned hand pump. A bottle-gas refrigerator stood on a cinder block next to a two-burner stove.

Jack stretched out on the bed, the springs twanging, and closed his eyes, but couldn't stop his racing mind.

CHAPTER SIX

1

Ringing woke Jack, who stumbled out of bed and fumbled in his pants pocket for his cell phone.

"Slidell."

"Sorry to wake you," Sciortino said. "Forty minutes ago, the hooker died. The boys are on their way out to pick you up."

"Accessory, manslaughter 3?"

"You wish. You're a lawyer. They figure you should've known better. It's man 2."

Jack hung up the telephone.

2

Sciortino walked with Jack from the Columbia County Court House.

"At least," Sciortino said, "you made bail."

"I get arrested once more," Jack said, "I'll have to start using credit cards. What do we know about the girl? Her name? Fingerprints? Record? The bouquet? Anything?"

Sciortino shrugged.

"We got a couple of guys on it," he said. "It's an open case, Jack, I can't mouth off to you."

"You remember when I was in law school?"

"You worked harder than anyone I know. Eighteen, nineteen hour days. Classes. Hitting the books. Then, hauling on the docks."

"For what? To get caught in someone else's mess, see everything I worked for go down the tubes?"

"We got nothing, Jack."

Jack stopped. So did Sciortino.

"Prints don't match up to any in the records," Sciortino said. "No lead on the bouquet. The nurses on duty said it just appeared. We asked around the crib joints, escort services. From Albany to Springfield. No one says any of their girls are missing. Our CIs on the street, no one heard anything."

Jack started walking again. Sciortino called after him, "We'll turn up something, Jack. These things take time."

Sciortino watched Jack get into his car, start the engine, and drive away.

3

Jack headed across the cemetery toward his car. The wind had dropped, although on his way to the funeral Jack had heard that the hurricane was moving up the coast. They'd been lucky so far, but the storm that had been threatening for days would eventually hit. Jack wondered how bad it would be and if he should tape the windows in his shack.

The still air carried the priest's words from Frank's grave: "God loved the world so much, He gave us His only Son that all who believe in Him might have eternal life."

Jack felt rather than heard the bass thud from the sound system of a car passing on the mall road skirting the cemetery.

"Have mercy, Lord. . . ." The priest's words were lost in the still air.

Caroline left her uncle Dixie and sister Nicole, who were at Frank's grave, and hurried to catch up to Jack, who stopped when he saw her coming.

"Are you okay?" she asked.

"Yeah," Jack said. "I'm okay."

"That's it?" Caroline asked.

Jack shrugged.

"You never struck me as a quitter," she said. "I can see you walking away from the job, from me, even from yourself, from everything you worked for. But from Frank?"

She walked beside Jack toward Jack's car.

"The way I hear it," she said, "you got out of law school and sent out . . . what was it? A hundred, two hundred résumés? They used to joke about it in the office. *Jack Slidell, the guy who doesn't give up.*"

"The human pit bull, huh?" Jack said.

"That's right," Caroline said.

"I never liked that," Jack said.

"Two hundred résumés," Caroline said. "And one hundred ninety-nine rejections."

"Never liked that either."

"When no one else would give you a break, Frank hired you."

Jack opened his car door.

"Someone murdered Frank," Caroline said, "and framed you."

"We don't know that," Jack said.

Caroline waited.

"Frank's dead," Jack said, sliding behind the steering wheel. "And I don't have a lot more to lose."

"Then what's stopping you?" Caroline asked.

Jack started the car and, without even a wave, drove away.

CHAPTER SEVEN

1

Caroline headed up the dirt road, her car bouncing in the ruts. When she turned through the broad leaves that splayed across her window and first saw Jack's shack, she stopped for a moment before driving the last two dozen feet and parking in the mud next to Jack's car. From beside her on the front seat she took a large manila envelope and, getting out of the car, climbed the cinder block steps to the front porch.

The front door was unlocked. She entered. The late afternoon sun slanted through the dirty lace curtains, casting reptile scales across the doorsill.

"Jack," Caroline said, "there are a few cases I thought maybe you could help me with—"

She stopped, staring at Jack who stood in the midst of devastation. The cabin was torn apart. Furniture, lanterns, smashed. Everything that could be destroyed had been.

"Either someone decided I needed to redecorate," Jack said, "or someone's trying to warn me off looking into Frank's murder."

2

Jack fixed a broken table leg as Caroline swept up shattered glass. The night was humid. Jack wore a T-shirt and jeans. Where Caroline's dress was sweaty, it clung to her body.

"Maybe you should get a gun?" Caroline said.

"I've got one," Jack said. "I keep it unloaded. That way things don't get messy."

Caroline approached Jack, drawn to him.

"Neatness," Caroline said, "is an overrated virtue."

"All virtues are overrated," Jack said.

They stood so close, Jack could feel the heat coming off her body.

"Why'd you come here?" he asked. "What do you want?"

"To help you."

"I usually handle things by myself."

"Even big jobs?"

"All my jobs are big."

"What about this one?"

"Biggest I've ever had."

There was a moment when they could have ended in each other's arms, but Jack broke the tension.

"And," Jack said, "the most dangerous."

"I've got a stack of what Robert calls *fix-me* cases . . ."

"Which you're going to toss my way?"

"I can use the help. You can use the money."

"You know I can't practice law."

"You can do research."

"I'm not an investigator."

Caroline nodded toward the files, which lay in a small stack on a side table.

"There's one," she said, "a client's convinced his wife is sleeping with his brother."

"I thought you wanted me to go after whoever killed Frank."

Caroline picked up one of the files.

"There's a girl who got a speeding ticket."

"Screw the files."

"She claims she was five miles below the limit."

"I was raised to do anything, even steal, rather than take charity, Five Spot."

"You spend a night going over these cases, you won't think it's charity."

"When I was a kid," Jack said, "payday was Friday. By Thursday, we'd be broke. I'd go with my dad to the market and watch him shoplift cans of sardines for dinner. My mother wanted more for me. Kept telling me, *fly, fly higher.* I got a scholarship, CCNY, then Fordham Law School. . . . And, when I started flying, she stood there below me, looking angry, because she couldn't fly, too. Every morning, she'd start with an eight-ounce glass full of gin. One day, it turned out to be Clorox."

"Jack," Caroline said, "whoever trashed your place . . ."

"Is more afraid of me than I am of him."

"You want help?"

"It's not your kind of work, Five Spot."

"I'm a quick study under the right teacher."

"How are you on top?"

"Even quicker."

"You're not going to like everything you see."

"Jack, after working with you, I'm used to that."

Caroline put her arms around Jack's neck and kissed him. Jack put his arms around her, pressed her damp body toward him. Caroline ran her hands up and down Jack's body.

"This is why I don't carry a gun."

"Yeah, it might go off unexpectedly."

Jack untwined her hands and gently, kindly pushed her away.

"Even twelve-speeds have to put on the brakes going downhill," Jack said. "And where we're going to find Frank's killer is all downhill."

3

Jack and Caroline crossed the street toward Empire State Florists.

"The girl who was with Frank," Jack said, "when she was in the hospital, someone sent her a bouquet. With a flower in it I've never seen before. We find out where it came from, Five Spot, maybe we find out who sent it."

A bell rang as they entered the shop.

The florist, a young woman with a crest of dyed white hair that made her look like an egret, studied the book of flowers Jack had brought in.

"You're sure the bouquet included this?" the egret asked.

Jack nodded.

"*White fringed orchid,*" the egret said. "We don't see that in bouquets that often. If at all. Not around here anyway. There's a specialty shop in town might handle it. Afton Florists."

Mr. Afton, an elderly man in a cream cardigan, tapped Jack's book of flowers with his forefinger.

"The man who bought the bouquet asked for something special," Mr. Afton said. "That's why I included the white fringed orchid."

"What did the man look like?" Jack asked.

"Ask me about flowers, I can describe plants I haven't had in stock for a decade," Mr. Afton said. "But people . . . ?"

He shrugged.

CHAPTER EIGHT

1

The alley off Columbiaville Street was lined with peep shows and cheap shops selling drug paraphernalia and porno. A two-block red-light zone in upstate New York. For years, Mycenae had been the drug depot of the mid-Hudson, peddling dope from Albany and Troy to the west, to the Berkshires to the east. An area filled with the hopeless poor and college students with more money than sense.

A few hookers strolled, giving the come-on to the even fewer down-state weekenders, most of whom were male couples. In the 1980s, Mycenae had become a popular gay community with regular Thursday evening tea dances and a local transvestite coffee house, Coffee Grounds, where, early in the morning, men in 1940s dresses and spike heels shambled in, unshaved, for breakfast.

A bar blared recorded Zydeco music: Queen Ida and Clifton Chernier's "Allons a Grand Coteau." The bar light cast a paradoxically nursery glow on the surroundings, all pink and baby blue.

Caroline followed Jack. The music from the bar changed to Richard and Mimi Farina, Sixties head music. Jack stopped at the doorway of the town's only topless joint, where an old man wearing electric blue polyester pants and a striped pajama top, Skinny Wecht, lounged. When he spotted Jack, he grinned, showing a mouthful of gold teeth.

"Hey, Jackie-boy," Skinny said, "long time."

"I've been busy, Skinny," Jack said. "Mama Lucky in?"

" 'Til she dies," Skinny said.

2

Inside Mama Lucky's Topless, three girls wearing not much more than a smile shuffled on top of the bar. In the corners, a few girls were lap dancing. A man sitting by himself patted Caroline's ass as she passed. She glared at him and moved closer to Jack.

"You spend a lot of time here?" Caroline asked.

"Skinny taught me how to play pool," Jack said.

"What else did he teach you?" Caroline asked.

"You notice his teeth?" Jack asked. "Got them all drilled and filled with gold. That's where he carries his stake. Figures that way he'll never get his pocket picked."

"He bets the gold in his teeth?" Caroline asked. "What happens if he loses?"

"Skinny never loses," Jack said.

A blond, six-and-a-half feet tall, stood against the wall. She gestured to Caroline.

"Honey," the blond asked, "do I have anything on the back of my dress?"

Languidly, the blond turned around.

"A smudge?" she asked. "Some soot? Nothing? Could you just smooth it out in back?"

Uneasy at the request, Caroline glanced at Jack, who shrugged.

"It gets so wrinkled in this heat," the blond said.

Caroline straightened the back of the blond's dress. The woman undulated under Caroline's hand, like a cat arching. Caroline stepped back.

"You look uncomfortable," Jack said.

"It was just so odd," Caroline said, "having a woman react that way to my touch."

"Don't worry," Jack said. "Tiny there isn't a woman."

Caroline took Jack's arm. Jack glanced down at how she was clutching him and smiled as they passed other women and transvestites, who all greeted Jack: "Hey, there, Jackie . . . Hey, Jack . . . Jack, boy . . . !"

At the back of the room, two thugs flanked a door. When Jack and Caroline approached, the thug on the left murmured, "Where you been?" The thug on the right murmured, "Hey, you, Jack. . . ." They stood aside to let Jack and Caroline pass.

Through the door was a dark stairway. As they started climbing, Caroline pressed even closer to Jack.

"You're popular around here," Caroline said.

"I once did someone a favor," Jack said.

"I shouldn't ask, right?"

"Right."

3

On the other side of a metal door at the top of the stairs was an office. Despite the desk and file cabinets, the place looked more like a bedroom. Dominating the space was a huge bed, and in the bed was the fattest woman Caroline had ever seen. Mama Lucky. Propped up on half-a-dozen pillows and sweating profusely despite the air conditioning and the five electric fans, which were arranged around her in a semicircle. Near her was a magnum of Jack Daniel's.

"That you, Jack Slidell?" Mama Lucky said. "I won't ask how the hell you been. You been up to your stubble in trouble, and you come to Mama Lucky like they always do for a little consolation and advice." She nodded to a chair. "Put it down."

Jack sat, gestured for Caroline to sit, which she did, primly. Mama Lucky stared at Caroline. Hard.

"Girl," she said to Caroline, "you too good for him. Never been a girl that wasn't."

"You're looking well, Mama Lucky," Jack said.

"You always was a liar, Jack Slidell," Mama Lucky said. "How much longer do I have? Five, ten more years. Sometimes I want to die just to get over the suspense."

"You're going to live forever, Mama Lucky," Jack said.

"Don't threaten me, Jack Slidell. I seen too much, heard too much."

"What have you heard about a girl beaten up at the Dutch Village Motel?"

Mama said to Caroline, "That man always do come right to the point." To Jack, she said, "You come right to the point with this gal, Jack Slidell?"

Mama Lucky took a swig from the big square bottle of Jack Black and handed it to Jack.

"Someone sent her a bouquet in the hospital," Jack said.

"You want a fortune-teller, you go out Avondale way," Mama Lucky said. "You know the place."

"Mama Lucky knows more than any fortune-teller," Jack said.

Mama Lucky wheezed a laugh.

"Ain't that the lick that killed Dick," Mama Lucky said. "Jack Slidell, you're a bucketful."

Jack took a swig from the whiskey bottle and handed it to Caroline, who looked at it as if Jack had just given her a live snake. Jack noticed and was amused by her hesitation to drink. He gestured for her to go ahead. Caroline wiped the mouth of the bottle. Twice. And using two hands to raise the heavy bottle took a hesitant swig.

"Ain't no one taught this girl how to put down a thirst?" Mama Lucky said. "Aim it at the sky, girl."

Caroline tilted the bottle higher, got a mouthful, and forced herself to swallow. Trying to suppress a gag, she handed the bottle back to Mama Lucky, who, gently mocking, wiped the bottle mouth just like Caroline had.

"No insult, girl," Mama Lucky said, "but I don't know where your lips have been."

One-handed, Mama raised the bottle and took a few gulps.

"That stuff who was beat up," Mama Lucky said. "She wasn't no regular trade. A college student, they say."

"You know what school?" Jack asked.

"Yale, Princeton," Mama Lucky said. "Local talent, sent off for a proper education. What she learned, she'd be better off ignorant. Kicked out, they say. Chipping for nickel, dime bags, she was. At school, then down home." To Caroline, she said, "Stuff like that give the good girls on the corner a bad reputation, don't you say so, honey?"

Caroline stammered, "I . . . I . . ."

"Speak up, girl," Mama Lucky said. "Didn't your mama teach you nothing 'bout conversation?" To Jack, she said, "I'll bet that gal knows how to dance. You always pick the dancers. But she don't know how to sing."

"The blow Frank was doing," Jack said. "It had cyanide in it."

"What folks won't do these days to get high," Mama Lucky said.

"Or dead," Jack said.

"Come to the same in the end," Mama Lucky said. "No, nothing on the street about that. But, Jack Slidell, you know people don't get their highs just from the street. Your boss—you ask his clients, his friends about him?"

"That's a long list, Mama Lucky," Jack said. "Frank had a lot of friends."

"Then," Mama Lucky said, "I don't care *how* he died. He was a lucky man!"

On her massive bed, Mama Lucky leaned forward and said, "You unwax your ears, Jack Slidell. About that bouquet. Go listen to Lafayette King, Gainsvoort Gardens." To Caroline, Mama Lucky said, "That's what they call an old folks' home. Where I should be. A better waiting room for heaven than this dump."

Jack stood.

Relieved, so did Caroline.

"Nothing happens around here that you don't know, Mama Lucky," Jack said, leaning over and kissing her on the cheek.

"You get your paw out of the snare, now, Jack Slidell," Mama Lucky said. "Then, keep your pants with a crease and your collar turned down, you hear." To Caroline, she said, "Trouble with that boy, he wanted to get rich. And, in this world, there's only two ways to make a fortune: Be born rich or be born brutal. Jack Slidell was neither. Never will be."

CHAPTER NINE

1

As Jack and Caroline walked away from the red light district, Caroline glanced at Jack, looking at him in a new way.

"How come the police couldn't get the information?" she asked. "If you know who to ask, why don't they?"

"They know who," Jack said. "But not how."

"Mama Lucky reminds me of Santa Claus," Caroline said.

"Yeah," Jack said, "if Santa came down the chimney carrying a chain saw."

A weathered blue-and-white historical marker at the beginning of the long drive up to Gainsvoort Gardens declared that Queen Beatrix of the Netherlands had once stayed there. Not, presumably, as a patient. Or resident, as the facility called its clients. In the distance, they heard a low roll of thunder.

The main house was a thirty-six-room castle with turrets, many chimneys, and a wraparound porch that gave it the look of an ocean liner aground on a rise, like a Catskill Noah's Ark. The house had been built in the 1880s by Wallace Beach, a tin magnate, for his daughter and her new husband, an English lord who thought he was broke and found out six months after the wedding that he'd inherited a fortune from some collateral relative. Everyone assumed he'd married for money and, newly rich, would vanish. He had married for money, but discovered he enjoyed his pug-nosed bride's sense of humor. They went off together to live on some property in Scotland, and Beach's castle was closed up for ten years before it was sold to the first of a series of not-rich-enough owners, all of whom unloaded the pile after a couple of winters. Expensive to heat, more expensive to keep up the grounds. In the 1930s, the place was boarded up. Shingles flaked from the roof. Windows cracked. Mice nested in mattresses. Bats hung from the ceiling of the baronial dining room. Pipes burst and water cascaded down the grand staircase. For generations, in winter, the steep, sloping lawn in front of the abandoned house became a favorite spot for sledding. As night fell, the packed snow went from blue to purple to black. The moon reflecting on the icy surface gave the estate a fairy-tale look. Lights sometimes flickered from the broken windows as teenagers wandered through the echoing rooms, their flashlights searching out corners in which to make out.

In the late-1960s, Billy Livingston, a descendent of one of the oldest and richest Hudson River families, bought the Beach Castle, cleaned and repaired half a dozen rooms, and used it as a commune until a girl on LSD took a wedge of pizza from the cardboard box in which it had been delivered and, convinced an ever-thinning thread of cheese connected her slice to the box no matter how far away she walked, wandered up stairs and down corridors until in an attic room she stepped on a rotten floor board and plunged into a third-floor bathroom, breaking her neck.

Livingston abandoned the commune and the castle, which six years later was bought by some Boston investors who gutted and renovated the place and turned it into Gainsvoort Gardens, a very expensive *retirement facility*. They kept the high ceilings, the half-dozen unbroken Tiffany glass runners in the living room windows, and the massive fireplaces, big enough to stand in. But building fires in the fireplaces was forbidden.

A nurse in a crisp white uniform padded down a hall, leading Jack and Caroline past half-open doors, behind which ancient men and women lay in beds with half-opened mouths, dying fish.

"This late, visits are against the rules," said the nurse, one of Jack's old high school friends. "But these old ones, they don't sleep much. It'll help him pass the time."

As she moved, the starched cloth of her uniform made a sound like ripping paper.

At a door, she stopped.

"He's in here," she said.

Jack and Caroline went into the small room. In the hospital bed, a wizened man was propped on pillows, wide awake. Lafayette King.

"Mr. King?" Jack said.

King blinked at Jack.

"My name's Jack Slidell," Jack said.

"I'm ninety-six years old," King said. "July 6th."

King's voice was strong. Melodic. Humorous.

"Congratulations," Jack said.

"Why?" King said. "Life's not an endurance contest. Or is it? I don't care. I'm not going for any record. You Billy Slidell's boy?"

"My people," Jack said, "you wouldn't know them."

"Billy Slidell was the best tennis player I ever met," King said. "Tried to teach me the backhand. I played tennis for seventy-five years and never did learn a decent backhand." To Caroline, he said, "Young lady, when I was a boy in school I once knew a girl as beautiful as you are."

"Thank you," Caroline said. And introduced herself, "Caroline Wonder."

"I knew a Caroline Wonder," King said. "A long time ago. Colonel Wonder's daughter."

"That was my grandmother," Caroline said.

"I think she would have married me," King said. "But I was too shy to ask her. In this life, by the time you're not too shy, you're too old. To what do I owe the pleasure of your company?"

Caroline glanced at Jack, who nodded for her to go ahead. Columbiaville was his world. This was hers.

"We heard a rumor," Caroline started.

"You look *bien elevee*," King said. "You should know better than to trust rumors."

Again, Caroline glanced at Jack, who gave her his poker face.

"You're right," Caroline said. "I once heard a rumor at work. One I shouldn't have trusted."

"Rumors are like cut flowers," King said. "Dead things people use to brighten up drab lives."

"This one, though, is important to Mr. Slidell," Caroline said. "Important to both of us. Someone said you know about a bouquet sent to a girl in a hospital."

King looked benignantly on Caroline, saying nothing.

"Please, Mr. King," Caroline said.

King sighed.

"I'm a gentleman," he said. "Another gentleman came to me to ask a favor. Could I have one of the boys here buy a bouquet, something special, and deliver it to a hospital."

"Who asked for the favor?" Jack asked.

"He didn't want anyone to know," King said. "That's why he asked me."

"Mr. King," Jack said.

"I gave my word, Mr.—"

"Slidell."

"That's right. Mr. Slidell."

"Two people have died. . . ."

"Look around you, Mr. Slidell. This place is filled with death. Do you think death matters that much?"

"Yes," Jack said.

"To me, honor, my word, matters more," King said. "You said I wouldn't know your people. Maybe that's the difference between your people and mine."

2

Another gentleman came to me to ask a favor. Could I have one of the boys here buy a bouquet, something special, and deliver it to a hospital.

"All we have to do," Jack said, "is figure out who that other gentleman is."

"That should be easy," Caroline said. "There aren't a lot of gentlemen left in the world."

Jack and Caroline walked down the long, sloping drive from Gains-voort Gardens to the parking lot off Route 203.

Caroline said, "A dead end."

Jack shook his head *no* and said, "We've been stirring up trouble."

"I thought," Caroline said, "we were trying to get *out* of trouble."

"If you expected a cotillion," Jack said, "you should have stayed in the ballroom."

"Given the results, I don't see it would've made any difference."

"I'm the one in the jackpot, not you, Five Spot. You want to sit this one out, it's okay with me."

"Five Spot. Why do you call me that?"

"In fifth grade," Jack explained, "I hung out in a store, the Acre General Store out on Route 66. It had a pinball machine called *Five Spot*. Cost a nickel to play. I used to save up. On the display, there was a picture of a woman I fell in love with."

"You fell in love with a picture?"

"I figured someday I'd meet someone who looked like her." Jack smiled.

"I look like a pinball bimbo?" Caroline asked.

"That tickles you?"

"You have no idea."

"When I got supplies the other day, when I moved into the shack down by the boat basin, I stopped in the store. The machine's still there."

"Five Spot, huh?" Caroline said.

3

The woman on the pinball display was dressed in a harem costume, beaded and fringed top covering nose-cone breasts, a voluptuous belly with a green jewel in her navel, and translucent pantaloons covering a skimpy bikini bottom. Her arms were raised to her right, hands palms out, obviously in the middle of a belly dance.

"Still costs a nickel," Caroline said.

"The good things never change," Jack said.

Caroline stood at the old pinball machine, her hands on the flipper buttons. Jack stood behind her, his hands over hers.

"This is the way you used to do it?" Caroline asked.

"Not quite," Jack said as Caroline moved her body back against Jacks. Bells rang and lights flashed. On the machine.

"Do you always hit the target?" Caroline asked.

"Every time," Jack said.

At the shack, Jack parked, got out of his car, and started for the door. Standing first on one leg and then on the other, Caroline paused to take off her shoes—to save them from the muddy path. She was looking down when she heard the noise, a thud, like a bat against a softball.

Jack was falling as a man, face hidden in the dark, raised the two-by-four he had used to crack Jack's head.

"Jack," Caroline cried, running half on, half off the planks toward where the stranger was beating Jack with the two-by-four.

The stranger gave Jack one last thwak in the ribs before running to a pickup truck and roaring off.

Kneeling in the mud, Caroline cradled Jack, half conscious from the beating, in her arms.

CHAPTER TEN

1

Kerosene light flickered on Jack's bruised face. One eye was swollen half closed. His upper lip crusted with dried blood. His shirt was off. Tiger-like welts striped his side, ribs. Caroline was sponging the wounds on his chest. Open beside her on the side table was her car emergency Red Cross kit.

"You've got great bedside manner," Jack said.

"This isn't exactly how I imagined we'd end up in bed," Caroline said.

She touched a raw spot. Jack winced.

"Sorry," Caroline said.

Caroline wrapped gauze around Jack's chest.

"Is all that necessary?"

"Think of it as a fashion statement."

Caroline touched a cut on Jack's lip.

"This might need special treatment," she said.

She ran her fingers over Jack's mouth. Closed her eyes and leaned forward to kiss Jack, who, taking a deep breath, pulled back.

"You're a good nurse," he said.

"Doctor," she said.

"You practice a lot?"

"I don't have a lot of patience."

"Which kind?" Jack asked.

Caroline kissed Jack again.

"I can tell you don't have a lot of patience," Jack said. "Did I tell you I can read minds?"

"Yeah?"

"You're going to say, *I'm not going to help you get killed.*"

"And you're going to say, *If they wanted to kill me, you'd be in mourning by now.*"

"And you're going to say, *Let's leave all this to the cops.*"

"And you're going to say, *Go back into Frank's files, everything from the past six months, everything.*"

"We know each other so well," Jack said, "maybe someday we ought to go on a date."

"I don't date corpses," Caroline said.

"Why not?" Jack said. "You know what they say about necrophilia? *At least, you don't have to worry about hurting your partner's feelings.*"

Caroline closed the first aid kid. Angrily.

"I thought you wanted me to find out what happened to Frank."

"That was before this."

"They stole my job—" Jack began.

"They?" Caroline asked.

"I worked hard to get where I am," Jack said.

"Where are you, Jack?" Caroline asked.

"Back where I began," Jack said. "That's what I mean. If it hadn't been for Frank's murder—"

"You don't know he was murdered," Caroline said. "As for screwing up your life—if it hadn't been Frank's death, it would have been something else."

"My fate, huh?"

"Your character. They pulled you in for obstructing justice. Resisting arrest. It's amazing you weren't disbarred years ago."

"So my fate's this car heading at me—"

"And your character is you being so stubborn you decide to play chicken when the driver of the car has had a stroke and can't turn the wheel away. You think he's trying to prove he's more macho than you, Jack. But he's dead. And you'd rather crash than get out of a dead man's way."

"But if he was alive . . ."

"You'd still be a fool to play chicken," Caroline said.

She grabbed her bag and headed for the door.

"At least," Jack said, "we now got a clue."

"What are you talking about?" Caroline asked.

Gingerly, Jack touched a bruise and said, "Whoever hit me was a professional."

Caroline slammed out.

2

Caroline balanced a doubled cardboard coffee cup, which splashed hot coffee onto her knuckles as she crossed the square in front of the Mycenae County Courthouse. Thrusting out his chin so he wouldn't drip on himself, Robert took a sip from his cardboard cup.

"Smart move," Robert said, "cutting free of Jack. That relationship wasn't going anywhere."

"Don't get me started," Caroline said.

"Does he have any idea who's trying to scare him off?"

Caroline shook her head *no,* took a careful sip of coffee.

"Jack's going to destroy himself," she said.

They passed a stranger slamming his fist against one of the last public pay phones in town.

"You see that, chief?" the stranger said to Robert. "I work hard for my money, and the goddamn phone stole my quarter!"

The stranger kept hitting the telephone. Caroline and Robert walked on. Robert shaking his head.

"There was a time in this city when people were courteous," Robert said.

"Long before our time," Caroline said.

"—when the air here was sweet with the smell of the honeysuckle they dug up when they redid the square," Robert said.

"Robert," Caroline said, "you're such a romantic!"

"If the commercial expansion of the seventeenth and eighteenth centuries hadn't happened," Robert said, "if the commercial expansion hadn't given impetus to capitalism, if the rise of capitalism in France hadn't outstripped the country's slower, natural social and political change, if that imbalance hadn't helped cause the French Revolution, if the Revolution hadn't created an opening for Napoleon to seize power, if Napoleon hadn't tried to conquer Europe, if the wars in Europe hadn't given the United States a chance to take over shipping between Europe and the West Indies, if America's expansion into shipping didn't cause Great Britain to impress American sailors and interfere with American maritime trade, if Great Britain's interference with American maritime trade didn't encourage Jefferson and Madison to prohibit trade with Britain, if that prohibition didn't contribute to the War of 1812, if the War of 1812 didn't lead to the British blockade of American ports, if the blockade of American ports hadn't made Mycenae one of the few protected ports in America, sailors wouldn't have come here, if sailors hadn't come here, Mycenae wouldn't have become a center of prostitution, if Mycenae hadn't become a center of prostitution—"

"Maybe people would still be courteous?" Caroline asked.

Robert shrugged.

"You're still courteous, Robert," Caroline said. "The last gentleman."

"You grow up with someone like my daddy, who's still fighting Shay's Rebellion," Robert said, "it's hard not to get wrapped up in the history."

3

Geigerman's Gym was dirty. In one corner was a brass spittoon left over from the 1940s, still used. Young guys sparred, jumped rope, worked on the heavy bag. Two of the three rings were occupied. An older man was climbing out of the third ring after a workout. Honey LeVigne.

Jack came over to LeVigne.

"Just like Archie Moore," Jack said.

LeVigne glanced sideways at Jack as he walked across the gym.

"You went for the nerve point on his hip," Jack said. "A man'll feel that head to toe."

"You don't look like a fighter," LeVigne said, checking out Jack's wounds, black-and-blue marks. "Not a good one anyway, you don't."

"I got caught by surprise," Jack said. "I'm looking for a rematch."

LeVigne grabbed a towel and hooked it around his neck.

"Your friend," LeVigne said, meaning whoever had beaten Jack up, "he should've gone for the body. Like Hagler. Frazier. Work on the body, the guy won't last five rounds."

"He wasn't looking to win the match," Jack said, "just sign an autograph on my face."

"So you'd remember him, huh?" LeVigne said.

"But he knew how to throw a punch," Jack said. "You know anyone who does that for a living?"

"Freelance, any palooka'll grab a fifty, figuring he's just going to get a workout, save time in the gym," LeVinge said. "Shit, a twenty'll do it."

LeVigne disappeared into the showers. Jack watched a young kid on the speed bag.

"You the man looking for somebody?" someone said behind Jack, close to his ear. The voice was a hoarse whisper, as if the speaker had been punched in the larynx and never recovered. Kevin Hooper. A big man in gray sweats.

"How many fights you got?" Jack asked.

"In or out of the ring?" Hooper asked. "You want to go a round?"

Jack looked Hooper up and down. Tenderly touched a mouse under his left eye and said, "I don't have any sweats."

"I fought guys worse dressed than you," Hooper said.

CHAPTER ELEVEN

1

Caroline sat at her desk at Milhet & Alvarez, going over files, one file in particular. She read it, puzzled. Outside a young law clerk, Curtis Lee, passed, pulling his bow tie loose.

"Curtis," Caroline said.

Unbuttoning his top shirt button and stretching his neck in a circle, Curtis came into Caroline's office.

"These files," she held them out for him to see, "they were all Robert's, right?"

Curtis nodded. Caroline tapped the file that especially had caught her interest.

"This one," she said.

Curtis read, "*Gaynor, Jean.* Speeding ticket." He looked at Caroline. "What's the problem?"

"Is she one of our regular clients?"

"No."

"Her parents? Are they our clients?"

Curtis shook his head *no*.

"These little *fix-me* cases," Caroline said. "We do them as a courtesy for our regular clients. Why are we doing this one?"

Curtis shrugged.

"According to this morning's paper, she's the one found dead in Frank's motel room," Caroline said. "This address, Paul Gaynor . . ."

"Husband?" Curtis said.

"Could be," Caroline said. "I think I'll find out."

2

In the second ring at Geigerman's, Jack, gloved and in street clothes, circled away from Hooper, who, grinning, flicked a few feints. Jack back-pedaled.

"So we tango," Jack said. "What do you got for me?"

"I surely got something for you," Hooper said.

He popped Jack in his already bruised face. Jack jabbed, but Hooper was too fast. He got in under Jack's left and opened the cut over Jack's right eye.

"I meant information," Jack said, blinking away the blood.

Hooper cracked Jack's nose, which started to bleed.

Again, Jack jabbed and missed.

"When I was a kid," Jack said, "I used to be a street fighter."

"Pity we're not in the street," Hooper said.

Hooper got inside and hit Jack over the heart. Jack went gray.

"You want to know who beat you up?" Hooper asked.

He thumped Jack over the heart again. Jack rebounded off the ropes.

"Does this feel familiar?" Hooper asked.

He connected with a combination, Jack's kidney and an uppercut to Jack's cut lip, which opened up again.

"What happened to your two-by four?" Jack asked.

"Wouldn't fit in my glove," Hooper said.

He swung. Jack sidestepped.

"Who hired you?" Jack gasped.

Hooper hit Jack, a left to the head, a right to the body, another left to the head. Jack staggered back, trying to shield the blows. Hunched, Hooper came in for the kill. Jack put up his gloves.

"Wait," Jack said. "Wait a minute."

"Hurt?" Hooper grinned.

"No," Jack said. "Got to, got to . . ."

Jack yawned. A big yawn. Yawns are contagious. Hooper yawned—and Jack, who had faked the yawn, used the opening to hit Hooper.

A left to the heart, a right to the temple, a left to the jaw, a right to the jaw.

Hooper went down.

Jack hung over him, panting. Out of the corner of his good eye, Jack saw LeVigne, ringside, in a lime green shirt, mustard yellow slacks, and worn but polished tasseled loafers.

"Hooper never could take a punch," LeVigne said.

"Hooper?" Jack asked.

"Kevin Hooper," LeVigne said. "Piece of shit. Surprised you let him do you so much damage."

"He seemed to need the confidence," Jack said.

"What he needed," LeVigne said, "you just gave him. About time someone did. But you could've saved yourself a tag or two if you did like I told you and worked on the body."

"That'd take five rounds," Jack said. "I'm impatient."

Jack crouched over Hooper, dripping blood on Hooper's face, his knee on Hooper's neck.

"Now, my friend," Jack said, "we talk . . ."

3

Caroline walked up the flagstone path to the white suburban house in Colonie, outside of Albany, and pressed the bell. She heard a ring, muffled by the door. The air was filled with static electricity, which made her dress cling to her pantyhose. She rang the bell again. The door opened, revealing a man in his early sixties, wearing a blue-and-red Hawaiian shirt outside his gray slacks. He was barefoot and holding a newspaper, the *Times-Union*, next to his leg, a finger in the pages saving his place.

"Paul Gaynor?" Caroline asked.

Gaynor nodded.

"I'm looking for Jean Gaynor," Caroline said. Then, guessing, added, "Your daughter."

Again, Gaynor nodded.

"I'm a lawyer," Caroline said. "My firm is handling some business of hers."

"What is it this time?" Gaynor asked. "Prostitution? Or drugs?"

The small, neat living room was dominated by the huge head of a buck mounted on a walnut panel. A rail like a blackboard chalk tray ran along the bottom of the panel. In it were three arrows, which, Caroline assumed, had been used to bring the buck down.

Gaynor sank into an easy chair. No socks. His pant cuffs were pulled up over his purple-veined, pale ankles. Caroline sat across from him in the middle of the couch. On the coffee table between them was a clear pitcher of water and a pastel plastic dimpled glasses. Half full.

"When Jean got into trouble down in the City . . . ," Paul began.

"At school?" Caroline asked.

"Pratt Institute," Gaynor said. He pointed at a chalk portrait of himself, framed, hanging next to the deer head. "She had some talent. But a few months after she went down there, she came home. Or they sent her home. Do they do that today? Send kids home? When they get into trouble? At school?" He sighed. "I couldn't control her. In two months, she's been arrested twice for soliciting in Hudson and once in Mycenae for possession of cocaine."

"Your wife?" Caroline asked.

"Jean's mother died when Jean was eight," Gaynor said. "Ever since then, she's pretty much done what she wanted."

"You haven't heard from the police?" Caroline asked.

Gaynor shook his head *no*.

"Told her last time she got arrested, I was through. No bail. No help. No nothing. Even she could figure that one out. She must've called somebody else to spring her."

"I'm afraid," Caroline said, "Jean's dead."

"Maybe," Gaynor said, "that's what she wanted."

"You don't seem—"

"Surprised? A kid like Jean, I been expecting it. The phone rings, I figure . . ."

He trailed off.

"The police should've called," he said. "Maybe they did. I got one of those voice-mail services, but I never check it. What for? Just bill collectors and cold calls. They'll be by. For whatever it's worth. I got nothing to tell them. Or you."

"Your daughter—"

"My wife was pregnant when I married her. I knew about it. But, like her daughter, Jean's mother had a wild streak. I never adopted Jean. Not legally, I mean. But far as she knew, I was her father."

"Who was her real father?"

"A married man."

"Local?"

"Not quite."

"You ever find out his name?"

"I found out all about him. Long time ago. Wasn't hard. He's well known. Massachusetts big shot. Keating Flowers."

"Keating Flowers?" Caroline said.

"You know him?" Gaynor asked.

"I know his son," Caroline said.

CHAPTER TWELVE

1

Jack, his face purple and pulpy, right eye swollen to a slit, upper lip crusted with blood and peaked as if he'd been fishhooked, stood in front of Geigerman's Gym on the corner of Horatio Seymour Avenue and Seventh Street across from Seed's Autobody, a junkyard, which had painted on its high wooden fence in big, sloppy red letters *Save Local Businesses—Fight Prop. 65*, a rezoning plan that would close the junkyard on the grounds that it was a blight and allow the adjacent County Hospital complex to expand.

Two nurses, in their crumpled whites, both in their forties, one tall and blond, carrying a Mexican cloth bag as a purse, and the other short with hennaed hair, clutching a small gold purse, stood at the nearby bus stop, ignoring Jack's ruined face.

"Laurie went to Albany Hospital," the first nurse said.

"Yeah," the second nurse said.

"Gallstones."

"Who has gallstones?"

"Laurie."

"No kidding."

"From the cesarean."

"What cesarean?"

"Laurie's."

"Laurie had a cesarean?"

"Yeah. It gave her gallstones."

"Yeah?"

"Yeah. She had to go to Albany Hospital."

"Who?"

"Laurie."

"The one who had the cesarean?"

"And the gallstones."

Jack's head throbbed, and he tasted copper, blood in his mouth, and was concentrating on not throwing up when Caroline drove up to where he waited.

As Jack slipped into the passenger side of her car, Caroline tried not to stare.

"I found out who sandbagged me the other night," Jack said.

"Wasn't there a less painful way?" Caroline asked.

"They paid him a dime."

"Someone will do that to you for a dime?"

"A hundred dollars," Jack explained. "A blond guy with long hair, western boots, and a cowboy hat. Doesn't know why or who it was."

"Or so he claims," Caroline said.

"I believe him," Jack said. When Caroline made a skeptical face, Jack said, "People tend to tell the truth when you're kneeling on their windpipe."

"You wouldn't have really hurt him?" Caroline asked.

"Look at my face," Jack said. "Yeah, I would have hurt him. Gladly. What'd you find out?"

"The girl with Frank. Jean Gaynor. Turns out to be Robert's half sister."

Even Jack's swollen eye tried to open with surprise.

"His father's indiscretion," Caroline said. "He's been supporting her, but apparently not in the style which she felt she deserved."

"Not enough to feed her habit?" Jack asked.

"Either habit," Caroline said. "Dope. And hooking, which was more than an expedient. She seemed to get off on it. That's why Robert was handling a speeding ticket for her. One of those little *fix-me*s you thought didn't matter. Do you think Robert knows his father is involved in Jean Gaynor's death? In Frank's murder?"

THE EXTINCTION EVENT 73

"We don't know his father is involved, Five Spot."

"What else could it be? Her adopted father virtually disowned her. It can't be him."

"We don't know that either."

"Robert's father is a client."

"*Was* a client. That's one account Robert took with him."

"If Robert's father found out Jean was having an affair with Frank—"

"What?" Jack said. "He kills Frank?"

"Maybe," Caroline said, "he tried to drag Jean out of the motel?"

"She resisted," Jack said.

"He hit her?" Caroline said.

"Things get out of control?" Jack said.

"He keeps hitting her until—" Caroline stopped. "Frank's passed out."

"Dying from laced blow?"

"I don't think Robert's father would poison Frank's cocaine."

"We don't know that either, Five Spot."

"Do you think Robert's father is capable of killing Frank?" Caroline asked.

"Who knows?" Jack said. "I never met the man."

2

Flanking the entrance to Keating Flowers' place were two stone pillars topped by lion-headed grotesques, half Sphinx and half harpie. The left monster's face was speckled by what must have been buckshot, courtesy of some passing hunters, tempted by either the target or hostility to the sign of aristocratic pretentions. The right-hand monster's face, worn by weather, looked sad, its left eye as damaged as Jack's right.

Jack and Caroline turned off the road a few miles short of Great Barrington and bumped along the potholed drive, which had been paved in the past but hadn't been kept up. Overhanging tree branches clawed at the car's windshield and scraped along the car roof. After a mile or so, the road curved out of the woods and along the near side of a weedy lake. Across the water stood Flower's Folly, the castle built by Keating Flowers' maternal grandfather—and Robert's great-grandfather—Artemis Flower, who had made a fortune in concrete. His great-great-great-grandfather, also named Artemis, had made the original family fortune quarrying Massachusetts marble for the new capital in Washington. He had bought the quarry, which was near Hadley, Massachusetts, thinking that Hadley would be the site of the new government. To this day Hadley, a town between Amherst and Northampton, has a green stretching as long as Pennsylvania Avenue.

For years, the concrete business chugged along, making sundials and garden trolls and foundations. But, since 9-11, the business had boomed: The company couldn't keep up with the demand for Jersey barriers to protect government buildings and businesses. Even the Mycenae Town Hall put up a wall of concrete as if expecting a terrorist attack in the Hudson Valley.

The crenulated towers of the main part of the castle stood shadowed against the twilit sky. To the right, toward a jetty that extended into the water, the castle fell away in ruins. Jack and Caroline could see the fading light through arches and blind windows. As they drove in a long curve around the lake toward the castle, they skirted stone arches that looked like a miniature Roman aqueduct, bearded with ivy, flanked by dead trees. To the left, on a barren rise, a doe stood as still as a stencil. A wild turkey exploded from the underbrush, looking prehistoric, unlike the window cutouts Jack remembered from grade school. Somewhere ahead, they heard the *chuck-chuck-chuck* followed by an odd sound, almost like someone playing a musical saw, a mechanical noise on the verge of human speech, of some kind of woodpecker.

"I can't believe this is where Robert goes home every night," Caroline said.

"You ever spend time with him outside of work?" Jack said. "Yeah, I can believe he lives here." Jack looked around, nearly a three-sixty turn, and said, "A storm's been coming all week. We should be visiting here in thunder and lightning."

They swung into a graveled drive that circled a huge stone wishing well decorated with chipped satyrs and nymphs. The castle loomed above them. Neither immediately opened the car doors.

"I thought his family still had money," Jack said.

"That doesn't mean they'd spend it," Caroline said. "You know what it would cost to keep up this pile?"

"As much as it costs your uncle to keep up Tabletops," Jack said.

3

As they walked up the crumbling steps to the cathedral-size front doors, Jack said, "Ever since I was a kid, I've liked places like this. Too many Vincent Price movies."

"Vincent who?" Caroline asked.

The huge doors were unlocked.

"Why not?" Jack asked about the unlocked doors. "Who'd come here uninvited?"

"We did," Caroline said.

The door creaked.

"Inner Sanctum," Jack said in a Boris Karloff voice; and, before Caroline could ask him what *Inner Sanctum* was, Jack added, "Prehistory. Don't worry about it."

The central hall was stacked like a warehouse with moldy furniture: chairs with torn brocade; a bureau with a clouded and cracked mirror; two refectory tables, one upside down on the other like a mirror image; a forest of standing lamps; a rolled oriental rug, which, furred with dust, looked like a huge cocoon. Naked marble gods and goddesses with hairless pudenda stood like giant chess pieces randomly in the hall, gleaming in the dusty light from high smudged windows. A half-open steamer trunk revealed mildewed drawers. A grand divided staircase rose in front of them, leading to a balcony that ran around the second floor—a second floor thirty feet above the ground floor. The walls were covered in faded green cloth with darker patches where pictures had been removed.

"Hello?" Jack called. "Robert?"

His voice was swallowed by the vast space.

Hesitantly, they wandered through sliding double doors into a library, which smelled like old dog. Floor-to-ceiling bookshelves. Hundreds of books with rotting leather bindings. A mahogany ladder was hooked on to an overhead stained brass bar. Laid out on a long table was a Union uniform: red fez, blue jacket, red pants, New York's Zouaves. A captured Dufilho Confederate officer sword, unsheathed and gleaming, recently polished, lay across the arms of a tall chair at the head of the table. Logs blazed in a fireplace large enough for half a dozen tall men to stand in.

"Robert?" Caroline called. She lowered her voice, "Maybe they're out?"

"Why are you whispering?" Jack asked.

Caroline blushed. Or maybe her cheeks reddened from the fireplace heat.

"Yeah, out," Jack said. "Probably to Wendy's for burgers."

Caroline opened a door in the far wall. Jack followed her into a glass-ceilinged atrium enclosing a scummy half-filled reflecting pool, flanked by twin gargoyle-faced fountains set into the wall. Coppery stains in the gargoyles' mouths made the creatures look as if they had just feasted on flesh and blood. Their eyes were blind. Passing clouds shifted shadows across the room. In the corner, in a yellow-and-blue enameled pot, a dead palm rattled.

"Sounds like bones," Caroline said.

"You think we're scaring the skeleton?" Jack asked.

"Why not?" Caroline said. "They're scaring me."

"I don't see any skeletons," Jack said.

"The whole house," Caroline said, "is a skeleton."

A cracked glass door opened onto a small back parlor filled with oil portraits, surfaces spidery with cracks, stacked against the peeling wallpaper. Facing a window, which looked out onto an unkempt lawn rolling down to the stagnant lake, its back to Jack and Caroline, was a deep rust-colored upholstered wingback chair. An old man's bony elbow perched on one of the chair arms, the cloth of a white linen suit hanging from his gaunt frame.

"I think we found our skeleton," Jack whispered. To the figure in the chair, louder, Jack said, "Mr. Flowers . . ." Slowly, he approached. "Sorry to disturb you, sir. . . ."

Jack came around the chair and stopped, staring at what looked like Keating Flowers' mummified corpse, dressed and positioned as if alive.

"Oh, my God," Caroline cried.

"Looks like he's been dead for years," Jack said.

"Dead?" a voice behind them said. "Resin."

Jack and Caroline turned. Keating Flowers came through the cracked glass door from the room with the reflecting pool. He was dressed just like the resin-work figure and was almost as bony.

"Since I live in such Gothic surroundings," Keating said, "I figure I might as well use the setting to good advantage."

"You have an odd sense of humor, sir," Jack said.

"I can afford to," Keating said.

Jack studied the sculpture and said, "Nice work."

"I studied at the Arts Students League," Keating said. "A long time ago." Keating tilted his head as he studied Jack's bruised face. He asked, "Do you mind if I take a picture?"

Before Jack could respond, Keating took a compact digital camera from his pocket and snapped. Twice.

Jack blinked in the flashes.

"Quite a ruin," Keating said about Jack's face, slipping the camera back into his pocket. "I can use the picture for one of my fright masks."

Jack scooped a spiderweb away from the sculpture's face.

"I know a cheap cleaning woman," he said.

"Jack," Caroline said, putting a restraining hand on his arm.

"Light dusting," Jack said. "Vacuuming. I don't think she does windows."

"Pity," Keating said. "I'd like to let more light in."

"I think you need something more than light," Jack said.

"Light's a good start," Keating said. "Speaking of starts, I'm sorry if my scarecrow gave you one."

"The dead don't scare me," Jack said. "It's the living I find frightening."

"Do I frighten you," Keating asked, "Mr.—?"

"Jack Slidell." Jack held out his hand, which Keating ignored. "And," Jack dropped his hand, "I'm not related to any Slidells you'd know."

"No doubt." Keating turned to Caroline. "My dear?"

"Caroline Wonder." Having seen Keating snub Jack, Caroline did not hold out her hand. But Keating took it and raised it to his dry, cracked lips.

"Charmed," Keating said.

Jack said, "I'm sure you know her family."

"Your friend seems to feel that I'm not being a kind host," Keating said, "a presumption, considering you're both housebreakers."

"The door was unlocked," Jack said.

"Oh," Keating said, "you're standing on the letter of the law."

"The law's not a bad place to perch," Jack said.

"Commonwealth law." Keating was dismissive. "I prefer the law of hospitality. Which I extend to invited guests."

"Why do I think you're reluctant to call the cops?" Jack asked.

"Jack," Caroline said, "we did trespass."

"Forgive me my trespasses—" Jack started.

"As I forgive those," Keating said, "I guess that means you two—who trespass against me."

"We're looking for your son," Caroline said.

"You're welcome to play hide-and-seek with him in this old white elephant," Keating said. "We don't run into each other much in here."

"Family's all anyone's really got," Jack quoted Bix.

"Family is what we have to free ourselves from," Keating said. "I'm a good example of what happens when you don't. Robert, too."

"History's prisoners?" Jack asked.

"From an early age," Keating said, "a family like mine instills in you a powerful Stockholm Syndrome."

"You've got the key," Jack said. "Why don't you let yourself out?"

Keating turned to Caroline and said, "Your rude friend's people must have short memories."

"If you mean," Jack said, "we don't practice ancestor worship, you're right."

"You can't worship what you don't know," Keating said.

"Funny," Jack said, "from Robert's description I assumed you'd be a gentleman."

"I don't feel the least uneasy in your company," Keating said. "A gentleman," he explained, "is comfortable in any company."

"I thought," Jack said, "a gentleman makes any company he's in comfortable."

Keating nodded and turned his back on Jack and Caroline.

"I'll leave you to your pleasure," he said.

After Keating had left the room, Jack nodded toward the resin work. "I think I prefer his scarecrow's company."

"You didn't have to be provocative," Caroline said.

Jack shrugged. "I've got status anxiety."

CHAPTER THIRTEEN

1

"You want to play hide-and-seek with Keating in here?" Jack asked.

"I could use some air," Caroline said. "We can call Robert at his new job tomorrow."

They walked onto a terrace. The fading light came with a breeze and the beginning of a chill. A shadow like a shutter slid across the lake. The air was heavy; the storm was working its way up the coast.

Caroline shivered. Jack took off his sports coat and draped it around Caroline's shoulders. She protested, but, when Jack held it around her, she didn't shrug off his coat—or his arm.

They descended broken stone steps leading to a long arbor, dense with grapevines, heavy with grape clusters. The arbor smelled of wine. The dying sun's horizontal light flickered stroboscopically through the green leaves, casting a netlike shadow on them.

"Do you feel like Adam and Eve being driven out of Paradise?" Caroline asked.

"Some Paradise," Jack said.

"I don't know," Caroline said. "I always figured Paradise would be a little threadbare by now."

"And Robert's creepy dad is God?" Jack asked.

"Well," Caroline said, as they came upon another sculpture, of a ghastly woman, "he's creating a race of resin."

The resin woman was dressed in what looked like a diaphanous skirt, high-collar blouse, and wide-brimmed sun hat trimmed with plastic flowers and spattered with bird droppings. The top half of the face from the bridge of the nose to the lifelike, but dirty, forehead was lovely. Almond eyes seductively half closed. The bottom half of the face, the mouth and the chin, revealed beneath shreds of skinlike resin a grinning skull.

"Jack!" Robert's voice hailed them. "Caroline!"

Robert appeared, backlit, at the far end of the arbor, near where they had parked.

"Dad said he saw you wandering around," Robert said. "I thought, if I came around by your car, I'd head you off at the pass."

Robert was in gray slacks, a white business shirt, and a beige V-neck sweater vest. His carried his suit jacket slung over a shoulder, hooked on a finger.

"Creepy place you got here," Jack said.

Approaching, Robert waggled his head.

"Too much Poe, too early," he said about his father. "You should see the old wine cellar. He's got one of his sculptures half bricked up inside. *My Montresor*, he calls it."

"Hallowe'en must have been a gas," Jack said.

"Is he crazy?" Caroline asked.

"You know how much he gets for his sculptures?" Robert said. "Enough to keep this place the way it was when my grandfather was alive. If he wanted to. Collectors come and see his works in this setting, they pull out their checkbooks and start writing zeros."

"I can write zeros in my checkbook, too," Jack said. "Just can't put any numbers in front of them."

"I was delayed in town," Robert said, "new job and all. So tea'll be a little late today. Daddy likes it at five-thirty."

"I don't think I'm up for playing more games with your father, Robert," Caroline said.

"I'll give you something in the kitchen," Robert said. "The kitchen's right out of *House & Garden*."

"No ghouls?" Caroline asked.

"Or cobwebs," Robert said. "The freak show is all downstairs. In front. The rest of the house, the part we live in, is normal. Well, not exactly normal, but not designed for effect. At least, not on purpose."

"Robert," Jack said, "two nights ago, was your father at the Dutch Village Motel?"

"You'll have to ask him," Robert said. "No, I'm sorry. That came out wrong."

"You didn't like the question?" Caroline asked.

"I don't think you had to ask it," Robert said, looking at Jack. "We were watching TV. I'd TiVo'd *The Kid From Brooklyn*. My dad's a Danny Kaye fan. And I know that makes both of our alibis dependent on each other—except for the pizza boy."

"You have pizza delivered here?" Caroline asked.

"I give big tips," Robert said. "That's my vice. Frank's vices, if he hadn't given in to them, he'd be alive today."

"We know about Jean," Jack said.

"My sister," Robert said, "half sister, shouldn't have been in the room with Frank. Ever since Jean was a child, she's gotten into scrapes. That's what Daddy used to say. *Jean's in another scrape.* But whatever trouble she was in, Daddy always got her out."

"Does *Daddy* know she's dead?" Jack asked.

"He knows she's dead," Robert said. "Neither of us is wearing crepe. We did that years ago."

"When she started drugs and hooking?" Caroline asked.

"When she started shaking us down for money," Robert said. "Which we would've given her anyway. Gave her. We paid her mother. After she died, we paid Gaynor. For her food, clothing, school. And blackmail. So they wouldn't reveal her connection to our family. Oh, did he forget to mention that?"

"You were afraid Frank would spill the beans?" Jack asked. "That he'd tell everybody Jean was a hooker and a drug addict. And your half sister?"

Wryly, Robert said, "We're a respectable family."

"I can tell that from your happy home here," Jack said. "How'd they meet?"

"At an NA meeting," Robert said. "At least, that's what Frank told me."

"What else did Frank tell you?" Caroline asked.

"I didn't want to know," Robert said. "But Frank needed to, I don't know, get my permission? They both wanted me, us, to know."

"For different reasons," Caroline said.

"Maybe not so different," Robert said.

"*I'm as good as you*," Jack said.

"That's what Jean wanted us to know," Robert said. "And *I'm as bad as Jean*."

"That's what Frank wanted you to know," Jack said.

"Peck's Bad Boy," Robert said. "I guess that's what Frank felt like when he did drugs, hung out with hookers."

"Did he do that a lot?" Caroline asked.

"For all I know Jean was his first time," Robert said. He shrugged and turned to Jack. "You knew him better than anybody. What do you think?"

"Never made Frank for a druggie," Jack said. "He never missed work. Never needed money. Never acted like he had some secret life."

"Until he turned up dead," Robert said.

Caroline asked, "What happened when you found out they were—"

"Keeping company?" Robert gave a thin smile. "Daddy told me, *Jean's in trouble again*," Robert said. "*Help her out*."

"And you did?" Caroline said.

"Helped them both out, huh?" Jack said. "Jean and Frank?"

"I told you," Robert said, "I didn't kill Frank."

"You were watching Danny Kaye, yeah," Jack said.

Robert shot Jack a look.

Jack said, "I'm naturally suspicious, I guess."

"Of me?"

"Why not?"

"We're friends."

"When they found Frank, when I was the cops' Top of the Pops, you didn't come forward."

"My father's spent two decades hiding our relationship to Jean. I had to choose."

"Family won out, huh?" Jack said. "I can understand that."

"I haven't murdered anyone recently, Jack," Robert said. "Not even the motel clerk. If you don't believe me, why don't you give your detective pal a call."

"I was wondering why the cops hadn't contacted Jean's father," Jack said.

"Stepfather," Caroline corrected him.

"My father contributes to the Patrolmen's Benevolent Fund," Robert said.

"And helps out useful politicians?" Jack asked.

"The police apparently think it's just a case of a hooker and a junkie running into some bad drugs," Robert said.

"And Frank beat Jean up when he realized he'd snorted a hot toot?" Jack said. "As he was dying?"

"I went to Jean after work," Robert said.

"That night?" Caroline asked.

Robert nodded and said, "That night. To give her money. What she really wanted was to get what's in the trust Daddy'd set up for her. She got the income from it. Spent it. She's gone through a lot of money in the past few years."

"Did you know she was meeting Frank?" Caroline asked.

"She bragged about it," Robert said.

"How much did you give her?" Caroline asked.

"A couple, three hundred," Robert said. "But it wasn't the money. Jean liked selling herself."

"Especially," Jack said, "if she could let you know about it."

"Was she with anyone?" Caroline asked.

"Her room," Robert said, "Galvin Avenue. Number thirty-seven, second floor back. Bathroom in the hall. A curtained alcove for a closet. I didn't look under the bed, but I'm pretty sure she was alone."

"Thanks," Jack said.

"Maybe she was meeting someone," Robert said.

"Before Frank?" Caroline asked.

"As I was pulling away from the house," Robert said, "a car was about to turn the corner. I flashed my high beams. You know, what truckers do.

To let him know I'd wait. He could turn first. He flashed back. So I started across the intersection, and the son of a bitch hit his accelerator. He almost broadsided me. In the rearview, I saw him park in front of Jean's building and go in. . . ."

2

Galvin Avenue, thirty-seven, was a mustard yellow-painted red-brick Federal-style house, two stories, with a half third floor, featuring a row of eyebrow windows. Most of the windows were flanked with broken green shutters. Two stone steps led up to the front door, whose broken glass had been replaced by a cracked plywood panel. The red and-blue colored glass fanlight above the door was, surprisingly, unbroken. The building looked more like a small factory than the ruins of the elegant home it had been a century ago. A tree with gnarled branches had covered the front yard with rotting apples. In the streetlamp light, the orange-brown mash spotted with fresher red and yellow fruit looked like an oriental carpet.

Jack and Caroline got out his car into the light rain spattering the street.

The breeze was brisker. Colder. Beyond the rooftops, the scudding clouds revealed Jupiter, bright and low in the southern sky. The storm kept coming.

"Why don't you wait in the car?" Jack told Caroline.

"Afraid I'll get hurt?" Caroline said.

"Afraid you'll get in the way," Jack said.

"Romantic bastard," Caroline muttered, following Jack up the walk through the apple mess.

The front door opened into a urine-stinking hallway with broken metal mailboxes. Some of the box doors were peeled up, curling tongues. The ground floor had two apartments. The door of the one to the left was decorated with old Christmas lights and a soiled cloth Santa raising a happy right hand in greeting. As they passed, they triggered a mechanical *ho-ho-ho.* The other ground floor apartment was at the end of a long, dark hall. That door was decorated with an eighth-inch steel plate.

Jack and Caroline climbed the stairs to the second floor, where there were three apartments. One in the front. With a cracked wooden top panel. Through which Jack caught a glimpse of a skinny man in boxers facing away from the door and rummaging in a bureau drawer. The door halfway down the hallway, which on this floor was dimly illuminated by a sixty-watt bulb dangling on a plain wire, was newly painted a bright yellow.

They stopped at the apartment, second floor back. Jean's apartment.

The door had been kicked in and hung open, dangling from the top hinge. The bottom hinge lay in the doorway, one screw still in a hole. The other two screws were scattered somewhere. Not in evidence.

"No police tape," Jack noted.

"Robert's right," Jack said. "The cops aren't knocking themselves out on this one."

On the wall inside the apartment door, Jack felt for a light switch, flicked it on.

Jack expected Jean's room to be bare.

When he was in college, his junior year, he'd stumbled into an affair with an older woman, twenty-four, three years his senior. She had returned to school to get her BA, and her husband, an ex-Marine, was working in Washington, D.C. Her bra unsnapped in the front, very sophisticated, Jack thought. The morning after their first night together, Jack opened the refrigerator, he found nothing but one half-empty pint of milk.

"Whores have empty refrigerators," the woman said.

Jean, though messy, had tried to make her room comfortable. On one wall she'd hung a multicolored Indian fabric with dozens of tiny mirrors, which glinted in the light. A blue-and-rose scarf hung over a lamp. The window shades were stained and torn, but they were half hidden by new white-lace curtains. The new, white, Walmart chenille spread, rumpled and half off the bed, was already coming apart in places. The unraveling threads made the spread look as if it were covered with milkweed seeds. Beside the bed, on the floor, next to a pillow, lay a large stuffed dog and two smaller stuffed animals, a bear and a monkey.

The bureau drawers were pulled out and dumped. Sweaters and blouses, panties and bras and G-strings, socks and slacks and shorts. The wastebasket had been upended; a crumpled toilet paper wrapper, some balled-up paper towels, a rolled copy of *Cosmopolitan*, a tampon carefully folded into a tissue . . .

"The place has been tossed," Jack said.

Covering his hand with his handkerchief, he rummaged through the cupboards over the sink and stove.

Chipped cups, glasses and plates. A half-empty box of Cap'n Crunch—which somebody had pawed through. Peanut butter, grape jelly—which had also been examined. Kid's food.

A half-size refrigerator sat on the floor, supporting a small TV. The cable was connected. Still covering his hand with the handkerchief, Jack turned the TV on. It worked.

Jack found the remote and, using the handkerchief, ran up and down the channels.

"HBO," Jack said. "She sprang for premium service."

"No bills," Caroline said. "No check book. No personal papers of any kind."

Behind the scattered dirty laundry pushed under the bureau, Caroline found a plastic bracelet with Jean's name on it, a number, some other codes. The kind worn in a hospital.

"This can't be from after her beating," she said, handing it to Jack. "She never came back here."

Before he even read the markings, Jack recognized the typeface, the look, of the bracelet.

"Berkshire Medical," Jack said, examining it. "Whatever was wrong with her, she needed more than a Samaritan could give her."

3

"AIDS?" Jack asked. He was driving Caroline's car, heading to the Berkshire Medical Center in Pittsfield, Massachusetts. The rain was now coming down hard, drops ricocheting off the windshield like bullets. "Hepatitis?"

"Maybe she went in to detox?" Caroline said.

Jack let that sit.

After a long silence, Caroline glanced at him. Glanced away.

"Were you ever married?" she asked.

Jack kept his eyes on the road.

"It was a big mystery around the office," she said.

Jack cranked up the defogger.

"You had quite a fan club," she said. "They wanted to know."

After another long silence, Jack asked, "You?"

"You want to know was I ever married?" Caroline said. "But you're going to remain a man of mystery?"

"Fifteen years," Jack said, fiddling with the windshield wiper. "Right out of college. Off and on a commune. It was the Sixties. One kid. Not with my wife. She never knew. I never saw the kid. One night after a party, I couldn't sleep. Got up to pee. Realized my wife was crying. I moved out the next day."

They drove a mile in silence.

"I'm leaving a lot out," Jack said.

Another mile. The windshield wipers did their dance. Rain rattled on the car roof. They passed an abandoned industrial site: *Half-Moon Naptha and Petroleum*. Jack looked at Caroline: Had she been married? But Caroline didn't say anything.

"Maybe you haven't had a chance to be disappointed yet," Jack said.

CHAPTER FOURTEEN

1

The clerk in the intake office at the Berkshire Medical Center said, "I don't know if I can give you that information."

She was tall, rangy, with hair the unnatural red of supermarket beef. Her skin looked like hide, tough; she must have spent her childhood in the sun. She wore a blue sweater draped over her shoulders, held in front by a gold-colored chain. She frowned, unhappy not to be able to accommodate them.

"Can you at least tell us the name of the doctor who treated her?" Caroline asked.

Rain dripped from Caroline's hair, which was plastered to her face; from her chin, from her elbows. Her blouse and sweater, sopped, clung to her. So did her slacks. Jack admired the outline of her ass.

"I'm a lawyer," Caroline explained. "It's germane to a case I'm handling."

"I think you need something from the courts," the clerk said.

"It involves a murder," Caroline said.

"Then, the police, too," the clerk said. "I guess."

Jack had told Caroline he'd hang back, figuring she came across as more respectable, more trustworthy than he did.

"You think?" she had asked.

"It's your face," Jack had said. "The bone structure."

Caroline had put her hands on Jack's cheeks and had turned his head so he was staring at himself in the car's rearview mirror. They were parked in the hospital lot next to the Emergency Room. Outside, the rain swept across the asphalt in what under the sodium lamps looked like mica sheets.

"That face," Caroline said, forcing Jack to look at himself. "How could you not trust it?"

"I don't trust it," Jack said. "And I've been looking at it all my life."

Gently, he detached Caroline's hands from his face, not releasing them, holding them lightly in his upturned palms.

"When I was ten," he said, "maybe I trusted it then. But since puberty, no way."

"I trust it."

"That's news."

She nodded and said, "A recent development."

"I don't trust recent developments," Jack said. "Not in my emotional landscape."

"What's your emotional landscape look like?"

"Andros Island," Jack said. "In the Caribbean."

Puzzled, Caroline knit her brows. The three vertical lines forming between her eyes made it look as if someone had tugged a string on a sachet, furrowing the cloth.

"Mangrove swamp and clay," Jack said. "A few palmettos. Nothing can live on it. At least, not on the west side. I went there on vacation once."

"And my emotional landscape?" Caroline asked.

"Very green," Jack said. "An arbor. Covered with baby-blue trumpet flowers."

"A secret garden?" she asked.

"I saw it through a hole in your hedge."

"You've got a dirty mind," Caroline said, reaching for the door handle.

The rain slapped the sides of the car.

"Just like getting out in a car wash," Jack said. "Ready?"

Caroline nodded.

They opened their doors at the same time and ducked into the downpour.

2

Once the intake clerk had turned them down, Jack and Caroline ran back out into the rain, slammed into the car, and drove around to the hospital's main entrance. Again, dripping, clammy, their clothes sticking to them, they entered the hospital.

"Do you have a towel?" Jack asked a guard, who was so bony it looked as if he had a wire hanger inside his square-badge jacket. "My wife," Jack gestured at Caroline, who looked like a wet cat. Rain puddled where she stood. "She got a call, her uncle Monroe, they brought him in about an hour ago. Monroe Ruggerio?"

"I just got back from my break," the guard said. When his mouth was closed, his large teeth under his upper lip made his face look like a death's-head. As if someone had pulled thin rubber over the bone. He poked his thumb over his shoulder. "The ladies' room is down the hall. Around the corner. First door on the right."

"Honey," Jack took Caroline in his arms. Their clothes squished, drizzling between their bodies. "Why don't you dry off? I'll see what I can find out about Uncle Monroe."

Jack kissed Caroline on the lips, which tasted fresh. Rainwashed. Surprised, she opened her eyes wide, then relaxed, and stuck the tip of her tongue into Jack's mouth.

Jack watched her sway down the hall, leaving damp footprints.

"Men's room?" Jack asked the guard.

"Across from the ladies'," the guard said.

Jack caught up to Caroline around the corner, out of sight of the guard, and grabbed two towels from a supply cart. He tossed one to her, wiped his face, ruffled his hair.

"What's with the tongue?" Jack asked.

"Did it give you a thrill?" Caroline said.

From the cart, he took a white medical smock, which he slipped on.

"Upstairs," Jack said. "Find an empty room. Make a scene. *Where's my uncle?*"

"Uncle Monroe Ruggerio." Caroline smiled.

From her pocketbook, she took a comb, ran it through her hair, and handed it to Jack, who also combed his hair. Then, ducking into a dark room where two patients were sleeping, Jack grabbed a clipboard from the bottom of a bed.

"What if there's an emergency?" Caroline asked, nodding at the sleeping patient, whose chart Jack had stolen.

"There is an emergency," Jack said. "Two people have been murdered."

3

In the elevator, Caroline held her forefinger over the panel and gave a questioning look at Jack, who shrugged. Randomly, Caroline hit a button: the third floor. The elevator door slid closed.

The third floor was quiet. The neon lights under their marcelled ceiling panels buzzed. At the nurses' station, a woman with close-cropped blond hair, sitting at a computer, glanced at Jack and Caroline, both in their medical smocks, Jack holding a patient's chart.

"Rubinstein?" Jack asked.

"Not on this floor," the nurse said and went back to the computer.

"Third," Jack said.

"Not here," the nurse said.

Another nurse, a man rubbing his face, was going into the nearby break room. At the end of the hall to the left, a custodian was polishing the floor with an electric hum. Jack smelled the wax.

The hall to the right was empty.

Jack walk up to the nurses' station, tapping the chart he held.

"R-u-b-i-n-s-t-e-i-n," Jack spelled the name.

"I know how to spell it," the nurse said, concentrating on her typing. The more insistent Jack was, the more the nurse ignored him. "He's not on this floor."

"She," Jack said. "Sadie. Sadie Rubinstein."

Caroline walked down the hall to the right.

"I can't help you," the nurse said, not looking up.

"Could you check what floor she's on?" Jack asked. "They told me third."

The nurse sighed, typed, looked, typed again.

"No Rubinstein Sadie," she said.

Jack flipped through some pages on the clipboard.

"Find her records, would you please? She's got to be somewhere."

Again sighing, the nurse again typed, again looked, again typed.

"No record of Rubinstein Sadie," she said.

Which is when the nurse heard Caroline's scream.

Leaving the computer on the patient records file, the nurse jumped up and ran down the left-hand hallway, almost colliding with the nurse running from the break room.

"Uncle Monroe!" Caroline cried at the end of the hall. "Where's my uncle?"

Jack glanced at the custodian, who ignored everything, moving the polishing machine in circles across the right-hand hallway floor.

He slipped around the counter of the nurses' station and quickly typed in Jean Gaynor's name.

CHAPTER FIFTEEN

1

Caroline's car stalled half a dozen miles from Mycenae. Two miles from the closest house, they hit a puddle deep enough to swamp them.

"Just as well," Jack said. "Can't see anything in this rain anyway."

. . . missed Houston but ravaged the Beaumont-Port Arthur area in southeastern Texas yesterday, blowing down trees, knocking out power and interrupting refinery operations. The storm hit shore—

Jack cut the engine, turning off the radio.

Now that the car wasn't moving, plowing through the rain as if parting billowing curtains, the wipers were useless.

"If you get chilly," Jack said, "I'll turn on the motor. Turn on the heat."

During the forty minutes they'd driven from the Berkshire Medical Center, they had both dried a little in the blowing heat from the vents.

For the first half hour out of Pittsfield, they had discussed what Jack had found on the computer: Jean Gaynor had checked into the Emergency Room complaining of headaches, muscle aches, fatigue, dizziness, ringing in the ears, irregular menstruation, irregular heartbeat, hallucinations, difficulty in concentration.

"She was a drug addict," Caroline said.

"That's what the doctor who looked at her figured," Jack said, leaning forward and peering as he plowed through the rain, going no faster than ten miles an hour.

"A lot of symptoms," Caroline said, also peering through the windshield. "There's a stop sign. So many symptoms," Caroline continued.

"She said it started when she moved," Jack said.

"To the place that was searched?" Caroline asked.

"Another address." Jack handed her a slip of paper from the hospital. On it he had scrawled: *17-41 Rostyn.*

"Mycenae?"

Jack nodded.

"Where she was living when she went to the Emergency Room. At least, it was the address she gave. Said about three months after she moved there, she started feeling sick."

"So she moved out."

"To Galvin Avenue."

"Because she thought the place"—Caroline looked at the piece of paper again—"17-41 Rostyn was making her sick."

"That," Jack said as he hit the puddle that stalled them, "and the ghosts."

2

About three in the morning, the rain let up.

"Hey, Five Spot," he said gently. "Time to wake up."

Caroline blinked. Turned her head, gazed at Jack.

"I'm the guy who's driving," Jack said. "Remember?"

"I fell asleep," Caroline said.

Ahead, the setting moon hung close to the horizon. Jack's window was open. The air smelled of soil, manure, cinnamon. The wet road hissed under their tires.

Before Caroline fell asleep, the rain drumming on the car roof, Jack had told her about the notation at the end of Jean's hospital record: Along with physical symptoms, Jean had complained about seeing a ghost. A little girl bouncing on a bed and running through the halls of 17-41 Rostyn.

"Coke hallucinations?" Caroline asked.

"The doctor wasn't about to get out a Ouija board," Jack said. "Wasn't about to do any more tests once he realized how much blow, God-knows-whatever stuff, Jean was doing. A real humanitarian."

3

At Caroline's, dried off, the smell of fresh coffee from the kitchen, Jack watched while Caroline searched for Jean's symptoms on the Internet.

Caroline wore a blue terry cloth robe. Her hair was pinned up with a big red plastic clip.

"It sounds like she had serious neurological damage," Caroline said.

"Drugs'll do that," Jack said.

Caroline printed out the research. Each page crisply slid from her printer. Jack could smell the hot ink and paper.

"I was married," Caroline said, belatedly answering Jack's question from the car.

She collected the pages from the printer, not looking at Jack.

"For three years," Caroline said. "Until two years ago."

Jack sipped his coffee. It burned his lips. But he kept sipping.

"I still see him," Caroline said. "Occasionally."

"Do you still make love?" Jack asked.

"That's the question you want to ask?" Caroline said. "That's the question?"

Jack sipped the scalding coffee.

"Why do you want to know?" she asked. "You've got no reason to ask something like that."

As Jack stared at her over his coffee cup, the steam from the hot coffee made his eyes water.

"I was infertile," Caroline said. "Well, not at first. A tubal pregnancy. Four months. Sixteen weeks. How could I not know? But I didn't. I always was irregular. I always had lots of cramps. Lots of cramps. The tube burst. Internal bleeding. Very messy situation. The doctors took everything. Hollowed me out."

"That's why you left him?" Jack asked.

"He left me," Caroline said. "I needed time and assumed he'd under-stand. He didn't."

Jack sipped his coffee.

"I've had seven lovers," she abruptly said.

"Like Snow White?"

"Most were taller than five feet."

"Go figure," Jack said.

Part Two

CARO'LINE

CHAPTER SIXTEEN

1

Outside, Jack walked toward the river. The sky was clear. The stars bright as pain.

Twenty years earlier, Jack met a woman with hair as red as fox fur and luminous green eyes that rarely blinked. She had freckled breasts. Pale skin. And long, almost prehensile toes, which she used to pick up dropped hair bands, quarters, socks. Penny Robartes.

"Find a Penny, pick it up," Penny said to Jack after they made love for the first time, "and all the day you'll have good luck."

A month after they met, they moved into a farmhouse in Vermont. South of Brattleboro. A broken-down two-story building with peeling 1950s wallpaper—large yellow and red and white blossoms in the dining room; a repeating blue-and-white design of pagodas that looked like electric towers in the living room; Jack and Jill with their water pails walking up and tumbling down a green hill, a pattern of repeated failure, in the bedroom.

On the second day after they took possession of the house, they hired a local handyman to mow the backyard and weed the overgrown gardens. The handyman arrived as the sun was rising. When he started work his breath in the chill billowed from his steam-engine mouth as he mechanically moved through the yard, ripping out weeds, hacking away roots. By midmorning, beads of sweat riveted his forehead. At two, he'd come to the front door; and, having lost his larynx to cancer, he'd hold a device to his throat and ask, robot voiced, for his wages.

Penny owned a mutt, Sweetie Pie, who was a crotch dog. To keep him from burying his snout between her legs in the morning—they slept on a mattress on the floor of a bedroom with a bricked-up fireplace—Penny would strip off her panties and throw them to the dog.

A week after the handyman had started working for them, Penny stripped off her panties as usual and wandered through the house look-ing for her pet. Figuring the dog had gone out, Penny stood, naked in the kitchen doorway, left hand holding open the screen, right hand waving her panties, as she called, "Sweetie Pie? Oh, Sweetie Pie, come and get it."

From the flower bed in the backyard, the handyman watched Penny calling and waving her panties—"Oh, Sweetie Pie, come and get it . . ."—and came around to the front door where, holding the device to his throat, he told Jack, "Your girlfriend needs help. I quit!"

When, after a year, Penny left him, Jack vowed he would never fall in love again.

And he didn't.

Until that night he left Caroline.

2

The revolving police car light flickered on Jack's face red, blue, red . . .

"What's it this time, Al?" Jack asked. "I drop a Mounds wrapper back there or something?"

"Or something," Sciortino said, leaning across the passenger side through the open window. "Want a lift?"

"Is *no* an option?" Jack asked.

Sciortino's face was in shadow. A strip of light illuminated his eyes like a mask. His pupils were big. He blinked.

"Not tonight, pal," Sciortino said.

The police car door handle was so cold Jack felt a ping in his right wrist. As he slid into the car, he rubbed his hands together.

"This official?" Jack asked.

"Are you in cuffs?"

"So unofficially what's up?"

"Seems to me, Jack, you've got enough on your plate. What the hell you doing back at the buffet?"

"Who's talking to me?"

"Okay, so I'm a ventriloquist. A medium. Channeling people who don't like you for starters. And can hurt you bad."

"And you want—"

"To make sure you stay on the right side of the tracks."

"Al, you know, that's not where I feel comfortable."

"Next time I see you—"

"It'll be official?" Jack asked.

"It won't be polite," Sciortino said.

Jack opened the door.

"I appreciate the warning," he said.

"Be smart," Sciortino said.

The sound of the slamming car door was hollow in the cold night.

Sciortino watched until Jack turned down toward the Hudson.

"Fuck me," he said and slowly drove away.

3

Jack's house creaked in the wind. Through the cracked window opposite the foot of his bed, Jack watched the sky change from black to gray to purple to streaky red. He heard an owl hoot. In the distance, a truck downshifted. The damp morning air held a whiff of skunk.

Dragging the quilt off the bed and pulling it around his shoulders like a cloak, Jack, feet arching from the cold of the bare wood floor, walked across the room to the window and gazed out at the mist rising from the damp earth.

Through the cracked window, almost motionless in the rising mist, Jack saw two rabbits fucking.

One rabbit hunched over the other, which made spasmodic motions.

The rabbit on top had its teeth fastened to the back of the bottom rabbit's neck. Like cats. When they fuck.

With a shiver of revulsion, Jack realized he wasn't watching two rabbits fucking.

He was watching a weasel killing a rabbit.

CHAPTER SEVENTEEN

1

Jack parked in front of the lodge at Hague Fish & Game.

The hall smelled of freshly waxed floors. Stale popcorn, rancid butter. The grain of the knotty pine walls made swirls: galaxies, cyclones. . . . The room was filled with hunting trophies—a red fox with reflecting glass eyes posed on a birch log; the head of a six-point whitetail over the stone fireplace; a feral hog, its flat snout looking like industrial tubing; a huge walleye on a plaque; two raccoons; a bobcat snarling.

Guns and bows were hung on the wall to the right of the entrance. A couple of old couches and easy chairs faced the big flat-screen TV next to the fireplace. In front of the couch, on a coffee table made of a huge spool for electric power cables, were gun, hunting, and fishing magazines. A couple of old *National Geographics*. Some out-of-date Albany and local newspapers.

Weaver—a retired Sears appliance salesman; Jack couldn't remember his first name—was getting himself a cup of coffee from the stainless steel twenty-cup urn on the bar counter.

"I'm looking for my brother," Jack said.

Weaver nodded at the urn. "Help yourself, Jackie."

"I'm okay, Ned." Weaver's name came to Jack.

"Bix's on the trail," Weaver said, "fixing up the targets. Likes to keep them trim."

Jack nodded and left the lodge.

2

Jack walked up one of the trails behind the lodge. Here and there, leaves had begun to turn, yellow or tipped with red. To the left and right of the trail, deep into the woods, half hidden—if you didn't know to look, you might miss them—were life-size targets of rabbits, bobcat, bear, squirrels, deer, a curious wolf, halfway up a tree a porcupine. . . . A few of them, newly touched up by Bix, looked glossy. The air midtrail was touched with paint and turpentine.

Jack whistled two notes, high and low, their childhood signal.

From somewhere ahead, Bix whistled back. He emerged from a stand of pines, carrying in each hand three paint cans by their wire handles. One of the cans, empty of paint, held a quiver of paint brushes.

"You look like hell, baby brother," Bix said.

"I keep running into things," Jack said.

"Maybe instead of running into things you should be running away from things."

Side by side, they walked back up the path toward the lodge. Sunlight through the branches dappled their heads, shoulders. Over their heads came the metal-on-metal *whan-whan-whan* of a nuthatch, which seemed to keep pace with them, the call sometimes behind, sometimes ahead. A snake rippled out of the dappled path. Jack heard it whisper away into the underbrush to their right.

"Tell me what you need," Bix said.

"I need backup," Jack said.

"Over lunch," Bix said, "you tell me what kind of trouble you got in since I saw you the other night, okay?"

On the way to the Chief Taghanick Diner, at the intersection of Routes 203 and 66, Jack blinked his lights at a car heading the other way, which was about to make a left turn in front of Jack's car.

"What're you doing, Jackie?" Bix asked.

"Letting him"—indicating the turning car—"know to go first," Jack said.

"Where you been, kid?" Bix asked. "Can't do that anymore. We got Pakis up here now. You flash your light at them, they think you mean *you try to cross in front of me, you son of a bitch, I'll ram you, kill you, your family, anyone in your car.*"

"*As I was pulling away from the house,*" Robert had said, "*a car was about to turn the corner. I flashed my high beams. You know, what truckers do. To let him know I'd wait. He could turn first. He flashed back. So I started across the intersection, and the son of a bitch hit his accelerator. He almost broadsided me. In the rearview, I saw him park in front of Jean's building and go in. . . .*"

"Pakis," Bix said. "Crazy SOBs. We can't even drive like we used to."

"Let me give you a rain check on lunch," Jack told Bix. "I think I'm going to find something I've been looking for in our local Paki community. . . ."

3

The half a dozen Pakistani families in Mycenae lived together in a derelict 1950s motel off Route 9G, halfway to Kingston. Four generations, uncles and aunts, cousins, about fifty people all together, spread out in thirty-some rooms on the two floors of the old L-shaped building. In places the green stucco had flaked away from the concrete blocks beneath. The shadow of the second-floor balcony angled across the first floor façade. The empty pool had a scarlike crack in the bluish concrete. Old cars and trucks filled the parking lot. The motel office had collapsed in the middle as if a giant had stepped on it. The broken neon sign tilted, the arrow that used to point toward the rooms now aimed up past the electrical power lines at the sky.

"It's haunted, you know," said Kipp, the young Pakistani, who seemed to be the clan spokesman, a tall man with a neat mustache in a peach-colored V-neck sweater and chinos. "By the ghost of a little girl. Six, seven. In jeans and a T-shirt. Once, twice a week, she roller-skates down the halls, singing *Hound Dog,* you know the Elvis song."

In a sweet tenor, standing in the parking lot, one hand on the top of the chain-link fence around the ruined pool, Kipp sang the song's opening. Various relatives watched from the balcony. When he finished, they clapped. He mock bowed, right, left.

"The ghost got a better voice than me," Kipp said. "But loud. She wakes people up. Ever since we moved in last June. No one gets any sleep. Pain in the ass."

Jack showed Kipp the photo of Jean from the local newspaper clip about her death.

"I seen her," Kipp said. "With my nephew, Hussein, we call him Stickman. 'Cause he's so thin, you know. 'Cause he does so much drugs. He only comes home when he runs out of money. He only runs out of money when he's too strung out to rob some 7-Eleven. I say, Why you robbing 7-Elevens? Boy's crazy. He'll get caught. He'll want my help. Not me. I won't lift this finger. Petty larceny. I read the law books. Take night courses at Hudson Valley Community College. My family needs a lawyer. This country, every family needs a lawyer. Lawyer, doctor, teacher. And someone to slap the kids back in line. My brother, he's a big guy, tried to slap Stickman back in line. That's when he leaves. Good. What this family don't need is a thief."

"I want to talk to him," Jack said. "About this girl."

"This dead one?" Kipp said. "You think he can tell you how she died?"

"It's a shot," Jack said. "Someone may have seen him at her house just before."

Kipp shrugged.

"Try the auto body out on Horatio," he said, meaning Horatio Seymour Avenue.

"Seed's?" Jack asked. "He works there?"

"He sleeps in the junkers," Kipp said. "You see him, don't tell him we talked."

1

Seed's Autobody was hidden behind a seven-foot-high corrugated and galvanized fence, two blocks long and one block wide. Bucky Seed, the grandson of the original owner, was in his seventies, a spry, wiry bantamweight with faded tattoos covering both arms. Every day, he scavenged in the municipal trash cans. If you had an old box spring or refrigerator the town garbage collector wouldn't pick up, Bucky would load it on his pickup for anywhere from five to fifteen dollars and add it to his collection. The lot, which under Bucky's grandfather and father had been a garage and auto body shop, was now a junkyard. Behind the old garage, which hadn't been used for that purpose for thirty years, since Bucky's dad died, was a collection of old cars, motors shot, shattered windows, floors rusted out.

For a few years in the early eighties when Bucky, never married, inherited the place, he held nightly games of Magick, a sword-and-sorcery card game, which attracted the area's oddball teenagers, who, walking to the lot in their inevitable ankle-length coats, looked like big, ambulatory bats. The second time kids were busted for smoking dope at his place Bucky disbanded the games, which parents had objected to, assuming more than cards and marijuana were involved in Bucky's nights. No one ever proved anything, but the place developed a creepy reputation. Because Bucky never sold anything except the occasional cannibalized Seventies Datsun headlight, no one understood how he made a living. His expenses were minimal: He lived in the old shop, ate canned tuna—there were bins of dirty empty tuna cans behind the shop—and drank jug wine. But he always had money to gas up his truck. And once a week he frequented one of the Columbiaville Street whorehouses, where, rumor had it, he didn't fuck, but bathed.

Every two or three years, his neighbors signed petitions and tried to close him down. On his galvanized fence, he'd painted an American flag. With only forty-eight stars. Below the sloppily painted *Save Local Businesses—Fight Prop. 65*, was the recently added *Save Seed's Autobody— Authentic Historic Mycenae Landmark.*

Two Dobermans prowled the yard, but they had never attacked anyone, not even the kids who slipped past the fence to tease and torment Bucky. The new generation, if they played games like Magick, did it on the Internet.

Occasionally, if for example the kids were setting off cherry bombs, Bucky ran out of the shop, sometimes in his boxers, occasionally in pajama bottoms—once, for reasons no one could explain, in scuba gear— firing an old Saturday Night Special into the air.

Jack could easily believe Stickman slept in one of Bucky's junkers.

2

The moon glinted off the household appliances. Behind a row of dishwashers, rank upon rank, stood ovens, washing machines, dryers, refrigerators, top freezers in one line and side freezers in another. Beyond that, fading into the dark, were hot water tanks, radiators and, almost obscured in the shadow of the shop, a row of some large insectlike machinery Jack couldn't identify.

The junkyard smelled of scorched plastic, oil, and dog shit. One of the Dobermans pricked up its ears when Jack slipped through a break in the fence, raised its head to blink at Jack, and then went back to sleep, chin on forelegs. The other Doberman came around a pile of scrap metal, sniffed Jack's shoes, and raised its head for Jack to scratch behind its ears. The dog's breath smelled of tuna fish.

As Jack headed across the lot toward the old cars, Bucky came out of the old shop, dressed in a ratty L.L. Bean nightshirt with a Vermont Country Store nightcap on his head—Salvation Army seconds Jack figured. It was unlikely Bucky would have ordered them new.

"How're you doing, Buck?" Jack asked.

Bucky probably had no idea who Jack was, but Jack wanted to keep the encounter casual.

Especially since Bucky was holding a shotgun.

"Doing okay," Bucky said.

"You mind if I take a look at some of your cars?" Jack asked.

"You always do business this time of night?" Bucky asked.

The shotgun was still aimed at Jack's belly.

"Days get pretty busy," Jack said.

From the shop Jack heard the end of Gene Vincent's old rock-and-roll song "Race with the Devil."

"Golden oldies," Jack said, fixing a smile on his face. "Cruisin' one-oh-one point three on your dial."

Bucky raised the shotgun to Jack's head.

On the radio the The Dell Vikings' "Come Go With Me" started. Jack sang along.

Bucky blinked.

Jack sang.

Bucky lowered the shotgun.

Jack sang.

Bucky started nodding in time.

Jack started doing the Lindy he used to dance in junior high.

Bucky's whole body was moving in time to the music. His nightshirt swayed. The cone of his nightcap flip-flopped.

Jack reached for Bucky's hand.

Bucky dropped the shotgun and, grabbing Jack's hand, jitterbugged with him.

On the radio came the song's claps, catcalls, shouts.

Jack released Bucky's hand and slipped away into the dark toward the junkers.

Bucky sang along with the radio, dancing alone in the junkyard.

The two Dobermans stood, their heads cocked as if baffled at their master twirling under the moon, his white nightshirt and cap making him look like a rock-and-roll ghost.

3

The moon streaked the roofs of the broken-down cars. Jack wandered through the jumble of cars, peering into windows, looking for Stickman or signs of where the boy slept. But all he saw was sprung seats, animal nests, a condom where some teenagers had used a car to fuck.

Could have been Stickman, but Jack doubted it. If the kid was using that much coke, it was unlikely he'd be able to get it up.

And wherever Stickman was sleeping would have, Jack assumed, a blanket, something to indicate more than a brief tryst.

In the distance from the shack, Jack heard Thurston Harris singing "Little Bitty Pretty One."

Jack wondered if Bucky was still dancing. Or prowling after him with the over-under.

Jack tried to ignore the music and listen for footsteps.

Nothing.

He continued his search among the junkers.

In the back of a Nash Rambler, the same era as the rock and roll the radio was playing, Jack found two crumpled Walmart blankets, Day-Glo green and orange, and three blue-striped pillows without pillow cases. The front seat of the car was filled with old beer cans, cartons from Long John Silver's, Wendy's, Burger King, empty Chinese food containers, their wire handles reflecting moonlight through the window. The car smelled rancid: stale grease, human sweat.

The floor of the station wagon was littered with drug paraphernalia: tiny plastic vials with colored caps, empty crack containers; a few broken glass tubes; steel wool; used propane torches.

Outside the car were crusts of dried vomit. Beyond that, but not far beyond, were pools of Stickman's runny shit, stinking and buzzing with blue bottle flies.

No signs, Jack noted, of toilet paper. . . .

It looked as if Stickman had been here recently.

Jack held his hand over his nose and mouth as he circled the car, looking for other signs of the boy. Something that might indicate where Stickman might have gone. About five feet away from the car, Jack saw a sneaker, a worn Nike, lying on its side.

Jack walked toward it and, tripping over something, an overturned orange crate, he brushed his forehead against . . . what? Jack stepped back and glanced up where he saw, foreshortened, one bare purple foot so swollen there were no creases in the skin on the sole, and another foot so swollen it billowed over the edge of the other Nike, swollen calves, also dark-streaked from the blood that had settled to the bottom of the body, pale white thighs dangling from piss-and shit-stained boxer shorts, the left thigh crusted with dried semen. The red and blue veins marbling the bare chest looked like Bucky's tattooed arms, and the skin looked pockmarked, as if some kind of bird had pecked at it.

Jack retched.

He didn't need to look at the face to know it was Stickman.

CHAPTER NINETEEN

1

"So this gal picks up this guy at a bar and takes him home, and, when the guy goes into her bedroom, all he sees are fluffy animals, fluffy animals on the bureau, fluffy animals on the TV, shelves and shelves of fluffy animals. *So what?* The guy thinks. The gal's got great tits, a great ass—fuck the fluffy animals. After they make love, the guy turns to the girl and asks, *So how was I?* And she says, *You can take anything off the bottom shelf.*"

Jack sat on the bumper of a junked Honda Civic watching two patrolmen sip coffee from cardboard cups and trading jokes.

"A doctor tells this guy he's got maybe a day at most to live," the second cop said. "The guy goes home and tells his wife the bad news. She gets all bent out of shape. Weeping, the whole nine. In bed that night, the guy says to his wife, *Honey, since I'm going to die why don't we mess around.* The wife says, *Of course, darling.* And they fuck like crazy. One in the morning, the guy wakes his wife and says, *Honey, since I'm going to die, would you mind if we did it again?* The wife says, *Of course we can, darling.* And again they fuck like crazy. Three in the morning, the guy wakes his wife and says, *I'm sorry to bother you, honey, but since I'm going to die, you mind if we go one more time?* The wife sits up in bed, pissed, and says, *Look, you don't have to wake up in the morning.*"

The police photographer, a gawky kid, tall, just out of Columbia-Greene Community College, moonlighting from the local newspaper, took pictures of Stickman's body, still hanging from the tree branch. The flash lit up the corpse. Its fingertips as fat as balloon animals. The hands swollen, dark from pooled blood. The forearms as big as sausages.

Like Popeye, Jack thought.

The knot of the noose above the bulging Adam's apple forced the dead man's chin up. Lines of saliva from the corners of his mouth down his chin made his jaw look like a ventriloquist dummy's. From his nostrils, which were crusted with cocaine, tracks of bloody mucus gave Stickman what looked like a painted bandito mustache. His open eyes had black rims, more pooled blood, at the bottom. His swollen, congested face had squared off like an Incan idol.

"Looks like one of those Mutant Teenage Turtles," a Crime Scene Unit technician said.

"Those freckles on the face," the County Coroner said to no one in particular. "Punctuate hemorrhages. Tardieu spots. Due to hydrostatic rupture of vessels."

The corpse's tongue, black from dried blood, poked between fat lips as if Stickman were French-kissing Death.

Another photographer's flash lit the face horribly.

"Don't touch the body," Sciortino said to one of the local deputies who had just put his arms around the dead man's legs. To lift the corpse down. "'Til CSU gives you the go ahead."

The deputy opened his arms wide and skipped back, tripping over the orange crate. Which Stickman could have used to stand on when hanging himself.

But he'd lifted the corpse just enough for the rope, which was tied with a simple slip knot, to slide a quarter of an inch up the neck before the dropping body yanked the noose tight again.

"What's the matter with you?" Sciortino asked the deputy, talking around the dead cigar clamped in the side of his mouth. "Never been to a hanging before?"

"I was at that couple," the deputy said, twitching his right shoulder forward pugnaciously, "who hanged themselves with the same rope. Over by Stottville."

Sciortino ignored him and drifted over toward the County Coroner.

When the noose slipped, it revealed a parchment-colored furrow, which had an indented impression of the weave of the rope. As if a worm had burrowed under Stickman's skin.

The breeze slowly turned the dangling body. Another photographer's flash.

And in the flash Jack saw the dead man's chest heave.

"Oh, shit!" Jack said.

Stickman's face twitched. His arms and legs gave a marionette dance.

"Sciortino!" Jack shouted. He had jumped up from the junker he'd been sitting on and, his right hand reaching toward the cop, had taken a step toward the hanging man. "The son of a bitch is alive!"

The coroner looked back over his shoulder.

"Just contractions," he said. "Hey, Jack, what the hell are you doing here?"

"He found the body," Sciortino said. "He keeps finding bodies."

The coroner was walking in a circle around the body, which was slowly twirling in the breeze.

"All you need is eleven pounds to occlude the carotid arteries," he was telling a man from the Sheriff's office, two state troopers and three Mycenae city cops, who looked bored. "Same for the trachea. Eleven pounds. Jugular veins, a little less. Only four-point-four pounds. But vertebral arteries, that's a biggie. Sixty-six pounds."

"Our friend up there got to weigh a hundred-thirty," Sciortino said. "A hundred-forty."

"His weight's enough you mean," the coroner said.

The coroner, part-time in his county job, used to be Jack's doctor. Danny Troubridge. Every time Jack had a check up, Troubridge would ask, "Any VD, Jack?"

"I don't mess around," Jack would say.

"Everyone messes around," Troubridge would say. "One way or another."

2

"Pressure on the neck in the area of the carotid arteries can cause unconsciousness in ten seconds," Troubridge said. "Death is due to compression of the blood vessels of the neck so there's not enough oxygenated blood reaching the brain."

"Autoerotic?" Sciortino asked.

Troubridge shook his head *no*.

"Where are the traces?" Troubridge asked. "Where are the panties? The porno? The fetish gear? The mirror? The lemon in the mouth? No towel under the rope to protect the neck. Maybe he wouldn't have bothered with that though. The semen's nothing. Hanging, autoerotic or not, the guy's going to shoot off. But take a look. The noose, it's a simple noose. No complicated knots. Some of these kids, those Goths, you should see the knots they tie. Real elegant. Like Boy Scouts."

"Yeah," Sciortino said, picking a shred of tobacco from his upper lip. "They get their merit badges in piercing."

"And, see," Troubridge said, "he used . . . it looks like clothesline, plain rope he probably got at Walmart or Ace. Oridinary rope, electric cord, belts—the mark of an amateur suicide."

"Amateur suicide, huh?" Jack said.

"Didn't tie or handcuff himself—," Troubridge said.

"How many times do you have to hang yourself to become a professional?" Jack asked.

"—which people in autoerotic activities sometimes do," Troubridge finished.

"To keep them from changing their minds," Sciortino said, snapping open his Zippo lighter.

"And the knot is in front," Troubridge said.

Sciortino cupped the lighter flame and leaned into it to light his cigar.

"In autoerotic hangings," Troubridge said, "it's usually at the side of the neck. Or the back."

"What're you looking for, Jack?" Sciortino asked.

"Virtually all hangings are suicidal," Troubridge told Jack. "Obstruction of the airway is caused by compression of the trachea or, when the noose is above the larynx, elevation and displacement of the tongue. Because of the small amount of pressure needed to compress carotid arteries, you can hang yourself sitting down. Like this."

Troubridge sat on the bumper of a junker and pulled his necktie above his head. He rolled up his eyes so only the whites showed and lolled out his tongue.

"Beautiful," Sciortino said. "You look deader than our hanged friend."

"Had more practice," Troubridge said.

"Dying?" Jack said.

"Studying the dead," Troubridge said. "Six, seven months back, don't you know, this guy hanged himself from the bedpost while his wife was sleeping in the bed."

Troubridge beamed.

"Hanging's the second or third most popular form of suicide," he said. "Depending on the part of the country."

"What about in Columbia County?" Jack asked.

"Around here," Troubridge said. "It's number one."

"February comes around," Sciortino said, nodding, "and people get stir-crazy."

"Christmas bills come due," Troubridge said.

"Seems like it'll be dark forever," Sciortino said.

"Cold forever," Troubridge said.

"People run out of wood," Sciortino said.

"Or can't afford the oil," Troubridge said.

"Or gas," Sciortino said.

They stood, side-by-side, finishing each other's sentences like a vaudeville team. Mr. Bones and Mr. Interlocuter.

"Friday comes around," Troubridge said, "they check their pay envelope, see how little they made—"

"After they've given the vigorish to the Uncle," Sciortino said.

"They wonder why they're working so hard," Troubridge said. "For what? And—"

Troubridge again grabbed his necktie and yanked it over his head, ghoulishly grinning.

3

"Why're you so interested in maybe the hanging was autoerotic?" Sciortino asked Jack.

"I'm not so interested," Jack said.

Sciortino looked at him. Hard.

"It's just," Jack said, "if it wasn't autoerotic . . ."

"We're done here," one of the Crime Scene Unit technicians said.

"Okay," a state trooper said, "bring him down. Hey, Minutello, leave the knot intact."

"Hmm," Troubridge examined the body. "We got a fracture, don't you know. Of the thyoid cartiledge. The superior horns."

Jack watched Troubridge examine the corpse, which was lying on a gurney.

"Fracture of the neck is rare," Troubridge said. "Only with osteo arthritis, with a sudden drop, or obesity, or old age."

Jack approached the body.

"But his neck *is* fractured," Jack said.

"Ninety hangings," Troubridge said, "I only seen one fracture of the cervical spine. The woman weighed over three-fifty."

"How'd she get up high enough to hang herself?" a trooper asked.

"She looped the rope over the back of the couch and tied it to one of the back legs," Troubridge said, "then rolled off the couch."

"You think someone could've, what, Jack? Knocked out our friend and strung him up?" Sciortino asked. "Any lumps on the head, back of the neck, anywhere someone might've given the guy a whack?" he asked Troubridge. "Any contusions on the arms where someone held him against his will?"

"Not that I can see," Troubridge said, examining the body.

"Or maybe two guys snuck up on him." Sciortino pointed at the body with his cigar. "What do you think, Doc? Two guys maybe hanged this mook?"

Wiping one hand against the other, Troubridge stood. To Jack, he said, "It's virtually impossible for one or two healthy males to hang a third unless he's been beaten unconscious or drugged or drunk."

"Maybe there were three guys," Jack said. "Four."

"Why not five?" Sciortino asked. "A dozen? Maybe the Elks interrupted their monthly meeting and came to the junkyard? Or maybe he was attacked by a biker gang? Or Russian gangsters? Or the Mafia? Or the CIA? They forced him to drink a bottle of Jack Black? Made him snort lots of coke? Want to see what the tox scan says? Seems to me, Jack, your boy was probably always drunk and drugged. We pare his fingernails, look for some killer's DNA? You think we got a budget for that?"

"You're going to close the case, huh?" Jack said.

"Jack," Sciortino said, "it's over, done, finished. The boy hanged himself."

"Why?" Jack asked.

"Who knows?" Sciortino said. "The guy was a fruitcake. Look at the way he was living. A pig."

"And pigs always hang themselves, right?" Jack said. "He suddenly got real disgusted with himself and decided to end it all."

"You think that doesn't happen?" Sciortino said.

Sciortino grabbed Jack's arm and steered him away from the crime scene.

"It ain't murder, Jack," he said. "What the hell're you trying to do?"

"He knew Gaynor," Jack said.

Sciortino stared at Jack.

"Could've given her the drugs that killed Frank," Jack said.

"Could've, would've, should've," Sciortino said. "You want to take that to the DA? Get a true bill on *could've*?"

"It's a big coincidence," Jack said.

"Like someone finds you dead in your car, which accidently runs off

the road some night?" Sciortino said. "You know life is full of coincidences."

"Seems to me—," Jack started.

"Seems to me," Sciortino said, "you're not paying attention."

CHAPTER TWENTY

1

Jack, who made himself scarce after Sciortino's warning, got a flashlight from his car and, after the cops had left, circled back to the crime scene. He played the flashlight on the ground below where Stickman had been hanging, up at the branch where Stickman had tied the rope, and ran the beam along the branch, the light illuminating bark greenish and diamond-patterned, like a snake. When the beam came to the end of the branch, it dropped down the trunk, elongated, a finger of light, as if it were dripping liquid.

Jack aimed the light to the right and left and higher, picking out broken twigs and small branches, where Stickman might have climbed up to tie the rope.

Jack aimed wider and higher.

The area of broken branches extended three, maybe four feet, in each direction.

More than one man would make climbing a tree?

Or damage consistent with one or two men hauling up a third?

No, Jack thought, *I'm building a case. Anyway, if Stickman had been drugged, unconscious, and then hanged by others, only one guy would have to climb the tree and tie the rope. Then, climb down and put the noose around Stickman's neck. . . . No, two men. One to lift Stickman's body and a second to set the noose, then drop the body, fracturing the spine.*

Building a case . . .

"*Could've, would've, should've,*" Sciortino had said. "*You want to take that to the DA? Get a true bill on could've?*"

"It's a big coincidence," Jack repeated aloud and repeated Sciortino's answer:

"Like someone finds you dead in your car, which accidently runs off the road some night?"

"Yeah," Jack said, again out loud, "life *is* full of coincidences."

Like Frank getting together with Jean Gaynor, Jack thought.

2

"Let's say Robert asks Frank to do a favor," Jack said, leaning across the table in a booth at the Mohawk Trail Diner overlooking the river.

"To help Jean?" Caroline said.

"We could look in the court records," Jack said, "the cops must've pulled in Jean plenty of times. Frank puts in the fix."

"And whatever Robert or his father is giving Frank for doing the favor, Jean decides to sweeten the thank-you with sex and drugs," Caroline said. "That could explain how Frank started using."

"But not why somebody would kill Frank," Jack said.

"You're sure the bad coke wasn't an accident?" Caroline asked.

Like someone finds you dead in your car, which accidently runs off the road some night?

"Just a coincidence?" Jack said.

Life is full of coincidences.

"I wouldn't bet on it," he added, gesturing at the passing waitress for a coffee refill.

"You like long odds?" Caroline asked.

"I don't think the odds are all that long," Jack said. "Do you?"

Caroline shook her head *no.*

After the waitress topped off Jack's cup, he tore open a packet and poured sugar into the coffee, stirring.

"Three people are dead," Caroline said, not looking at Jack, who raised his cup and gazed at Caroline over the rim. "You've been attacked."

"Go back through Frank's papers," Jack said. "Whatever's left at the office. Think you can get into his home? Say you're looking for something relating to a case Frank left pending. I'll hit the library, see what I can find about Gaynor's condition. Her neurological condition. Why she went to the hospital."

3

The morning Jack started his research, sheets of rain swept over the façade of the public library, a Beaux Arts building four or five times larger than one would expect in a city the size of Mycaenae. Hunching his shoulders, clutching his turned-up coat collar, Jack ran from his parking spot a half block away from the library, up the library's six stone steps, past two human-size saucer-eyed Chinese guard dogs, baring ancient ceramic fangs, and through the new steel-and-glass doors, into the overheated library foyer, which smelled of damp wool. As Jack entered, the rain stopped and the clouds rolled away.

Jack pushed through double doors into the main room, which was flanked by half a dozen narrow two-story-high cathedral windows. In front of him at the far end of the room, towering over the wooden card catalog that no one used anymore, was a Tiffany window: A woman with shoulder-length auburn hair. Draped in what looked like a bed sheet, falling in peek-a-boo folds over her small bosom, she sat in an arbor. The sudden sun passing across the colored glass made it seem as if the grapes, which in the moving light turned from pale gray to purple, were ripening as Jack watched.

"Start with *Harrison's Principles of Internal Medicine* and Mosby's *Internal Medicine*," said the librarian, a red-faced, red-haired man who looked, Jack thought, like a short-order cook. The sunlight streaming through the windows made the thin red hair on his forearms glow as if they were lightbulb filaments. Each book was eight-and-a-half by eleven, three inches thick, one over two thousand pages, the other just shy of three thousand. Together they weighed twenty pounds.

Jack started with drug addiction—narcotics may suppress the production of endorphins or a craving for narcotics may be caused by a lack of naturally produced endorphins—and worked his way through Jean's symptoms: alcoholism; the causes of headaches from dilation of arteries to inflammation; headaches associated with the eyes or infection or hemorrhage; muscle aches, myalgic states, due to inflammation; systemic infection from Colorado tick fever to glanders (which sounded to Jack like a city in the Netherlands), an initial symptom of rheumatoid arthritis, or, according to *Harrison's*, "In thin, asthenic adults . . . the authors have found it difficult to exclude hysteria or other neurosis or depression," through the rest of the list: dizziness; ringing in the ears; irregular menstruation; irregular heartbeat; hallucinations; and difficulty in concentration. . . .

Each symptom branched out into multiple possible causes. Each cause ramified into other paths to research. Each path led to worlds of pain, misery, and disease. At times, Jack felt like an explorer hacking his way through a dense jungle, where he might find lost tribes or forgotten species. Prehistoric monsters. Insects of monstrous size.

Networks of nerves seemed like spiderwebs. Charts showing spikes of chemicals in the blood seemed like mountain peaks he had to climb. A diagram of "an approach to the evaluation of diarrhea and wasting in AIDS patients" could have been a constellation on a star map. The two ghostly ovals in an illustration of radioactive iodine scanning of the thyroid gland hinted at the wings of fraudulent fairy photographs or ectoplasmic emanations from a nineteenth-century medium. A picture of a "perivenular area with dense collagen (progressive alcoholic fibrosis)" looked pitted like a stretch of dead coral near the seashore on the part of Andros Island Jack had visited.

From *Harrison's* and Mosby's, Jack went on to other standard medical textbooks, working backwards from symptoms to causes like, he felt, Hansel trying to find his way home through a mazy wood where the birds had pecked up the trail of bread crumbs. Headaches behind each eye made Jack feel as if he were absorbing Gaynor's symptoms.

"That's one way to figure out what Gaynor was suffering from," Jack told Caroline at dinner, after his third day in the library. "Become her and look in the mirror."

"Don't be in such a hurry to do firsthand research," Caroline said. "Remember, Jean's dead."

Sitting in the library at a computer terminal, books stacked on either side of the monitor, Jack scanned dozens of journals on line: *The New England Journal of Medicine, JAMA, Morbidity and Mortality Weekly, International Journal of Medical Science, The Canadian Medical Association Journal, Annals of Internal Medicine, Alcohol and Alcoholism, The Lancet, American Family Physician, American Journal of Psychiatry, Journal of Clinical Investigation, Archives of Internal Medicine, Archives of General Psychiatry, Archives of Neurology.*

Half of what Jack read, he didn't understand. Even after leafing back through *Harrison*, other texts, and *Stedman's Medical Dictionary.*

Jack got up and walked toward the stained glass window, hands behind him on his lower back as he stretched and searched the face of the seminaked woman in the shimmering glass grape arbor. His eyes burned.

"I'm not a doctor," Jack told Caroline on Tuesday. "I flunked high school science. What the hell do I think I'm trying to do?"

"Solve three murders," Caroline said.

"One certain murder," Jack said. "Two maybes."

"Probables?"

"Most of the books I'm checking are ten, fifteen years out of date."

Jack gave himself to the end of the week. Then—

"What?" Caroline asked. "You give up?"

"I write off Gaynor's symptoms the same way the doctor at the hospital did," Jack said.

"Why do we even assume whatever's wrong with her can give us a lead?" Jack asked on Thursday night.

"Because otherwise we've got nothing," Caroline said.

"You haven't found anything in Frank's papers?" Jack asked.

"Not yet," she said.

"Diary?" Jack asked. "Date book? Phone book?"

"The police must have all that," Caroline said. "Along with his hard drive, his BlackBerry . . ."

"Safe-deposit boxes?" Jack asked.

"He apparently emptied everything out," she said.

"He must have known—"

"That someone was going to kill him? Why would that make him empty out his safe-deposit boxes—where things would be safe?"

"Maybe he hid things in a safer place."

"Or there's nothing there," she said.

"Or someone else got there first," Jack said.

"Where?" Caroline said.

"His office?" Jack said. "His files? Wherever he hid things?"

"I'm as tired as you are, Jack," Caroline said.

Across the table Caroline's face was lit by the flickering candle.

Leaning across the table, Jack kissed her.

"You're going to set your tie on fire," Caroline said.

Jack sat back in his chair.

"Tonight," Caroline said, "I think, we should—"

"Go right home," Jack said, studying her. "Me to mine, you to yours. That is what you were going to say, wasn't it?"

Caroline smiled and said, "You'll never know."

The next day, Jack found the article about the dead cows.

CHAPTER TWENTY-ONE

1

The cow, brown and white, a Jersey—Jack thought—lay on its side, legs stretched out, udder flopped on the dirt like a semi-deflated balloon, cow shit round as croquet balls on the ground by its haunches. In the photograph Jack couldn't see its head.

The headline: SAVE ANIMALS FROM ELECTRICITY.
Sub-head: A SUPPORT GROUP FOR FARMERS WITH POWER QUALITY PROBLEMS.

The posting from a group called SAFE, Save Animals from Electricity, on *http://www.safe.goeke.net* by Nancy Bellville, dated March 14, 2001, said:

> My name is Nancy Bellville; I am from Prescott, Mi. For the last 35 years, my husband Brian and I have been dairy farmers. In Dec. of 1998 we looked at our DHIA records and found that we had freshened 39 animals and had removed 45 animals. We no longer were able to maintain our herd size. We had 10 cows not milking waiting to gain enough weight to sell and 6 pens full of sick cows. We knew we had a problem and set about trying to discover what was causing such devastating losses. We discovered another farm in our area that was also experiencing the same symptoms that we were and he believed he had a 'stray voltage' problem . . . When the utility company uses the earth as the pathway to transmit the unused electricity back to their substations,

they cannot control where it might go and as a result it follows the path
of least resistance which in our case is in our barns.

Jack looked back at the photograph of the dead cow, two other cows
standing to the left of the picture turned away like bystanders who didn't
want to know. On the right, in the background, was a live cow looking
at the dead cow from a distance. Four other live cows stand by the dead
cow, their heads lowered like gossipy neighbors discussing the strange
death of a friend.

The stray voltage shocked the cows, which caused them to stop eating and drinking and to produce less milk. In some cases, the shocks
shut down their immune systems, causing them to die.

A later posting on the same site said:

> Along with sick animals there is also a human health epidemic. . . .
> No one wants to investigate why so many farm families and people in
> and around these farms are experiencing health problems.

The health problems included headaches, muscle aches, fatigue, dizziness, ringing in the ears, irregular menstruation, irregular heartbeat,
hallucinations, difficulty in concentration. . . .

Jean Gaynor's symptoms.

2

Grotesque masks covered one wall: A Jew with a hooked nose, a
drunken Irishman, a pinched German, an Italian, an African-American,
a Swede. . . . The paint was faded and flaking. The mouths stretched up
in ghastly grins or down in terrifying scowls.

"From vaudeville," the professor of biology at Highland Community
College explained. "Turn of the century. The last century. Performers
wore them when they did ethnic humor."

The professor—Dr. Matthew Shapiro—took down the mask of the Jew and held it in front of his face.

"A Jew comes home and finds his best friend screwing his wife. *Leo,* he says, *I have to, but you . . . !*"

Shapiro held the mask in his lap like a cat. "Nineteen-oh-one," he said, "that used to kill them."

"Electrical pollution," Jack said.

"My grandfather was the Goldman half of Goldman and Webber," Shapiro said. "Changed it from Gordon. Which was a Jewish name in Lithuania. Gordon. Don't ask. There were two famous Gordons in Vilna in the eighteen-eighties, sometime around then, both writers. A journalist and a poet."

"I found some of your articles on electrical pollution online," Jack said.

"Tell me, Mr. Slidell," Shapiro asked, "why would a guy change his name from Gordon to Goldman? In America? In the late eighteen hundreds?"

"You were an expert witness in a lawsuit against Mohawk Electric," Jack said.

"I helped bring the suit," Shapiro said. Fondly, he looked at the mask in his lap. "Goldman and Webber were one of the biggest comic teams in vaudeville until Webber got shot. A guy came home and found him schtupping his wife. Killed him while he was on top of her."

"I'm investigating a murder," Jack said. "Maybe more than one murder."

Shapiro swiveled in his desk chair away from Jack to face a window that opened onto the campus. The sky was low. A breeze that smelled of mud wafted in. In the window was Shapiro's face reflected, masklike. He leaned forward and pulled the window shut.

"My father started collecting the masks when his father, my grandfather, died," Shapiro said. "My wife won't let me keep them at home. She finds them offensive."

"I can see that," Jack said.

"They're history," Shapiro said. "People hear my grandfather was in vaudeville, they think, *How cool,* begin romanticizing the past." Shapiro nodded at the masks. "Nothing romantic about them." He swiveled his chair back to face Jack. "I'm sorry these people died, but I'm not a cop."

"One of the victims was complaining of symptoms that sounded like electrical pollution," Jack said. "Like what you reported in your research." He flipped open his notebook and read, "Headaches, muscle aches, fatigue, dizziness, ringing in the ears, irregular menstruation, irregular heartbeat, hallucinations, difficulty in concentration . . ."

"A lot of things could cause those symptoms," Shapiro said.

"I wish you could be more help," Jack said.

"The last time I tried to help somebody prove electrical pollution," Shapiro said, "I lost my federal grant."

"This is life and death," Jack said.

"And my job," Shapiro said. "At Cornell. I'm lucky to have landed here. Since then, I mind my own business. And teach freshman courses. Twenty-six, twenty-seven in a class. Do you know how boring it is to teach freshman bio?"

"The girl with the symptoms was living under high-tension wires," Jack said.

"When I was six years old," Shapiro said, "I discovered the pond at the bottom of the backyard. In the dingle. I'd lie in the ferns at the edge of the scummy water and watch water skimmers, dragonflies hovering over the surface. Underneath the water were shiners, some gold, some silver with blood-red fins, their scales flashing in the sunlight, darters disappearing like fishy magicians under lily pads. Frogs and peepers, the hum of insects, the small sounds of the pond lapping the mud under my chin . . . Everything smelled full of life, a dark, rich, bitter, sweet stink I loved. Deep in the weeds, all around me, the sun looked green. I could feel my shirt and shorts wet against my skin, the heat on the back of my neck. On my lids when I turned over and closed my eyes. Everyone must have some heaven in their childhood. That was mine. I began studying pond life: the beetles that looked black until you saw the black was green and purple and red and gold. For my eighth birthday, I got a microscope. Not a fancy one. Through it I could see transparent creatures. I decided all I wanted to do with my life was study biology. Which I did. Until three

years ago when I got involved in that lawsuit against Mohawk Electric."
Shapiro covered his face with the mask, which grinned horribly at Jack.
"Suddenly, no more research. All my work shit-canned. And I'm teaching
students who make fun of the subject. They make fun of me."

Jack looked at the mask, which still hid Shapiro's face.

"I'm sorry," Jack said to the grinning mouth, the hooked nose, the
eyes blinking deep in the blank sockets.

He lifted his jacket, which he'd slung over the back of his chair.

At the door, Jack stopped at a sepia photograph of a burlesque dancer.

A beautiful woman naked to the waist, her left arm, in a black lace
glove that reached her bicep, holding her tousled golden hair in a pile on
her head, her gloved right arm bent, her fingers spread just below her
breast, her thumb dimpling her side below the shaved hollow of her
armpit. She was sitting in white feathers. A lavaliere of sparkling white
stones hung between her breasts. Matching pendants sparkled from her
long earlobes. Her lips were parted, revealing even, damp, gleaming teeth.
Her nose was narrow, slightly snubbed, elegant. Her eyebrows were
plucked and arched.

"My grandmother," Shapiro said. "A big star at the Old Howard in
Boston. Where my grandfather met her. Right after World War One. He
was fifty-something. She was a teenager."

Shapiro picked up a wooden-framed color photograph of an older
woman in a peach sweater, cream-colored slacks, and pearls who looked
shrunken underneath her big straw hat.

"My grandmother last year at Tanglewood," Shapiro said. "Celebrat-
ing her one-hundred-and-third birthday."

He held the recent picture up next to the burlesque picture.

"No stopping time," he said.

3

The pylons supporting the electrical power lines straddled the hill behind the motel where Stickman's family lived, where Jean Gaynor had

lived with Stickman. Before she moved to Rostyn Avenue. The two uprights, with the cross beams reflected in the pale moonlight, looked like the spinal column of some giant, turned to metal by a spell. An Atlas holding up the electrical world. Or a crucifix for an alien martyr with six arms in a lurid Frank Frazetta sci-fi book cover.

"Sorry about your nephew," Jack said to Kipp, who shrugged.

"You surprised?" Kipp asked.

Jack shook his head *no.*

"This ain't a sympathy call, right," Kipp said.

"Tell me more about the ghost," Jack said.

Kipp sat in a rusty pool chair. The green webbing was frayed. Jack sat in another rusty chair, next to him. Kipp stared into the empty, cracked pool.

"What's to tell?" Kipp said. "She skates through. Singing. They say you found Hussein?"

Jack nodded.

"I helped you out," Kipp said. "Told you where."

Jack leaned to the left side and fished in his right pocket for some folded twenties.

"Don't insult me, man," Kipp said.

"Like you said, you told me where."

"Not the favor I want." Kipp leaned down and pulled up a sock. "You tell the cops how you knew?"

"No."

Kipp sat up, gave Jack a smile.

"That's the favor."

"Who needs the trouble is what I figured," Jack said.

"We got enough trouble," Kipp said. "Kids drive by. Shout things. Throw things. Someday they shoot things, huh?"

"You ever see the ghost?" Jack asked.

"I look like someone sees ghosts?" Kipp asked. "I see the ghost I kick the little pest in the ass, tell her to sing something else for a change."

"How many people have seen the ghost?" he asked.

"People talk," Kipp said. "Say they know somebody who knows somebody who saw something."

Jack looked past Kipp at the pylons.

"You ever get headaches?" Jack asked.

"Everyone gets headaches," Kipp said. "What's your interest in the ghost?"

"Muscle aches?" Jack asked. "Dizziness, ringing in the ears, irregular heartbeat . . . ?"

"What's your point?" Kipp asked.

"You moved in last June?" Jack asked.

"Ringing in the ears," Kipp said, "I guess everyone gets that one time or another."

"Did you have that, ringing in the ears, before you moved in?" Jack asked.

"Who can remember?" Kipp said.

"The electric wires up there," Jack nodded toward the pylons. "Were they here when you moved in?"

Kipp nodded.

"Did Jean complain of headaches, ringing in her ears, muscle aches, dizziness?"

"Like I said, who remembers?"

"It's important," Jack repeated.

"I didn't see her much, you know."

Jack waited.

"What you saying? I get ringing in my ears, headaches, because of the wires?"

"Maybe."

"Maybe means what? Yes?"

"I don't know."

"But you're asking, which means—"

"I don't know."

Slowly, Kipp smiled.

"You think we maybe got a lawsuit?" he asked.

"Jean Gaynor."

"I become a lawyer, maybe that's my first case, huh?"

"Jean—"

"Okay. Okay. You help me, I help you."

"If I find something, I'll let you know."

"Who do we sue?"

"If I find that out, I tell you, too."

"The Great American Dream, huh?"

Jack grinned.

"A scholarship to Harvard, winning the lottery, getting hit by a big corporation's truck, yeah."

Kipp called to some girls on the balcony, "You know Hussein's girl? Who was here? She ever complain about being sick?"

The girls looked at each other. Two giggled.

"Hey," Kipp shouted, "this man wants to know."

"She was always complaining," one of the girls called.

"About what?"

"Everything."

"Smart-ass, I'm asking you."

"She's right," another girl said. "She was always complaining."

"She couldn't sleep," a third girl said.

"You do that much coke," the second girl said, "who sleeps?"

"Kept telling us," the first girl said, "turn down the music."

"What music?" the third girl said. "We don't play any music."

"Maybe she meant the ghost?" the first girl said.

The girls laughed.

"Hey," Kipp called. "You think this is some joke? She's dead. Hussein's dead."

The first girl glanced at the others.

"I don't know," she said. "She was worried about her, you know, monthlies."

"Her period?" Jack asked.

"Always asking if someone has Tampax," the second girl said. "But what's the point? Between her legs, nothing."

"Like the pool," the third girl said. "Dry."

"And cracked," the second girl said.

"And growing moss," the first girl said.

Again, they laughed.

"Headaches," Jack said, "muscle aches, fatigue, dizziness, ringing in the ears, irregular heartbeat, hallucinations—"

"You talking about the ghost?" Kipp said.

"—difficulty in concentration," Jack continued, "and irregular menstruation . . ."

"We get that from the wires?" Kipp said.

"You do, you get your lawsuit," Jack said.

"How do we prove it?" Kipp asked.

"Like I said," Jack got up. "I'll let you know."

CHAPTER TWENTY-TWO

1

"Jury Awards Damages For Wisconsin Family," Caroline read the printout from *Agri-view,* a Wisconsin publication, which billed itself as *Your premier agricultural newspaper to provide up-to-date Capitol news, compelling livestock topics, current dairy coverage, timely crop reports and . . .*

"Eight hundred fifty thousand dollars," Jack said. "They sued the local power company for electrical pollution, stray voltage."

"Two brain cells from a rat exposed to a low-level electromagnetic field show significant amounts of damaged DNA," Caroline read from the next printout.

"And that's just from blow-dryers and electric blankets," Jack said.

Caroline flipped to the next printout and read, "Nighttime exposure to electromagnetic fields and childhood leukemia . . ."

And the next: "The Urban Decline of the House Sparrow (*Passer domesticus*): A Possible Link with Electromagnetic Radiation."

And the next: "A Possible Association Between Fetal/Neonatal Exposure to Radiofrequency Electromagnetic Radiation and the Increased Incidence of Autism Spectrum Disorders (ASD)."

And the next and the next and the next . . .

—During 1977 another U.S. Navy-funded researcher reported that his experiments of exposing primates to radiofrequency radiation resulted in "gross morphological damage to the brains" of the test subjects . . . Soon thereafter, this researcher's funding was canceled . . .

—Cluster of testicular cancer in police officers exposed to handheld radar.

—Children whose birth address was within 200 meters of an overhead power line had a 70% increased risk of leukemia.

—Scientists at the Pacific Northwest National Laboratory have identified a chemical reaction that may explain higher rates of illness observed among some people exposed to strong electromagnetic fields such as those produced by high-voltage power lines.

—A dose-responsive relationship between magnetic fields from power lines and asthma and combined chronic illness is identified in an August 2001 Australian study . . .

—There is solid evidence that secondhand smoke is less dangerous than magnetic fields.

—Area legislators are working together to safeguard neighborhoods that have been targeted for the expansion of a high-voltage electrical transmission line.

2

Caroline read the "The California EMF Program" report's chapter headings: *Leukemias, Adult Brain Cancer, Childhood Brain Cancer, Breast Cancer, Miscarriage, Alzheimer's Disease, Heart Disease, Suicide* . . .

"Did you see the report on electrical power lines and hallucinations?" Jack asked.

"Ghosts, fairies, UFOs," Caroline glanced over the printout. "Remember, twenty years ago the big UFO flap in the Hudson Valley?"

"You must have been a baby," Jack said.

"Every night I had a dilemma," Caroline said. "Keep the window open so Peter Pan could come get me or keep it closed so the aliens couldn't."

"How long did it take you to grow out of that?" Jack asked.

"When I hit puberty," Caroline said, "I traded aliens for vampires."

"Sexier," Jack said.

"I don't know," Caroline said. "All those alien anal probes . . ."

"See the report on how many people getting the electric chair see angels or devils before they fry?" Jack asked.

"Who says they're hallucinations?" Caroline said.

She turned to another printout and read: *"One of the issues confronting policymakers is the value of a human life. Does it make sense to spend $4 million to bury a line if the reduction in EMF will save [only] one life?"*

"Money," Jack said. "That's what it's all about."

"Says here *Slate* estimated a human life is worth between four and eight million," Caroline said.

"If someone grabs you," Jack said, "I wouldn't pay a penny over five mil."

As Jack said it, he felt a constriction of his heart, a physical reaction to fear.

"What if—?" Jack started.

"No one's going to bother me," Caroline said.

"They went after me," Jack said.

"I'm not backing off," Caroline said. "Even if you do."

3

They were driving past the Volunteer Fire Department sign, which this week said: *Welcome home, PFC Dwayne Prettyman, Iraq—Two Tours.*

At the junction of Route 66, Jack hung a sharp right and then turned left into the parking lot of the Jayhawkers Inn. Gravel crunched underneath the car tires.

Inside, the restaurant was dim, each table lit by a small lamp with a red shade. Three metal trays held corn relish, cottage cheese, and spiced crab apples. An ancient Wurlitzer finished playing a Peggy Lee song and started a Frankie Laine number, one after another, songs from the late Fifties, Snooky Lanson's *Your Hit Parade.*

"So where are we?" Jack said. "Frank's dead. Stickman's dead. Both were connected to Jean—"

"Who's also dead," Caroline said. "And who was a junkie hooker."

"And who was possibly suffering from electrical pollution," Jack added.

"And related to Robert," Caroline also added.

Jack smeared some corn relish on a water cracker, cracking it.

Jack was very aware of the flop of the new record on the Wurlitzer—Dinah Washington—the sound of some kind of food grinder in the kitchen, a murmur of voices from across the room—only one word, "bathtub," stood out—and a faint ammonia smell.

The waitress delivered their meals: Jack's jumbo burger special with extra crisp string fries, Caroline's rack of lamb with garlic mashed potatoes and creamed broccoli.

"You're not supposed to pick up your lamb chop unless it's wearing those little paper panties," Caroline said, "but I figure I'm wearing panties, so—"

Caroline picked up a chop with both hands and, pulling back her lips, baring her teeth, began ripping off the meat and gnawing on the bone. Jack could hear the bone cracking.

When she smiled at Jack, he saw a string of lamb caught between her top front teeth.

Jack tapped his own top teeth with a fingernail and handed Caroline a napkin, which she used to wipe her mouth.

"Frank had files and files on Robert's family," Caroline said. "Going back generations."

Jack shrugged.

"Frank was their lawyer," he said.

"The files he had seem like overkill," Caroline said.

"Maybe they just thought family papers would be safer in his office than at home," Jack said.

"Did you know Frank was so involved with the Flowers family?"

"There's a lot I didn't know about Frank," Jack said.

"Then, there's this," Caroline said, putting the lamb bone onto her plate and taking some folded papers from her pocketbook.

Jack recognized the dark blue stripe across the tops of the pages.

"Frank's phone bill?" he asked.

"Jean's cell." Caroline handed the bill across the table. "Frank was paying her bills. I've got more in the car. Take a look at the second page."

Jack did. Caroline had left a lamb-grease fingerprint on the paper.

"A lot of calls to a 415 number," Jack said. "Western Mass."

"I checked," Caroline said, picking up the lamb bone. "It's in Great Barrington."

"Robert's number?" Jack asked. "Keating's?"

Caroline nodded, looking up at Jack over the bone she gnawed, whites showing under her rolled-up eyeballs.

"Three the night Frank died," Caroline said. "I figured she was calling for help."

"*Before* she met with Frank?" Jack asked.

"Or to rub Robert's or Keating's nose in the fact she was meeting Frank?" Caroline said.

Jack gestured for the check.

"I'm still eating," Caroline said. "And dessert comes with the meal."

"You said the files are in the car?" Jack asked.

Caroline nodded.

"You drive," Jack said, "while I go through them."

CHAPTER TWENTY-THREE

1

The silhouette of Caroline's head was outlined by oncoming headlights. Her frizzy hair looked electrified.

The intermittent rain spattered the windshield.

Jack sat in the back seat next to two brown-and-white cardboard bankers boxes. When Jack took off the top of the closest, flakes of brittle, browning paper puffed up, making him sneeze. The files seemed to be in chronological order. Jack slipped the front manila folder out, opened it, and in the car's yellow ceiling light read,

"*Legation of the United States*

"*Madrid, March 4, 1844*

"*My dear Commodore:*

"*Ill health, which has made me rather irregular in my correspondence, has prevented . . .*"

Jack glanced down to the signature at the bottom of the paper—

"*I am, my dear Commodore,*

"*Ever very truly yours,*

"*Washington Irving.*"

—and the addressee below the signature:

"*Commodore M. C. Perry*

"*Commanding African Squadron.*"

Perry, yeah, Jack thought. Robert had mentioned he was an ancestor.

The following file had a letter written horizontally and then, when space ran out, sideways up the page, crossing the horizontal lines. Reading it was a trick, Jack thought, like the psychology experiment in which a picture, focused on one way, was a vase and, focused on another way, became two faces looking at each other. It was from Commodore Perry to what seemed to be his daughter, Bell, Robert's Perry ancestor.

"*Navy Yard, Vera Cruz*

"*November 2, 1847*

"*My dear child:*

"*I was very much gratified last evening by the receipt of your truly affectionate letter of the 3ʳᵈ of last month and am very glad that your mother has entrusted your education to the charge of Madame Cheganay for whose attainments and ability, and estimated—*"

Jack figured the word should have been *esteemed*.

"—qualities I have always entertained the highest respect."

A different world, Jack thought, glancing at Caroline's haloed silhouette in the front seat. A truck went by fast. The passing airstream slapped their car so hard it rocked.

Caroline turned on the radio, which was tuned to the local NPR station.

"Songs of the Auvergne" filled the car.

Jack would have looked for a rock station. Rhythm and blues. Or jazz.

Songs of the Auvergne . . .

Jack wasn't a reverse snob. He'd learned to appreciate, even like, classical music, although his taste—Wagner, Richard Strauss, Bruckner, Sibelius, Tchaikovsky, Liszt, Puccini's *Turandot*—tended toward the lurid or sentimental. But, when tired or stressed, he gravitated to the music of his youth: the Dell Vikings, Jerry Lee Lewis, Chuck Berry, John Lee Hooker, the Blues Project, Mingus. . . .

Songs of the Auvergne . . .

Jack smiled.

The music of Caroline's youth?

As Jack worked his way through college and law school, struggling not to get good grades, which he found easy to do, but to civilize himself, he often regretted that he didn't have Caroline's kind of background, picking up art, classical music, great books from the very air she breathed at home. Junior year of college, when Jack knew enough to realize he was missing references others found obvious—Sinbad, "My Last Duchess," Ratty and Mole, "The Pied Piper," the Jabberwocky—he bought himself a used copy of *Journeys Through Bookland* and read it, volumes one through eight of the faded blue-covered books, from Mother Goose to Peter Stuyvesant. He'd smoke dope and spend hours gazing at the color-drenched illustrations of *The Water-Babies* and *Robinson Crusoe*. He bought a child's version of the Greek and Roman myths. A book about the Norse myths and one about the legends of Charlemagne. He got to know all the common store of references that a cultured person in the first half of the twentieth century might know.

But he *knew* them.

That was the problem.

He hadn't *lived* them.

He could never catch up—any more than Caroline could catch up with baseball statistics, games Jack had listened to in the dark in his bedroom, the radio dial glowing the color of the gold-brown old letter from Frank's files in his hand.

See for yourself why over five million glasses of Ballantine beer are enjoyed every day. . . .

Jack could remember the ads, remember Mel Allen and Phil Rizzuto's voices:

Our broadcast today will be joined by the Armed Forces Radio Service, short-waving this broadcast around the world to our troops. . . .

Jack was a Red Sox fan. South of Albany right over the Massachusetts border, there were pockets of Sox fans, although most of the kids in his neighborhood were Yankees fans. Every season, Jack got into half a dozen fistfights.

The final game of the season . . .

October 1, 1961.

JFK was in the White House, and the Sox were at Yankee Stadium.

No TV. Jack had to listen to the game on a New York AM station, which faded in and out. He was too far west to get a Boston station.

1961—the year that looked the same when turned upside down.

And there's the pitch. It's in there. Strike one. . . .

A couple of weeks earlier, Jack—who was a UFO buff as a kid—had followed the news about the first report of a Gray alien. Maybe one of the spacemen Caroline was afraid might sneak through her opened window . . .

And the pitch. Curve inside. . . .

Between the commentary, the fans in the bleachers made a background *churr* like the cicadas outside Jack's window.

. . . swung on and fouled off. One and two. . . .

Roger Maris was one home run away from beating Babe Ruth's record.

. . . strike three. . . .

Jack had a buried affection for Maris, because the other Yankees ostracized him; they didn't consider him a real Yankee.

Here's the pitch to Maris. Left field. Going back to Yastrzemski. And he manages a one-handed catch. . . .

Jack liked Yaz. Instantly liked him—even though this was his first season. Shit, he was born on Long Island, Southampton, wherever that was, and yet he was a Red Sox, playing left field just like Ted Williams.

When Maris got up at bat again, it was his last chance to break the Babe's record.

Last time up, Roger hit deep to left field. . . .

The fans stood up to see if Maris could pull it off. Hit number sixty-one.

Way outside . . . Ball one. . . .

It was the middle of the afternoon. Jack lay on his back on the bed, staring at the brown water stains in the ceiling.

There's the wind up . . .

. . . and it's a hit to deep right. . . .

The crowd went wild, drowning out the sportscasters.

Who was the pitcher? Jack tried to remember.

Another standing ovation for Roger Maris. . . .

Stallard. Yeah, Jack thought, Stallard.

I've got a headache. . . .

Which one of the announcers said that? Rizzuto? Allen?

You still have it?

I still got it. . . .

An odd personal exchange, caught on radio, remembered vividly almost half a century later—remembered more vividly than Maris at bat, about to beat the Babe's home-run record.

The sweet summer smell of grass had seeped in through Jack's window, which he left open, not for Peter Pan like Caroline, but for a breath of air in his small, hot room in the old shack.

Songs of the Auvergne . . .

. . . qualities I have always entertained the highest respect . . .

How alien Caroline's world seemed to Jack. Not like the aliens Caroline feared, but real, physical beings, people Jack saw on the streets in clean, pressed clothes that fit them. People driving in new cars. People at home reading in the glow of a lamp, seen from the sidewalk through their windows at night. People who didn't have to worry about whether there would be food in the house on alternate Thursdays, the day before the pay envelope came home.

Because the '61 season was eight games longer than seasons before, they tried to say Maris's sixty-one home runs didn't count.

They always try to screw the underdog, Jack thought.

Caroline swerved, swerved again, her fingers gripping the steering wheel.

"I can't stop killing them," she said. "They're all over the road."

2

In the headlights, Jack saw what Caroline was trying to avoid hitting: The road was swarming with tiny frogs, which the tires were squashing.

"I can't help killing them," Caroline said, "but I don't have to kill us."

Jack watched as Caroline grimly plowed through the plague of frogs.

"It's a massacre," Caroline said

Although Jack could see her eyes bright with tears in the light reflected back from the road, she started laughing, a low, almost animal bark. Not quite hysterical, but—Jack thought—close enough to hysteria.

Jack wanted to touch her, to put a hand reassuringly on her knee, but knew the gesture would be misinterpreted.

After a while, where the road was drier, the frogs thinned and then disappeared.

"You okay?" Jack asked.

"Why wouldn't I be?" Caroline asked back.

Jack studied her.

She felt him studying her. Her right eye twitched.

3

Jack went back to examining the bankers boxes.

A faded diary of a cruise up the Nile, written by Robert's great-great-great aunt, Edith, who apparently was sinking into depression.

A sheet of soft, thin paper—"a flimsy"—with a rusty pin in the upper left hand corner. Whatever had been attached was missing. The ink looked blurred, furred from where it had bled through onto the copy, the nineteenth century equivalent of carbon paper or a photocopy.

The next: "*Great Barrington, Apr. 27/62*

1862.

"*My dear Barlow, The conduct of the Administration against McClellan is really disgraceful + wicked—it shows once more that instead of patriots and statesmen we have only partisans at the head of government. . . .*"

Next: A paper book sewn together with brown thread: "*Official Proceedings of the Democratic National Convention, Held in 1864, At Chicago,*" printed a third of the way down the fading cover.

Flipping through the documents, which, in the second bankers box, ended a month ago, Jack felt he was seeing a panorama of American history.

Jack felt that, unlike the Flowers and their relatives and friends, who had such an intimate connection with the historical events, he had no part of that history. He was excluded. Like a child in his bedroom, vaguely hearing the sounds of an adult party downstairs.

Maybe, when he was a kid, Jack should have closed his nighttime window against aliens after all. . . .

From the last folder, Jack took a slip of paper, the torn bottom of a yellow legal sheet, which had written on it in Frank's hand, underlined and circled three times: *07-2376.*

"A docket number," Caroline said when she glanced at the paper Jack held out to her. "One of Jean's cases?"

Jack shrugged as he studied the number.

"The *07* indicates the year," Jack said.

"Not so long ago," Caroline said.

"It's got its own file," Jack said, looking ahead at the car's headlights on the curving road.

"Frank must have thought it was important," Caroline said.

"It's in the Flowers files," Jack said. "Maybe Keating can help us with that, too."

CHAPTER TWENTY-FOUR

1

The stone sphinx and harpy flanking the entrance to the Flowers estate dripped rain. It looked like the creatures were weeping.

As Caroline drove up the winding way through the grounds towards the big house, Jack noticed in the wet, jade green undergrowth huge concrete turtles with waffle-patterned backs, one of the Flowers company's big sellers thirty years ago for playgrounds and school yards.

Yellowing vines climbed up trees and covered the branches like giant spiderwebs.

Low clouds scudding across the sky looked like curdled milk.

Through the car windows came the reek of chicken shit—sharp, a yellow stink, more unpleasant than the maroon odor of cow or horse manure. Worse than skunk.

The smell made Jack's eyes water.

They parked on the circular gravel drive in front of the chipped and cracked stone staircase leading up to the house.

You'd think a family in the concrete business could keep the staircase patched, Jack thought.

Withered rolled-up morning glory blossoms, looking like joints, littered the ground near the entrance.

"What's that?" Caroline asked.

She was looking at the left side back panel of the car.

Jack walked around to her and followed her gaze.

In the metal was a round hole.

Jack touched it with his forefinger.

"Someone shot at us?" Caroline asked.

Jack didn't answer.

"When?" Caroline said. "Not while we were in the car. We would've noticed."

Jack was silent.

"And why would they shoot when we weren't in the car?" Caroline said.

Jack walked away from the car. Up the chipped stone steps.

"It's probably not a bullet hole," Caroline said, following him.

"It's a bullet hole," Jack said.

2

Someone shot at him? At Caroline? At the car?

Jack assumed it was to discourage him. Them. From trying to find out who killed Frank.

But that question ramified into questions Jack couldn't even frame. A constellation of unknowns and uncertainties.

Don't get distracted, Jack told himself. Keep it simple. *Who killed Frank?*

But how could he untangle that from who killed Jean? Who killed Stickman? And why?

And what all that had to do with Robert and his father?

Caroline watched Jack charge up the steps and throw open the huge, heavy, oak front door, which was half again their height, as if designed for a generation of giants.

Jack's face was pale, drawn, his eyes narrowed. A vein throbbed in his forehead. Not the good-looking, battered face she'd gotten used to, but fierce. She felt a stirring in her belly and realized she was getting wet.

Inside the gothic front hall—its vaulted ceiling disappearing into shadows—was the double staircase like calipers curving down to measure the stone floor on which they stood.

The right staircase was rigged out with an Easy Climber, a track with a seat driven by a cable, so Keating—Caroline assumed it was Keating— wouldn't have to climb the steps.

Keating hadn't seemed that infirm to Caroline.

"Mr. Flowers!" Jack called, his voice echoing. "Robert!"

Jack strode from one side of the hall to the other, glancing through doors, calling: "Mr. Flowers! Robert!"

Jack froze.

In a corner, on a chair, sat Jack.

Or rather, one of Keating's simulations.

Keating had used the photograph he'd taken of Jack to make a duplicate.

Jack took the left-hand stairs two at a time. Caroline followed.

At the top of the steps, Jack vanished down the hallway. Caroline faintly heard a song—a CD? Radio? TV?

A big band swing sound. Lots of brass.

Hoagy Carmichael? she thought. Johnny Mercer?

Under the music was another sound coming from an open door. A bestial noise. A growl, snarl of anger, followed by a grunt—a second voice—and a cry, a whimper, also the second voice.

When she got to the door, she saw—inside the room—Robert half sitting, supporting himself on one elbow on the floor, his white terry cloth bathrobe splayed open, revealing his pale belly, an almost hairless crotch, and a flaccid fat cock. His lip was split. His tongue, pink and quick, licked the blood dripping down his chin.

Jack stood, humpbacked, like a werewolf, above Robert.

"I've been suspected of murder, I've lost my job, I've been beaten up, I've been shot at," Jack said very softly to Robert, "and far as I can tell it's got something to do with your family."

Robert was wiping the blood on his face with the back of his hand.

"I want to know what's going on," Jack said.

"Jack!" Caroline said. Horrified at his violence.

But the flutter in her belly didn't go away.

3

Caroline helped Robert up.

Jack glared at her.

Robert shook off her hands, cinched the bathrobe, tight, around him, crossed to a mirror, and examined his wounds.

"What the fuck's the matter with you?" he asked, catching Jack's eye in the mirror.

"Where's your father?" Jack asked.

"Some political event," Robert said. "The Van Buren Testimonial Dinner." Robert dabbed a forefinger on his lip, blinked with the pain. "He's on the Eleanor Roosevelt Legacy Committee. The governor's there. The attorney general . . . Maybe you should go over there and punch Dad out, too."

"Jean called here three times the night she died," Jack said.

Robert crossed the room and opened a window wider, closed his eyes as he let the breeze hit his face.

"I keep telling Dad, we should get central AC," he said.

"Why did Jean call?" Jack asked.

Robert kept his back to Jack.

Behind Jack, Caroline could see Jack's shoulders, still hunched.

Robert's shoulders, pulled back, looked like the stubs of emerging wings. Robert's head was erect, his chin raised—reminding Caroline of a history book photograph of Mussolini on a balcony posing for the crowd below.

Robert pulled his bathrobe belt tighter.

He's embarrassed, Caroline thought.

The rain had stopped.

Beyond Robert, through the window, the sky was lurid. Just above the treetops, the clouds momentarily parted. The moon was huge, as if it had moved close to the Earth.

Too close.

The lawn, which looked black, not green, in the night, extended the length of a football field on this side of the house. And it was filled with an army of . . . children? Right arms stretched forward in a . . . Hitler salute?

No, Caroline thought, not children. . . . Midgets? Dwarves?

She moved closer to the window, crowding Jack who stood with his fists balled at his side.

Not people, Caroline realized. Not humans.

The lawn was filled with plaster jockeys, arms out to hold missing lanterns. White faced. An army of concrete mimes.

More of the Flowers company products.

Were they being stored on the lawn? Caroline wondered. Or did Keating like the display?

Or Robert?

Robert turned to face Jack.

Jack's right hand shot out—as if he'd become one of the plaster jockeys—and grabbed Robert by the throat.

"Why?" Jack asked again.

Robert gargled in Jack's grip.

Caroline realized she was backing up—until she was now half a room away from the two men.

"Why?" Jack whispered, relaxing his hold.

"Who knew you were such a violent man," Robert croaked. He looked over Jack's shoulder at Caroline. "Did you?"

Without releasing Robert, Jack glanced back at her.

Her eyes were wide. Her mouth open. Lips so dry they looked cracked—as if she too were made of plaster.

As she looked into Jack's eyes, she licked her lips. Unconsciously. Slowly.

"Get the fuck out of my house," Robert said to Jack, who swung his head around to Robert as if he'd forgotten about him while he'd gazed at Caroline's tongue wetting her lips.

"120.10," Robert said. "*Assault in the first degree.*" Lawyerlike, he quoted the New York State Penal Law: *". . . with intent to cause physical injury. To destroy, amputate, or disable permanently a member or organ of his body . . ."*

Jack kneed Robert in the balls.

Robert gasped. The blood drained from his face. He tried to bend over, but Jack held him up by the throat.

"Why?" Jack repeated.

Robert gasped for breath. His eyes watered.

"I'm not going away," Jack said, "until you tell me."

Robert moaned. Breathed a stink into Jack's face. Meth breath? Jack wondered if Robert was also using drugs. More likely Pritikin breath, the stench of vegetable compost.

Jack pulled Robert towards him, twisting as he did so, and slammed Robert's head so hard against the wall next to the window that the plaster cracked.

"Jack," Robert gasped.

Jack kneed Robert again.

Robert made a sound like a deflating balloon.

"Why did Jean call three times the night she died?" Jack asked.

Robert's face, no longer pale, was now flushed. He tried to take a breath.

Jack released him.

Robert crumpled. On the floor, he curled up like a worm on a hot sidewalk.

Jack squatted beside him.

Robert turned his head to look at Jack with watery, glittering eyes.

"Prick," Robert croaked.

On the breeze coming through the window, Jack smelled something like lemon peel. Tart, bittersweet. Wondered what it could be.

Robert pushed himself into a semisitting position.

"What if I call the cops?" Robert said.

"Who's your witness?" Jack said.

Robert turned his gaze on Caroline, who looked from Jack to Robert and back to Jack.

"You wouldn't perjure yourself in court?" Robert said to Caroline.

Caroline stood very still.

"For him?" Robert asked.

The breeze fluttered her hair.

"Under oath?" Robert added.

CHAPTER TWENTY-FIVE

1

Jack looked around the room.

Lying on a long library table was a green fiberglass fishing rod and an old creel, the wicker dark with age. Lined up next to the rod were an assortment of lures: jigs, plugs, spoons. One of the spoons, dimpled silver, glinted in the lamp light.

On the other end of the table, under a library lamp with a green shade, were a few magazines: *Horse & Rider, Dressage Today, The Practical Rider.* . . .

Buying A Weanling: Great Tips For Getting A Good One . . . Over Fences Training: On Course Confidence . . . 27 Grooming Tips From The Pros . . .

Leaning against a straight-back chair was a shotgun: very expensive looking, walnut stock and gold chasing. On the chair seat were two closed boxes of shotgun shells and one open box, shells spilling out, the brass bases catching the light, the paper shells dried-cranberry red. Slung over the chair back was a threadbare green hunting sweater with a worn leather shoulder patch.

On the rug, by one of the chair legs was a dead . . . mouse? Vole? A paw open, claws spread.

The windows lit up—lightning cut across the sky like a knife slashing a painting.

Jack turned his attention back to Robert, who was biting a strip of skin from his thumb.

"What time is it?" Robert asked.

Caroline slipped her cell phone from her jacket pocket, glanced at it.

"Nine-oh-seven," she said.

"A digital answer," Robert said.

Thunder cracked.

"I don't want to keep you, Jack," Robert said.

"I wasn't going," Jack said.

There were plaster flecks in Robert's hair.

Behind Robert, on the wall where Jack had slammed his head, was a squashed-spider-shaped blood spot.

"Then, excuse me if I leave you," Robert said. "I'm going to my room to lie down." He started for the door. "I've got a terrible headache."

Jack took a vase off a side table.

"Beautiful piece," Jack said.

Robert blinked at Jack, who held the vase up to a light.

"Not a flaw," Jack said.

"My great-great-something grandfather brought it back from China," Robert said.

Jack threw it against the wall, shattering it.

"Shit!" Robert said.

Jack picked up the creel, dropped it on the floor, and stepped on it, splitting the wicker.

"What the fuck did you do that for?" Robert asked.

"This looks like an antique," Jack said, picking up the shotgun and, grabbing its barrel in two hands as if it were a bat—*Maris beating the Babe's record?*—he raised it over his shoulder about to swing against the stone fireplace.

"Jean was arguing about money," Robert said. "As usual. When my father refused to talk to her—she kept calling back—I had to. She was going on about Frank, how she was going to meet him—apparently, my father had asked her to meet him, don't ask me why—and he'd given her some money to arrange it. And she wanted more—more than he promised. I told her I didn't know anything about it. I didn't. I don't. Frank had been up to the house a few times in the weeks just before all this happened—talking to my father about something, something my father wasn't happy about."

"Your father was unhappy about what Frank wanted," Jack said, "and was using Jean to set Frank up."

"You can't think Robert's father arranged Frank's murder," Caroline said.

"Maybe he was trying to get something on Frank," Robert said, "to blackmail him. To get him to back off. And things went wrong."

Jack didn't say anything. His head was tilted to one side, studying Robert, who held out his hand for the shotgun, which Jack didn't relinquish, still holding it by the barrel, but no longer threatening to smash it against the fireplace.

"It's a Purdey," Robert said. "1872. One of only a hundred-seventy-five. When Rosebery was in the States, he gave it to Tilden. Jack, Rosebery became prime minister. Tilden became—"

"I know who they were," Jack said.

Robert gave a small smile.

"Somehow it ended up belonging to Horace Howard Furness, the Shakespeare scholar. Story is an uncle, a great-uncle, won it on a bet from a groundskeeper at the University of Pennsylvania, I don't know how it ended up with the groundskeeper. My grandfather taught me how to shoot on it. . . ."

Robert's hand was still out.

"Hunting season," Robert said. "Bow, gun, muzzle loader. I've never tried a muzzle loader. . . . They still make them, you know. For hunters, re-enactors who aren't obsessed with authentic equipment. Or who can't afford the antiques."

Robert's hand was still out.

"A guy I knew—a reenactor—collected Civil War pornography," Robert said. "It wasn't all Matthew Brady. . . . Just like the Internet—the minute there were photographs, there were pornographic photographs."

Robert's hand was still out.

"The gun is worth a lot of money," Robert said.

"Fuck you, Robert," Jack said—but handed the gun to Robert, who held it protectively. He was sure Robert's interest in the gun was only sentimental.

"Last Christmas," Robert said, "I got a new Evans, a St. James, beautiful gun, over/under, twenty-bore, but I never use it."

Holding the Purdey in the crook of his left arm, Robert knelt and picked up what was left of the creel, looked at the shards of china from the vase.

"You didn't have to do that, Jack," he said.

Robert stood, put the creel on the table, and almost casually scooped up two shells from the chair seat.

Jack took a step forward, but before he could get close enough to stop him, Robert had cracked open the shotgun, loaded, snapped it shut, and aimed it at Jack.

"Get undressed," he said.

2

"You come into my home, knock me down, bare-assed, in front of Caroline, and think I'm going to show you nicely to the door and kiss you good night?" Robert said. "Get undressed, or I'll blow your head off. No," he said, swinging the gun toward Caroline, "I'll blow her head off."

Robert took a step toward Caroline and pressed the shotgun muzzle against her head.

"Before you try to jump me, Jack," Robert said, "the questions you have to ask yourself are: Am I crazy? Am I trying to protect my father? Am I just pissed off at you?"

Jack stripped. He stood naked in the middle of the room. Felt a chill at the small of his back.

There was another flash of lightning, followed this time almost immediately by thunder.

"Your turn, Caroline," Robert said.

"You shit," Caroline said.

Caroline kicked off her shoes and unbuttoned her skirt, which she let drop to her feet. She crossed her arms, took hold of the bottom of her sweater and pulled it over her head, revealing her shadowed shaved underarms. She reached behind her back, unsnapped her bra, and shrugged it off. Her breasts were covered in goose bumps. Her nipples were the rusty rose of the shotgun shells. She took off her panties.

"Pick up your clothes," Robert said, "go out the door and turn left down the hall."

3

At the end of the hall, Jack and Caroline, followed by Robert and the shotgun, took two steps down to a landing, feeling dwarfed by the landing's cathedral-size window, which overlooked the swimming pool in the side yard. In the pool, Jack saw a body floating facedown.

Another corpse?

Jack stopped to take a closer look.

Or one of Keating's resin constructions?

"It's a float," Robert said.

When Jack looked at him skeptically, Robert added, "Made to look like William Holden at the beginning of *Sunset Boulevard*. One of my father's least successful business ventures. Along with the bobble-head Katharine Hepburn car doll."

In the sky, a thunderhead veined with lightning looked like an electrified brain.

"Down the rest of the steps," Robert said, "and through the door."

The crack of thunder made the glass in the window vibrate. Rain spattered against the side of the house.

Naked, side-by-side, Jack and Caroline continued down the stairs to the first floor and out the massive door, down the steps outside, and onto the driveway. "Robert," Jack asked, "did you ever hang out with your sister?"

"Half sister," Robert said. "Once or twice."

"Did you do drugs with her?" Jack asked.

"Once or twice," Robert said.

"Did your father know?" Jack asked.

"No," Robert said. "Are you constructing a motive for murder, Jack?"

"Did you ever fuck her?" Jack asked.

Caroline shot a glance at Jack.

Robert sucked his thumb where he'd bitten off a strip of flesh.

"Nervous?" Jack asked.

Jack felt Caroline's hand searching for his.

"Get the fuck out of here," Robert said.

CHAPTER TWENTY-SIX

1

Clutching Caroline's hand, Jack led her into the shadows under the huge trees, inching his way forward, feeling his way, one hand stretched out— like one of the plaster lawn jockeys.

Halfway to their car, Jack and Caroline stopped and dressed.

While kneeling to tie his shoes, Jack looked back at Robert, who was filling his car—a dark blue Honda Accord—from an old-fashioned Esso gas pump outside the property's six-car garage.

With his free hand, Robert flipped open his cell phone, punched in numbers, with his thumb hit *call*—and blew up in a fireball that splintered the high window and filled the air with a black, hot, gasoline-smelling cloud.

2

"A spark from his cell phone," Jack said.

The air stank of burning chemicals and rubber, scorched metal, which made Jack and Caroline's eyes sting and their throats burn. Caroline put her left hand on Jack's shoulder to steady herself as she leaned sideways, away from Jack, and retched.

The breeze blew the hair hanging forward from her forehead, the locks moving like snakes.

Under the other smells was the aroma of cooked meat. Sweet. Like pulled pork. Robert's flesh.

Once more, Caroline retched.

She straightened up, wiping away a thread of spittle hanging from the side of her mouth with the back of her hand.

Without looking at her, to give her privacy, Jack handed her his pocket handkerchief.

The wind swept the sky clear of curdled clouds.

Directly above them, at the pivot of the sky, were Vega and the other stars that suggested the two parallel lines, the two strings, of the constellation Lyra.

To the north was Draco, the Little Dipper, the Big Dipper—more familiar to Jack than Lyra. To his right were constellations he didn't recognize.

Jack kept staring at the sky until he thought Caroline had a chance to collect herself. They were walking away from the burning car. The stench was less powerful.

Caroline swallowed.

"Do we call the police?" she asked.

"I've had enough to do with the police lately," Jack said. "And I'm not ready to explain why we came."

Caroline hesitated—both in answering and in walking toward their car.

"Are you?" Jack asked. "Ready to explain?"

"I don't think I could," Caroline said. "What about our fingerprints?"

"We've been here before," Jack said. "There's nothing to tie us into tonight."

They were at their car. Upwind of the fire.

Caroline gulped air.

"But Robert—," she started.

"He'll be found soon enough," Jack said. "There's nothing we can do for him."

"And Keating?" Caroline asked.

"There's nothing we can do for him either," Jack said.

Caroline ducked her head to slip into the car. Her shoulders heaved. She started sobbing.

Lightly, Jack rested his hand on her back. Felt her body shake.

He forced himself to say nothing.

She stopped crying as suddenly as she started. And swung around to sit in the car.

Moonlight, shining through the windshield, bathed her left cheek. Turned her face into a half-dark moon.

She turned her head more to her right. To look beyond Jack at the trees, Jack thought. Maybe at the sky.

And more of her face was shadowed. Her cheek was now only a sickle moon.

Diana, Jack thought. The Virgin Goddess of the Hunt.

Diana killed Orion, Jack couldn't remember why. Caroline would know, though this wasn't a good time to ask.

Jack searched the sky for the constellation of Orion. The three stars that made up his belt, but Jack couldn't find them.

As a kid, Jack wanted to know all the stars, the names of all the plants, all the creatures around him.

Diana also killed Actaeon.

Jack remembered that story because in his old mythology book with the orange cover there was a picture of Actaeon, his dogs at his heels, peering through the trees at Diana, who was bathing, naked in a stream.

In the illustration, Diana had small breasts and a hairless crotch.

Because of the hairless women in Greek and Roman mythology and in the statues of goddesses he saw when he was taken on a class trip to a museum in Springfield, Jack wasn't prepared for his first girlfriend's pubic bush, a dark, curly, moist tangle that delighted him.

But he thought Actaeon got a raw deal.

Being turned into a stag and torn to pieces by his own dogs just because he stumbled on a goddess.

No, Jack changed his mind—that seems right.

Every time in his life that he had stumbled on a goddess—in the guise of girls or women he'd fallen in love with—there always came a time when he felt the girl—the woman—would sic his dogs on him if she could.

3

Caroline faced front in the car. The moonlight made her face silvery. A metal mask. Expressionless.

Jack shut her door and came around to the driver's side, opened his door, slipped in, glanced once at Caroline whose face was immobile, now all in shadow. A cloud had covered the moon. He turned on the ignition, put the car in reverse, backed in a semicircle, put the car in forward, and descended the long drive away from the Flowerses' house.

Part Three
KEATING

CHAPTER TWENTY-SEVEN

1

As the car bumped down the long rutted road from the Flowerses' house to the highway, Jack saw through the trees, on a ridge, backlit by the moon, the silhouette of a giraffe followed by two elephants.

Caroline followed his eyes and said, "They're from the next farm. It belongs to one of the Ringlings. The circus family. They used to have eight elephants. They're down to two. You know, retired from the ring. There's always something in the papers. Usually some animal-rights group. I'm surprised you don't know about them. Could you go a little slower? God knows why they keep them up here instead of Florida."

A quarter of a mile down the road, Jack saw what looked like two centaurs. From their human waists to their horses' hocks they were masked by tree branches, but above and below they were clearly visible: Their heads and naked chests—his chest hairy, her small breasts mango shaped. The horses' elegant legs picked their way through the woods.

"Are they from the Ringlings' farm, too?" Jack asked.

Startled, the centaurs reared and galloped away. No longer half hidden behind tree branches, they lost their magic—just two people, riding naked in the night.

Why not? Jack thought.

As the riders disappeared into the trees, Jack saw a mist rising, swirling as if turning to face Jack, who shivered.

A hawk, its wings crimped up at the tips, swooped over the trees from the left and sailed ahead of them.

"Dixie always said hawks coming from the left are a bad omen," Caroline said. "But leading you is a good omen."

As they turned onto the highway, they saw on the road's shoulder a dead stag, probably hit by a truck, its intestines coming out of its side like toothpaste from a tube.

"What kind of an omen is that?" Jack asked.

2

At Dixie's house—Caroline's house—Jack parked in the wide driveway leading to the garage, beside a battered Volvo and an old but well-kept Mercedes.

The house, much smaller than Keating's, had its own eccentricities: turrets and bay windows, gingerbread details, a wraparound porch.

On the way back to Mycenae, Jack and Caroline had been silent. Neither one turned on the radio.

The car passed phallic cattails. Vaginal-looking split milkweed pods.

Caroline let them in through the unlocked side door into a mud room, the floor cluttered with clogs and boots and sneakers; two unmatched ski poles leaning in the corner; pegs hung with a brown corduroy jacket, a denim jacket, a tweed sports coat, two identical gray hoodies with large blue lettering, so hidden by folds Jack couldn't make out what the letters spelled, a black watch cap, a battered fedora, a cracked straw planters hat, furry red ear muffs, leftover from the previous winter or waiting for the next winter.

In the kitchen, Caroline took a kettle off the old stove—although none of the appliances was newer than the mid-Fifties, all were in impeccable condition—and held it under a faucet that was fitted with a cylindrical Brita filter.

"Do you want some tea?" she asked.

Jack asked, "Where do you keep the liquor?"

"Through the pantry," Caroline said, "on the side table in the dining room."

The pantry—an old-fashioned butler's pantry with glass-fronted cupboards, plates zipped up in quilted cloth storage bags, and a collection of glasses: cut crystal and old jelly containers, tumblers—one with Foghorn Leghorn, another with Bugs Bunny—a Hopalong Cassidy teacup, and a Flintstones mug.

"You haven't been here before, have you?" Caroline asked.

Blue ceramic canisters, with Scotch-taped labels—*sugar, brown sugar, lentils, flour, whole-wheat flour, granola, French, Viennese, Colombian* coffee beans—were lined up below the cupboards on a wide shelf that also held mixing bowls, a food processor, an old Hamilton Beach blender, two juicers—one ancient lever-action—the other modern and motorized—a new four-slice toaster, a bright brass La Pavoni espresso maker and its companion coffee grinder. . . .

In a shelf corner, plugged into a three-pronged outlet, was a circuit-breaker strip with a staring red light.

Another wall had open shelves, filled with canned goods, pasta, staples. . . .

"Are these your leftover Y2K emergency supplies?" Jack asked.

"Dixie's still waiting for the apocalypse," Caroline said.

Below the shelf were more cupboards—with wooden doors one of which, warped, didn't quite close.

The recently polished oak floorboards had a matte finish. Jack could smell the wax. Which mixed oddly with the taste of pennies leftover from the burning car.

The pantry hadn't been painted in decades. But it was immaculate.

Old money, Jack thought.

In the center of the long and narrow dining room was a wooden table that would easily seat twenty. The centerpiece, on a blue-and-red cloth placemat, was a large blue vase holding a dozen or so dying, drying red roses. A few brown-fringed petals had fallen to the table.

Nineteen chairs were antiques with scroll backs and fraying gray-and-rose silk seats. The twentieth chair was relatively new, wooden, straight back, cheap, from Walmart, Jack figured.

To the right of the dining room table, loomed a ceiling-high breakfront with more dishes and glasses, a random mixture of old, expensive china and new, plain plates. On top of the breakfront were a silver toast holder, an unmatched collection of candlesticks—silver, wooden, glass—and a Chinese urn with a thousand-deer pattern.

To the left stood a massive sideboard displaying polished silver chafing dishes.

Above the sideboard was an oil painting in a gilt frame of an elderly man in a three-piece suit, gold watch chain, wing collar.

"My great-great uncle," Caroline said, watching through the two pantry doors from the kitchen, where she stood at the stove, waiting for the kettle to boil. "Under-Secretary of Something in the second Cleveland administration."

Caroline's great-great uncle, the Under Secretary of Something, had lush, silver hair, bushy eyebrows, smiling eyes behind circular steel-framed glasses, a fleshy nose, and a mustache and goatee, both darker than his hair.

"He looks like Colonel Sanders," Jack said.

"Do you always have to be so negative?" Caroline said.

"Getting fired helps," Jack said. "So does getting beat up. Getting shot at."

"You're not the only one who was shot at," Caroline said.

"We don't know you were shot at," Jack said.

"Fuck you, Jack," Caroline said.

"You're not negative," Jack said. "You're Little Mary Sunshine."

The kettle Caroline was watching sent up a trail of steam, which to Jack, from the dining room, looked like the spectral mist in the woods.

Jack took another look at the Under Secretary of Something.

"When I was a kid," Jack said, "*my* great-uncle stood up—he'd been sitting on the side of the bed, shaving with an electric shaver, that was his one big luxury—and hit the floor. Just toppled. Face first. Broke his nose when he landed. He was hemorrhaging—a stomach ulcer. We got him to the hospital. The doctor said he needed a transfusion. Fast. He had an hour, maybe two. He was in the Carpenters Local. He said, *I don't want no scab blood in me. You find me a union donor—and I want to see his card—or you let me bleed to death.*"

"You think anyone with money is corrupt?" Caroline said. "Don't you?"

"What's the old line?" Jack asked. *"Behind every great American fortune is a great American crime . . ."*

"Then," Caroline said, "I'm an accessory after the fact. My great-great uncle, Voorhees—"

"That his name?" Jack asked, looking back over his shoulder at Caroline. "Voorhees?"

"—didn't have any children. That's where I got most of my money."

"How much money do you have?" Jack asked.

"Next," Caroline said, "are you going to ask my age?"

"Don't get coy with me, Five Spot," Jack said.

Caroline shot Jack a curious look.

"You haven't called me that for a while," she said. "Are you trying to apologize or pick a fight?"

"Apologize for what?" Jack asked.

Using a purple oven mitt, Caroline took the whistling kettle off the stove.

"Sometimes," Caroline said, "you can be a real prick."

"Sounds to me like you're the one trying to pick a fight," Jack said.

On a low table under the far window, facing the street, between garnet-colored drapes, was a silver platter holding half a dozen bottles: three Scotch—Lagavulin, Teacher's, and Talisker—Six Grapes port, Calvados, Wild Turkey. Beside the tray was a bottle of B & B.

Jack took the bottle of Wild Turkey by the neck. As if he were about to ring a bell.

On his way back to the kitchen, he grabbed a jelly glass from the cupboard.

3

They were both silent as Caroline steeped her tea and Jack sipped his bourbon.

"Why the hell am I drinking tea?" Caroline said.

Jack poured another four fingers of bourbon into his glass.

Caroline opened the refrigerator and took out a can of beer, which she put on the table next to her teacup. She turned back to the fridge and, leaning over, found another two cans of beer on the bottom shelf.

Jack realized he was staring at her ass.

"You planning a party?" Jack asked, as Caroline straightened up and popped open a can. "A little game of beer pong?"

"In LA," Caroline said, "we used to call it *Beirut*."

"Why?"

Caroline shrugged.

"Maybe it was less offensive than calling it *Baghdad*?"

"Why not call it *Bel Air*? Or *Passaic*?"

"Why don't you go home?" Caroline said.

She had glugged the first beer and had popped open the second.

"I don't need a baby-sitter," she said.

Jack poured another glass of bourbon. He eyed the bottle.

"I hope you've got more of this in this great, big house," Jack said.

Caroline had a dimple in the left corner of her mouth, and her right eye was slightly crossed.

Jack had never noticed that before.

"You really want me to go?" Jack asked.

Caroline's shoulder-length hair was a little darker in the part, not dark enough to suggest she'd changed her hair color. Jack didn't think she was the kind of woman who'd dye her hair.

"You're too drunk to drive now," Caroline said.

Jack went back into the pantry and studied the rows of cans.

"You shouldn't have hit Robert," Caroline said.

From the open shelves, Jack took down a can, Dinty Moore beef stew, and read the label.

"*Nutrition facts,*" he said aloud. "*Total fat ten grams.*"

"Did you think that would make him cooperative?" Caroline asked.

"*Cholesterol thirty milligrams,*" Jack read.

"That was a real smart move."

"*Sodium nine hundred seventy milligrams.*"

"Hurt him—"

"*Total carbs. Six percent.*"

"—humiliate him—"

"*Dietary fiber one gram. Protein eleven grams.*"

"What the fuck were you thinking?" Caroline asked.

"I guess," Jack said, "you've decided to blame me for Robert's death."

In three strides, Caroline was in the pantry.

Her slap knocked Jack's head back.

Jack put the can back on the shelf and said to Caroline, "Take off your sweater."

Caroline glared at him.

"Take off your sweater," Jack repeated. Softer. More dangerously.

"You do a pretty good imitation of Robert," Caroline said. "But, if I'm remembering correctly, you got undressed first."

Locking eyes with Caroline, Jack methodically stripped.

When his clothes were on the pantry floor, Jack nodded. Her turn.

Caroline pulled her sweater over her head.

"I wouldn't give my ex blow jobs," Caroline said.

She unhooked her bra.

"I played the English horn," she said, "and I was afraid of ruining my embouchure."

She unbuttoned her skirt and let it fall.

"I gave up the English horn," she said.

She stepped out of her panties and kicked off her shoes.

"My ex was a cellist," she said, putting Jack's hand on her cunt. "Have you ever watched a cellist's fingers when he's playing vibrato?"

"You don't want to make love to me," Jack said. "I've got gray pubic hair."

Caroline arched her back as Jack fingered her.

"You want to talk about it first?" Jack asked.

Caroline said, "No."

Over Caroline's shoulder, Jack saw a can of chicken soup with stars.

"Not here," Caroline said, "with Dixie asleep upstairs."

CHAPTER TWENTY-EIGHT

1

Their clothes bundled in their arms, just like when Robert forced them out of his father's house, Jack and Caroline, naked, shivering in the chill, went into the field behind Dixie's house. Beyond the gaze of anybody accidently glancing out a window. The grass was damp. The sky was starless. Muddy. With a red seam along the horizon.

Some of the flower beds were already mulched, early, for the coming cold weather. A few plants were tented. In the rising light, a tree showed a scarlet clump of early turning leaves.

Holsteins were standing in the pasture beyond the field, half of them typically aligned north to south, the other half lying down, a fifty-fifty sign another storm was coming. A few cows were still trailing up from the barn.

The sky grew lighter.

They found a spot in a thicket. On a deer track. Bordered by goldenrod and purple loosestrife. Asters, white speckled like nonpareil candies. Dandelion puffs like hair electrified straight out from the head by a Tesla coil. Horse chestnuts lay scattered around. Glossy brown with cream-colored circles like dead eyes. There was a patch of mushrooms, which looked like nipples—a dozen nipples from a many-breasted fertility goddess.

Mother Earth.

Jack remembered a woman he dated in the Seventies, who used to say, *The Great Goddess is coming back, and, boy, is she pissed.*

Caroline hugged herself.

Jack draped his shirt over her shoulders.

"You have a someone?" Jack asked.

"I don't love him," Caroline said.

"But you fuck him?" Jack said.

"Not for months," Caroline said.

Jack spread out their clothes to make a nest.

"We should have brought a blanket," Caroline said.

They knelt face-to-face. Their chests touching. Their thighs touching. Jack pushed his shirt from her shoulders, so she would be like him, completely naked.

"Goose bumps," Caroline said in a childlike voice.

Later, when she lay in his arms, both gazing at the brightening sky, he said, "My grandparents used to burn cannel coal for heat. The pieces cracked like a gun shot. The biggest treat I used to get was a Hoodsie Cup, vanilla ice cream in a small cardboard cup. On the bottom of the cardboard lid was a picture of a ball player. You'd lick the ice cream off to see what player you got. The knife-and-scissor man still came around, shouting, *Sharpen your tools . . . Sharp tools make work easy.* Coal chute. I remember the iceman, the straw sticking to the ice blocks to keep them from melting together, the smell of the peroxide from the permanents in the department store beauty parlor, the X-ray machine in the shoe store where you could look at the bones in your feet. . . . Milk delivery was a luxury. As I grew older it become a necessity, then old-fashioned, then an embarrassment."

"I don't think you're too old for me," Caroline said.

"Do you know who The Great Gildersleeves is?" Jack asked. "Henry Aldrich? Little Annie Roonie? Frank Pangborn?"

"I've watched Preston Sturges movies," Caroline said.

In the dawn light, the ghost of the moon vanished.

"For my first science fair in junior high, I built a dinosaur," Caroline said.

Jack levered himself up on an elbow and smiled at her.

"Life size," Caroline said. "A brontosaurus."

Jack kissed her upturned face.

"Out of two-by-fours, chicken wire, and papier-mâché," Caroline said. "No, I didn't realize how heavy it would be. And it never occurred to me that it wouldn't fit through the bulkhead. Dixie helped me cut it into three parts. The neck and head. The body. The tail. Which we just managed to get out onto the driveway. With lots of help. We then hooked the three parts together. Using pulleys and cables. Put it on wheels. We cut a view port just under where the neck met the body. I recruited half a dozen friends to go inside the body with me. Together, we pushed it down the streets, a mile, to school. I couldn't understand why I didn't win a ribbon."

Jack kissed her again. This time on the mouth. He covered one breast with his hand—and felt Caroline go rigid.

"It was around the time I was waiting for my first period," she said. "The boy I was in love with—he used to dry hump me under the school stairwell. But when I raised my skirt and hooked my finger under my panties to pull them aside, he wouldn't fuck me."

Caroline, lying legs straight, arms close to her sides, looked past Jack to the sky.

"It wasn't his fault," Caroline said. "I don't think he had a clue. But I wanted revenge. For two weeks, I went everywhere with Kotex. Just in case. At a dance, when I felt myself getting moist down there, I took him into an empty class room, lifted my skirt, stepped out of my panties, and sat on his lap. The front of his khakis were covered with my blood."

Jack touched her cheek, but she turned her head away.

"I stood," she said, "clipped on the Kotex, pulled up my panties, and smoothed my skirt. He look down at his lap. Horrified."

She met Jack's eyes.

"I'm a difficult girl," she said.

2

"Bleeding on that kid's lap isn't exactly a sin," Jack said.

"Shouldn't we say a prayer for Robert?" Caroline asked.

"Maybe when I'm not so angry," Jack said.

Caroline started to say something else. Jack put his finger to her lips.

"As Bette Davis once said about Joan Crawford," Jack said, *"just because someone's dead doesn't mean they've changed."*

3

The sunlight came at a low angle across the fields.

When Jack climbed on Caroline again and started making love to her, he became aware of something approaching, coming out of a spinney along the deer track on which they lay. He raised his head, raised his chest from Caroline's, and saw a young man in Nikes, gym socks, gym shorts, and T-shirt heading toward them—his face, as he noticed them, turning into a mask of woe.

Too embarrassed to stop, unsure what to do about the two naked, coupled bodies in his path, the cross-country runner jumped over Jack and Caroline.

And, before Jack and Caroline could rise, roll out of the way, hide in the thicket, a second, appalled cross-country runner leaped over them. A third. A fourth. Each one, as they saw the fucking couple, stricken with expressions ranging from embarrassment to glee. A fifth. A sixth . . . A dozen runners in all.

After the last runner jumped over them, they lay still for a long while. To make sure no one else would appear on the path.

Jack's head was still up, his back arched as he watched for oncoming cross-country team members. When he was sure the coast was clear, he forced himself to look down at Caroline—who, instead of being humiliated, was trying to suppress giggles.

They lay on the cross-country route that they had mistaken for a deer track, semi-coupled, surrendering to mirth.

CHAPTER TWENTY-NINE

1

07-2376.

The docket number found in a file in Frank's collection of the Flowers papers.

Although it didn't have an initial federal court ID number, Jack was pretty sure it was a New York case.

Jack no longer had access to a PACER account or a valid New York State Unified Courts System eTrack registration, so he called in a favor from an assistant district attorney in Morgenthau's office in New York City, a guy he'd gone to law school with, who looked up the complaint.

Jack expected it to involve Jean. Some case Frank fixed for her—probably, Jack thought, on Keating's behalf.

But Jack's law school pal—Vincent Tremain—called a day after Jack asked him to look up the case and said, "It's an assault beef. Some guy named Shapiro took a swing at a guy named Flowers."

"Shapiro?" Jack asked. "Dr. Matthew Shapiro?"

"Matthew Shapiro, right," Tremain said. "I don't know about the *doctor* part."

"Took a swing at Robert Flowers?" Jack asked.

"Hang on," Tremain said. "No, not Robert."

"Keating?" Jack asked.

"That's it," Tremain said.

2

Jack caught the 12:20 Amtrak from Hudson to New York City, to talk to the lawyer who had defended Shapiro. Paul Guzman. From a reputable firm: Traylor, Wein, and Castello.

He wanted to get information on the case—especially why Shapiro had attacked Keating—before he confronted Shapiro or Keating.

Caroline reminded Jack to be back in time for Robert's funeral.

"You really want to go?" Jack had asked her.

"Don't you think it would look suspicious if we weren't there?" Caroline asked.

"The paper reported Robert's death as an accident," Jack said. "And no one's reached out to us. No reason for them to do so."

"He was a colleague," Caroline said. "And a friend."

A tall, cowboy-looking guy with long blond hair, wearing pointy brown boots with decorative stitching, jeans, and an olive work shirt under a denim jacket, followed Jack into the coach car and sat two rows behind him on the other side of the aisle.

Hooper—the guy who beat Jack up—said the guy who paid him looked like a cowboy with long blond hair.

Jack studied him.

Could be the same guy.

An artsy-looking forty-year-old woman with white-streaked hair in overalls and two twenty-something girls, each plugged into their own iPods, entered the car and found seats.

When the Cowboy followed Jack into the café car, Jack took more interest in him.

The café was closed.

Jack had gone there to make a cell phone call.

Why had the Cowboy gone into the café car?

The Cowboy studied the café menu.

When Jack returned to his seat, so did the Cowboy.

Curious, half an hour later, Jack again went into the café car and this time pretended to make a cell phone call.

Again, the Cowboy followed and studied the closed café menu.

When Jack got off at Penn Station, the Cowboy followed him up the escalator and out onto Eighth Avenue. As Jack waited in the taxi line, the Cowboy, standing behind him, studied a Nokia ad on a billboard.

Jack left the line and, instead of taking a taxi, headed down Eighth Avenue.

The Cowboy strolled after Jack, checking out a barbecue joint, a shoe store, a bead store, looking at everything except Jack.

Whoever hired him, Jack thought, hired an amateur.

Or someone so professional and protected he didn't have to be invisible.

3

Guzman's law firm, Traylor, Wein, and Castello, which Tremain had said was reputable, was on the twenty-second floor of a steel and glass building on Lexington Avenue between 52nd and 53rd Streets.

Jack took a circuitous route, down 8th, east on 27th, up 6th, passing a former bank building, which looked like a Greek temple and was now a pharmacy, and, catty-corner across the intersection, a former pharmacy, which was now a bank.

When did we replace worshipping money with worshipping health? Jack wondered.

To make sure the Cowboy was following him, Jack stopped at X-Cite XXX, where he browsed the sex toys, the lubricants, the aisles of porn films, identified like sections in a supermarket: *Bondage, Lesbian, Interracial, Barnyard. . . .*

The Cowboy studied whips and handcuffs, leashes and collars, C-clamps and dildos that looked like chew toys.

The feathered masks and restraints seemed like artifacts of some dead religion. Or like things you would find in a pet store or hardware store.

"Last night," a customer in hospital greens was saying to the Pakistani or Indian clerk, "this guy comes into the emergency room with a lightbulb up his ass. He apologizes. I tell him, *Honey, you don't know who you're talking to. . . .*"

"You going to buy the magazine, too?" the clerk asked.

"This guy," the customer said, "was ripped. Gorgeous."

"The magazine?" the clerk said. "I should ring that up?"

"Ever think that's an odd term for muscle definition?" the customer said. "Ripped!"

The clerk shrugged, rang up the magazine, and put it into a brown paper bag with a DVD.

"Some nights," the customer said, "I mean, honey, this is St. Vincent's, the Village, there are so many people in the ER with body art, the place looks like a tattoo convention. Twenty, thirty years from now, I don't want to see these people with their clothes off."

A woman in a G-string the green of a Japanese beetle was taking a break next to her one-on-one booth and talking to another woman in a sheer white bodysuit. G-String, who had high-piled auburn hair, wore green spike heels. Bodysuit, who had a Louise Brooks helmet of glossy black hair, wore fuzzy slippers with cat-face toes.

G-String nodded at Bodysuit's slippers.

"Those'll get you in trouble for sure," she said. "Attract a Furry. You know, one of those freaks into dressing up like a cartoon animal."

The cell phone in her clear plastic pocketbook made a chattering sound, like a toaster having a nervous breakdown.

Jack walked toward the back of the store.

A half-dozen men were studying photographs on the covers of porn movies or porn magazines with rapt attention, as if they were worshipping.

In a way they are, Jack thought. Worshipping what's between a woman's legs.

The source of life.

The Great Goddess is coming back, and, boy, is she pissed.

Jack went into a booth. He put a dollar into a slot, which, with a whirr, inhaled the bill.

The split screen offered four previews. The booth smelled of disinfectant.

Jack heard the door of the next booth close.

Jack slipped out of his booth, left the shop, and was halfway down the block before the Cowboy came out of the peep show and spotted Jack turning a corner.

The Cowboy's indifference about being spotted struck Jack as dangerous.

At a Papaya King, Jack ordered two chili dogs.

He took one and told the henna-haired clerk to give the other to the Cowboy—which she did when the Cowboy made his demonstration stop at the counter.

The Cowboy touched his hat brim in thanks—and followed Jack over to Lexington, as they both ate their dogs.

Just before entering Guzman's building, Jack folded the paper napkin, which smelled of the chili, dabbed at the corners of his mouth, balled it up, and walked to a trash can—where he was joined by the Cowboy, who also tossed in his balled-up napkin.

The Cowboy smiled.

Jack smiled back and, pointing with his thumb over his shoulder at the office building, asked, "You going in?"

The Cowboy shrugged.

"I'm going in," Jack said. "Traylor, Wein, and Castello."

The Cowboy stuck out his lower lip and nodded, another thanks.

"Figure I'd save you the trouble," Jack said.

The Cowboy nodded.

"Twenty-second floor," Jack said.

Again, the Cowboy nodded.

"Figured you'd find out anyway," Jack said.

The Cowboy nodded.

"You going to follow me in?" Jack asked.

The Cowboy nodded.

"You'll have to sign in," Jack said. "You got a name?"

The Cowboy shook his head *no*.

Jack went into the building, showed his driver's license, and signed in.

Waiting for the elevator, Jack glanced back at the Cowboy, who flashed some kind of ID and was waved through without having to sign in.

Amateur or protected?

Jack had his answer.

Protected.

CHAPTER THIRTY

1

The receptionist in the office of Shapiro's lawyer, Paul Guzman, checked and told Jack that Guzman was in court.

As Jack left the office, the Cowboy leaned over the receptionist and flashed his ID.

The receptionist looked sideways at Jack. Suspiciously. And repeated for the Cowboy the information she had just given Jack.

Whatever ID the Cowboy possessed impressed people.

Jack and the Cowboy waited for the elevators side-by-side, facing forward. Not talking.

Side-by-side, they entered the elevator, simultaneously turned to face-forward as if they were a double act in vaudeville, and rode down to the lobby in silence.

Jack hailed a cab.

"Can I give you a lift?" Jack asked.

The Cowboy nodded and got in beside Jack.

Together, facing forward, still in silence, they rode down to 100 Centre Street.

Jack smelled the Cowboy's very uncowboylike aftershave, a light, almost lemony scent. Expensive. Not something you'd pick up in a drugstore.

Jack checked out the Cowboy's fingernails, which were manicured.

Why the cowboy outfit?

Why not?

Jack was still studying the Cowboy's fingernails, when the Cowboy unconsciously flexed his left hand.

Those long tapered manicured fingers were deceptive. Those hands could belong to a strangler.

2

"Docket ending 971," said the bridgeman standing at the front of the courtroom. "The People versus Fritz Donas on a 230.00, Prostitution, 115.05, Criminal Facilitation in the second degree, 100.10, Criminal Solicitation in the second degree, 220.41, and Criminal sale of a controlled substance in the second degree."

Jack whispered to a man carrying a briefcase in his left hand and a brown overstuffed expanding file under his right arm—undoubtedly a lawyer—"They told me Paul Guzman's in this court."

"Counsel," the bridgeman was saying, "do you waive the reading of the rights and charges, but not the rights thereunder?"

"Biland," the man with the briefcase and expanding file said. "Roger Biland. I'm not your guy, Guzman."

"What I meant," Jack said, "do you know Guzman?"

"What's your guy, Guzman, charged with?" Biland asked Jack.

"He's a lawyer," Jack said.

"Lawyer?" Biland said. "It's not good when one of us gets nailed."

"I'm not a lawyer," Jack said. "Not anymore."

"But you're representing your client," Biland said. "This guy Guzman."

"I'm not representing him," Jack said.

"Who is?" Biland asked.

"Nobody," Jack said.

"Let me give you my card," Biland said. "If he needs a lawyer, he could do worse than me. A lot worse."

"Your Honor," the defense lawyer was saying, "the bottom charge, criminal sale of a controlled substance in the second degree—"

"Your plea, Counselor," said the judge.

"Guzman's not charged with anything," Jack said.

"Then why are you here, trying to get him representation?" the man asked.

"I'm not," Jack said. "I'm just trying to find him."

"Keep the card," Biland said. "If you ever need a lawyer . . ."

Tucking the overstuffed expanding file tighter under his arm, Biland continued around to the right aisle of the court and sat in the back bench, where he put his briefcase on one side of him and his file on the other side of him and started taking papers from his pockets.

The bridgeman was calling another case:

"Docket ending 694. The People versus Francisco Franco on a 120.04, Grand Larceny in the fourth degree on the complaint of Officer Leonard Cruz."

At the back of the courtroom, a man with white hair was jotting something in a reporter's notebook.

"Francisco Franco . . . ," the judge said. "You've got a notable name."

Jack figured the white-haired man for a journalist. If the court was his beat, he might know Guzman.

"*Los Cuatro Generales, Los Cuatro Generales,*" the white-haired man was singing under his breath. "*Los Cuatro Generales, Mamita mia, Qué se han alzado, Qué se han alzado . . .* "

"What's that?" Jack asked as he eased next to the white-haired man, who gave him a side-long glance.

" '*The Four Insurgent Generals,*' " the man said. "It's a song from the Spanish Civil War," he said.

"I didn't know the Spanish Civil War was a musical," Jack said.

The white-haired man held out his hand and introduced himself, "Leo Diamond."

Jack took his hand and introduced himself, "Jack Slidell. Are you a reporter?"

"I write about the courts," Leo said.

"Do you know a lawyer named Guzman?" Jack asked. "Paul Guzman?"

"The short, bald guy on the right," Leo said.

Jack nodded his thanks and started toward Guzman, but Leo touched his arm.

"If you're looking for a lawyer," Leo said, "he's a pit bull."

The Cowboy watched Jack talk to Leo.

A woman in a tan, tailored suit passing Guzman asked him, "Where's your client?"

"In LA," Guzman said, "doing hard time at the Beverly Hills Hotel."

"Mr. Guzman," Jack said, "can I talk to you for a minute?"

It took Guzman a moment to figure out which case Jack was asking about.

"Shapiro," Guzman said when he placed the case. "Right, the college professor who attacked the guy, what's his name, Flowers, and got fired."

3

"Keating got Shapiro fired?" Caroline had said on her end of the phone call as Jack, followed by the Cowboy, walked up Broadway toward the bowling alley.

The wind kicked a discarded cardboard coffee cup down the street. The sky was a sulfurous yellow-green. Clouds boiled, racing up Broadway. An off-duty cab passed, its scram light on. On a construction site, six identical posters advertised an all-female, all-nude production of *Waiting for Godot.*

"Why would Keating get Shapiro fired?" she asked.

"Find out," Jack said. "What's Keating's connection to the college?"

The neon sign for Cosmic Bowling was made up of a crescent moon, stars, comets, zigzags indicating extraterrestrial forces.

Inside, the bowling alley was lit like a nightclub. A spinning disco ball sprayed the room with splinters of light. A throbbing bass beat below the eerie 1950s science fiction music of a theremin. Phosphorescent nebulae glowed on the ceiling. Black lights illuminated fluorescent blue-and-pink pictures of colliding galaxies on the walls.

Jack rented a pair of bowling shoes and sat down on an orange plastic chair.

The Cowboy sat in a bright blue chair in the next lane, also tying the laces of rented bowling shoes.

Jack hadn't bowled for years.

His backswing was jerky. He tended to start the ball behind his back, not straight by his side. He released the ball too far from his body, and his wrist felt loose. He got a couple of bad splits

When the Cowboy held the ball, his thumb was at about twelve o'clock. He had a smooth four-step delivery. When he released the ball, his thumb was at eleven. Perfect.

His loft averaged twelve feet from the foul line.

Jack bowled a 115.

The Cowboy bowled a 137.

Jack left his ball and returned his bowling shoes to the clerk at the counter, a sandy-haired, young-looking middle-aged man who was reading a comic book. When the man looked up to acknowledge Jack's return of the shoes, Jack thought his eyes looked as galactic as the black-lit spirals on the walls.

The guy's tripping on something, Jack figured.

The Cowboy left his ball and returned his shoes and followed Jack out of the bowling alley.

When they both had left, Jack's law school friend, Vincent Tremain, got up from the table in the Cosmic Bowling restaurant, where he'd been nursing a cup of black coffee. As he'd planned with Jack over the phone, he wrapped the Cowboy's bowling ball in a pillowcase, brought it to the clerk, and asked, "How much to buy this thing?"

"That's an Ebonite Maxim Captain Midnight," the clerk said. "New, it'll run you seventy bucks, something like that."

Noticing how quickly Tremain pulled out his wallet, the clerk added, "I'll sell it to you for a hundred,"—which Tremain paid.

An hour later, while Jack was waiting in Penn Station for the Empire Service north to Hudson, Tremain called.

Jack answered his cell.

"I delivered your friend's bowling ball to the lab," Tremain said. "There's a cop who works there who owes me big. Says there won't be a problem getting prints off the ball, in the finger holes."

CHAPTER THIRTY-ONE

1

On the train back to Hudson, the Cowboy sat across the aisle and two rows behind Jack.

The car was half full.

Jack's seatmate was a big, florid man, sixty-something, in relaxed-fit jeans and a blue denim work shirt patched with a piece of duct tape. Yosemite Sam mustache. Hair in a ponytail.

An old hippie, Jack figured.

For the first hour, the hippie didn't speak.

When the train stopped between stations for fifteen minutes, the hippie said to himself, "In the summer, the heat makes tracks buckle. In the winter, the cold freezes the switches. Too cold. Too hot. Just right. The Goldilocks Line."

Jack had the inside seat, next to the window, on the river side of the train.

Through the reflection of the old hippie in the glass, Jack watched the moonlit landscape rush past.

Across the Hudson, lights of a town twinkled.

The hippie, looking across Jack, gazed out the window, too.

When the train passed a NYC street vendor's falafel cart washed up on the shore of the Hudson, the hippie said, "Hudson River's an estuary. Tidal saltwater runs one hundred fifty-three miles upriver."

In the window reflection, Jack saw the hippie shake his head sadly at the cart.

Jack wondered how it got there.

The hippie clearly saw it as merely one more example of the struggle to keep the Hudson from pollution.

"Used to freeze over," the hippie continued. "You could walk across the river from Mycenae to Catskill."

Jack turned to face the hippie.

"Four hundred years ago," the hippie said, "when Hendrick Hudson discovered the river, it all looked different. Now, the elms, gone. Chestnut trees, gone. The 1938 hurricane leveled forests."

At Poughkeepsie, a dozen people got off.

"The storm last week headed out over the Atlantic," he said. "But this new one, it's like three systems going to hit us at the same time."

Jack didn't respond.

"It's all the same thing," the hippie said. "All one system. Global warming, yup."

Jack checked over his shoulder. The Cowboy sat straight in his seat, military posture.

At Rhinecliff, almost everyone got off the train. Only Jack, the Cowboy, and the hippie were left in the car.

"You know how many people get killed by trains every year?" the hippie asked.

Jack didn't answer.

"A lot, let me tell you," the hippie said. "The engineer sees someone on the track, but can't stop in time. They have kind of a lottery, see who kills the most."

When Jack gave him a skeptical look, the hippie said, "True. My father was a conductor." Then: "PCBs in the river," the hippie said. "Lakes clogged with milfoil. On this trip, look out the window during the day. One pond after another, the surface is so green it looks solid. Some imports, they're lovely, like the hibiscus. Red blooms. Big as a kid's head. Globalization brings in new species like Queen Ann's lace. Snakehead fish in the watershed out-compete the local fish. Zebra mussels, same problem. Predator invasions. Like lionfish. They're natives of the Indian and Pacific Oceans, but are now in the Atlantic. And," the hippie leaned closer to Jack, "they have no known enemies."

Jack realized he was being as silent with the hippie as the Cowboy had been with him.

"There are six billion people alive right now," the hippie said. "To survive, to make the world habitable, we need to lose four billion."

The hippie snapped his finger as if the gesture could annihilate people the hippie considered dispensable.

"I'm the guy," the hippie was saying, "who was at Newport when Pete Seeger asked for an axe to cut the cables of Dylan's electric guitar. . . ."

The car vibrated with thunder.

"Forty-eight billion text messages in December 2007 alone," the hippie said. "It's End Times, I tell you. I'm a Buddhist, but I'm not going to put up with this shit."

Jack climbed past the hippie's fat thighs and headed up the aisle to make a cell phone call from the empty café car.

"I'm a good person," the hippie was saying to himself, "but I'm going to fuck him up so bad."

As the automatic door hissed closed behind Jack, the hippie was talking in a louder voice about "high-steel Mohican workers" and a shad bake.

Behind Jack, the door hissed open.

The Cowboy entered the space between the cars, and, before Jack could turn, wrapped his forearm around Jack's neck, choking him, and kneed Jack in the small of the back.

Jack dropped.

The Cowboy put his hands together as if in prayer and hit Jack on the back of the neck.

Jack had always heard about people who'd been hit on the head who saw stars, but he'd assumed it was an exaggeration.

Jack saw stars.

It was like being back in Cosmic Bowling.

He barely felt the Cowboy kick him in the side.

Oddly, he also felt clearheaded as if part of his consciousness had left his body and hovered somewhere in the upper right corner of the space between the cars—a viewpoint from which he saw the Cowboy take from his pocket a large key, which he fit into a keyhole on a panel and turned.

The Cowboy opened the outside door.

Framed in the doorway, woods rushed past.

Jack smelled fresh air and earth.

Everything had happened so fast. Less than a minute.

The Cowboy now held, not a key, but a straight razor.

And was leaning over Jack's body.

Abruptly, Jack's consciousness was back in his body—and Jack was gazing into the Cowboy's impassive face.

The Cowboy flipped open the razor. And was about to slash Jack's throat—when Jack kicked out, once into air, a second time, hitting something solid, a wall, and pushed himself across the floor.

The Cowboy brought his right hand, his razor hand, across his chest, and leaned closer to Jack. With his left hand he went to push Jack's face back to raise Jack's chin, exposing the neck.

Jack slammed the heel of his right hand against the Cowboy's oncoming fingers.

There was a snap.

The Cowboy's left eye twitched. Otherwise, he showed no sign of pain.

But it gave Jack enough time to kick out again, harder, scooting himself backward across the floor.

Jack felt nothing but rushing air under the back of his head.

The Cowboy slashed his razor—and would have slit Jack's throat if Jack hadn't kicked again, shooting himself through the open train door.

For a moment, Jack felt suspended in space.

He felt as if someone had drawn a piece of ice across his thigh.

Cold.

Then, wet.

He cut me, Jack thought.

A wall of noise was passing as if Jack, suspended in space, calmly watched a hurricane pass.

Or like Moses; hidden in a cleft of rock, watched the Eloheim pass.
Stars winked in the sky. Not as gaudy as the sky at Cosmic Bowling.
Maybe the noise was not the train.

Or not just the train.

Thunder?

The ghosts of Hendrick Hudson's men bowling?

Jack felt as if he could sleep forever.

He landed in a marsh, cracking his head on something. A log? Twisting his neck.

He couldn't sort out the pain from the Cowboy's attack from the pain of falling from the train and hitting mud, rocks, branches. . . .

He wondered—almost disinterestedly—how badly his thigh had been cut.

The stars receded.

Fast.

Faster.

Streaking away from him. Or toward him as if he were a starship hitting warp speed in the movies.

And there was no sound.

No sound.

Had the shock made him deaf?

Or had he shocked all the marsh creatures by dropping into nature?

Very near his left ear, he heard a chirp.

That's when he lost consciousness.

2

The stars were back in place.

The marsh was crazy with noises. Peepers, rustling reeds, an owl—all nature unnaturally loud.

The marsh smelled fetid.

Or maybe it was Jack himself, stinking worse than the hippie on the train.

Jack felt as if he'd slept for hours.

But off to the right he saw the winking lights of the train disappearing around a bend, heading towards Hudson.

He must have been out for less than a minute.

Painfully, Jack pushed himself out of the mud. To any observer, he would have looked like human life emerging from the primordial slime.

His right pant leg flapped.

At first, Jack thought it was his own flesh flapping.

He touched his cut, realized how deep it was, and retched.

Well, Jack thought, if I'm going to vomit, this is the perfect place to do it.

The Cowboy had a key to open the train door.

He had planned to kill Jack on the train home all along. Toss him into the woods. Be gone with the train to Albany? Where he would get off. Anonymous. Vanishing into the city.

If someone had seen him, would he have waited for another opportunity?

How long had he been waiting for *this* opportunity?

While Jack thought he was playing with the Cowboy, the Cowboy was playing with Jack.

How long would it have taken for Jack's body to be found?

If it was ever found.

Throat cut, kicked off the train, maybe Jack would have sunk into the marsh, becoming food for the noisy creatures around him.

Jack felt as if he were trying to fit pieces from one jigsaw puzzle into another.

When the Cowboy had attacked, Jack had been holding his cell phone. But he had no idea what had happened to it.

Was Caroline okay?

Jack had to get to Caroline.

He forced himself to move. He stumbled through the woods, roots tripping him, leaves like reptile fins slicing his mouth. . . .

The razor hadn't crippled him, Jack figured.

Jack looked around. Looked at the sky. Disoriented.

Was he stumbling in the right direction to get to Caroline's?

Hudson was behind him. North. Northish.

That made sense.

That's the direction the train had been going.

Jack realized he was not thinking as cogently as he had assumed.

Caroline's house—her uncle's house—was north of Hudson.

Through Mycenae. Along the river.

Jack's head throbbed. His ribs, his back, his side—everything hurt.

Without looking down, he touched his thigh. His hand came back wet with blood.

Jack leaned against a tree and took deep breaths.

The only thing to do was to keep walking.

3

The woods ended with a scrim of pillarlike trees, backlit by a moonlit backyard. A hand-painted sign shaped like a pointing hand said *See 3.6 Million Year Old Hominid Fossilized Footprints Next to Dinosaur Footprints: Proof Man Lived With Lizards—$10.*

A homemade exhibit.

Jack blinked at the fossils next to a slab of concrete with the imprints of a high-arched human, modern foot, maybe thirty years old.

The sign looked worn.

On the other side of the footprints was another worn sign that asked: *What killed the dinosaurs?*

The sign was decorated with a faded cartoon of two running velociraptors, a tyrannosaurus, a brontosaurus, and three pterodactyls, all fleeing from a bloody-looking comet with a face and fangs.

The exhibit might have been popular twenty years ago. Maybe.

Closer to the house was a broken seesaw and a rusty swing set. The breeze rattled the chairs as if ghostly kids were pushing each other.

The house was dark.

Beside the side door was a propane canister, looking like a space probe.

On the road in front of the house, Jack checked his watch and headed north—past a closed farm store with its empty plywood bins, past *Harvey's Meat Company*, past the twenty-foot tall ad for *Stan the Vegetable Man*, a figure made up of zucchini legs, pumpkin chest, corn arms, grinning tomato head. A *Knish-O-Rama*, abandoned by a couple from the Catskills across the river who thought to expand their franchise.

Walking along the Taconic Parkway, Jack saw a car driven by an elderly man, sharp chin, leaning back in seat with, in the seat behind him, a huge, stuffed toy gorilla in a porkpie hat.

A battered pickup truck stopped on the other side of the road.

Jack half ran, half hobbled to the median, glanced to his right—no oncoming cars—and approached the truck.

The driver—a kid with a soul patch on his chin—leaned out his window and asked, "You need a lift?"

Jack, his throat bruised, croaked *yes*.

As Jack climbed into the passenger seat, the kid surveyed him, "Looks like you've had an interesting night."

Jack nodded.

"I'm going as far as Hudson," the kid said. "Warren and Fourth. I can drop you off at the police station."

"No police," Jack croaked.

"Didn't think so," the kid said, grinning.

In Hudson, Jack hailed a taxi.

CHAPTER THIRTY-TWO

1

The trees around Caroline's house were hung with bars of deodorant soap to discourage the deer. Unsuccessfully.

Half a dozen deer stood in the yard. Like Balinese shadow puppets.

The front door was unlocked.

Jack entered.

In the living room to his right, Caroline, Nicole, and Dixie were playing chamber music. Caroline played a violin. Nicole leaned over a cello like an animal over a scrap, scraping away ferociously. Dixie, in a tattered, old-fashioned, red smoking jacket, played the piano, working the pedals as if he were taking a curve in the Indianapolis 500.

Her back to Jack, Caroline said, "It's harder to get my fourth finger on the F-sharp. Bach is still Bach."

The piano was painted bright red. The room's drapes were red. The walls were red. On the piano, lying in front of the score, was a red Pentel pen.

"My better-red-than-dead red," Dixie said, serenely catching sight of Jack with his peripheral vision.

"My God," Caroline said.

She put down her instrument and ran to Jack.

Her knees clutching the cello and pointing her bow at Jack, Nicole, thinking she was joking, said, "You look like someone tried to kill you."

"The linoleum cutter slipped," Jack said, "and I fell down the stairs."

Nicole laughed.

She'd never been to Jack's shack and didn't know it had no stairs.

"And you came all the way over here for Caroline's care and tend-ing," Nicole said. "How touching."

"Caroline's a good nurse," Dixie said.

"I hope you left a trail of blood," Nicole said, "so you can find your way home."

"You should spend the night," Caroline said.

When Jack heaved himself up to go into the bathroom off the front hall, Nicole called after him, "We're trying to go easy on the environ-ment. I only use three squares of toilet paper for every flush."

Under his breath, Jack said, "I'm glad I don't have to do your laun-dry!"

2

After Jack showered, the blood from his razor cut circling, diluted, down the drain, he toweled off, soaking a towel with blood—even though he had made a tourniquet from his ripped shirt.

When Caroline handed in a white terry-cloth bathrobe, Jack said, "Better get me an old robe."

Caroline slipped into the steamy bathroom.

When she saw the blood pooling on the floor, she sagged.

Jack caught her.

"You have to go to the hospital," Caroline said.

"It's slowing down," Jack said.

"Please," Caroline said.

"If it's still bleeding in half an hour," Jack said. "Get me some hydro-gen peroxide. Gauze if you've got it. Adhesive tape . . ."

Caroline put her hands on Jack's cheeks and kissed him so hard she bruised his lips.

While she was gone, Jack, light-headed, sat on the closed toilet seat. He stared at the floor. At the molding. Which had a complicated pattern of grooves. Hard to keep clean. Maybe that's why rich people favored complicated molding? To prove they could afford to keep it clean?

The molding in the bathroom was immaculate.

The neon tubes flanking the mirror buzzed.

The shower dripped.

On the shelf above the sink, reflected in the mirror, was a glass bottle of Geo F. Trumper after-shave, some Flomax, and mint dental floss.

The shower dripped.

A branch tapped the window. As if trying to get Jack's attention.

Across the lawn, a deer turned its head. Reflected light gave the deer X-ray eyes.

Jack forced himself to examine the vaginal-looking wound. Something out of Dali.

Caroline came back with the medical supplies. She watched as Jack poured the hydrogen peroxide on the wound. The hydrogen peroxide foamed.

Jack put gauze on the cut and taped it into place.

The exposed edge of gauze was red, damp with blood.

"I should've killed the son of a bitch," he said.

"It's going to leave an ugly scar," Caroline said.

"I know." Jack grinned.

"Take two," Caroline said, spilling a dozen pills into Jack's hand. "Dixie's Percodan."

Jack popped three into his mouth.

He told Caroline what had happened.

"Have you noticed anyone following you?" Jack asked.

Caroline shook her head *no*.

"The police?" Caroline asked.

"I don't know if that would help," Jack said, thinking of Sciortino's warnings. "I need a drink."

"You just took three Percodan," Caroline said.

"I told you I didn't need a cop," he said.

"Hey, Jack," Caroline said, "I didn't throw you off the train."

"Nobody threw me off the train," he said. "I pushed myself off."

"Whatever," she said.

There was a silence.

"It's stopped bleeding," Jack said.

"Almost," she said.

Another silence.

"I just don't want you to die of an accidental overdose," she explained.

Jack grinned and said in a phony accent, "Strong like ox."

Caroline grinned and said, "Stupid like ox."

This silence had a different quality from the other two.

"Ox," Caroline said softly.

She knelt at his feet, wiping up the congealing blood. In the closed room, she could smell the blood's coppery smell.

"I want to lick the blood off your leg," she said.

"Now, I'll have to keep *my* window closed against vampires," Jack said.

3

Before they went out to Dixie and Nicole, Caroline told Jack that she'd found no connection between Keating and the college.

"He must have some other influence," she said.

"I'll poke around," Jack said, "call some old friends. Shapiro was fired after he got involved in that electrical pollution case."

"I'll see if Keating has any connection with the electric company," Caroline said.

"What are you two doing in there?" Nicole called.

She knocked on the door.

"Your sister's helping fix me up," Jack called back.

"I'll bet she is," Nicole said.

"I think she's jealous you have a boyfriend," Jack said to Caroline.

"She's jealous you have a wound," Caroline said. "She likes being the only martyr in the neighborhood."

CHAPTER THIRTY-THREE

1

Singing alternate dirty lyrics to "You're the Top," Dixie leaned over the piano keys and hit the last note with his index finger, his thumb cocked as if he were pretending his hand were a gun. Like Chico Marx.

"The lyrics Cole Porter used to sing at parties," Dixie said. "When he lived in Williamstown."

A trickle of blood wormed down Jack's leg, over his ankle into his shoe.

"*He* claimed they were written by Irving Berlin," Dixie said.

Jack took a clean rag from the pile Caroline had put on the arm of the horsehair sofa and wiped it away.

The wound was clotting.

"Thick blood," Jack had told Caroline. "Comes from growing up messing with cars. Some people have greasepaint in their blood. Some have printer's ink. I've got crankcase oil."

"I've got some filthy Larry Hart lyrics, never recorded," Dixie said.

"Jack doesn't want to hear your cabaret act, Dixie," Nicole said.

"Mabel Mercer—" Dixie started.

"Maybe I should put another towel down. Under my foot," Jack said. "I don't want to ruin your carpet."

"Rug," Nicole corrected him.

"—taught me the lyrics the night we all got drunk at El Morocco—"

"It's from Kurdistan," Nicole said. "See the tiny horses along the inside left?"

"Angelo, the maitre d', taught them to her," Dixie said.

"It's a Mina Khani pattern," Nicole said.

"I think Jack's got other things on his mind right now," Caroline said.

Jack felt a metallic taste rising in his throat.

"It belonged to Dixie's grandfather," Nicole said about the rug. "My great-grandfather."

Jack took a swig of his bourbon.

"That night," Dixie said, "we all drove up to Edna St. Vincent Millay's house in Austerlitz," Dixie said. "She'd been dead for years, but her sister still lived there."

"The rug's irreplaceable," Nicole said.

Caroline sighed and said, "I'll get another towel."

"We arrived at dawn," Dixie said. "She gave us breakfast and then showed home movies from when her sister lived in the same brownstone as Cary Grant—Archie Leach back then. He's trying to teach her to stilt walk."

The living room windows were double paned. Cloudy stains looked like nebulae caught between the two sheets of glass.

"You're looking at my collection of antique false teeth," Dixie said to Jack. "I specialize in pre-World War Two."

Jack—who hadn't noticed the collection—followed Dixie's glance to the fireplace mantelpiece, where a dozen pink-and-white dentures grinned, disembodied, at him.

Dixie got up from the piano bench and settled in one of the Duncan Phyfe Sheraton chairs flanking the fireplace.

"My nieces think my collection odd," Dixie said.

"Freaky," Nicole said.

Caroline came back with a dark red towel, which she spread over the blue towel under Jack's foot.

"If the blood stain doesn't come out," Caroline said to Nicole, "it will blend in."

"Bitch," Nicole said.

"Bully," Caroline said.

Jack took another swig of bourbon.

"But dentures are no odder than other things people collect," Dixie said.

"God, Caroline," Nicole said, "he's going to tell about the guy in New Paltz who collects the shit of famous people."

Jack's leg throbbed.

"I should go," he said, low, to Caroline.

"You can't walk," Caroline said.

"Then," Dixie said, "there was that rare-book collector in Philadelphia who bought Napoleon's penis."

"Caroline," Nicole said, "Dixie's talking about Napoleon's penis again!"

Jack finished his drink and poured himself another brimful glass.

"It'll dehydrate you," Caroline said.

"It'll help kill the pain," Jack said.

"You already had three Percodan," Caroline said.

"My roommate at Deerfield collected Tijuana bibles," Dixie said. "Pornographic satires of comic strips. Blondie and Dagwood. Blondie has the biggest bosom of any cartoon character."

"I should go home," Jack said.

"Bigger than Tootsie," Dixie said.

"You should go to the emergency room," Caroline said.

"Art, rat, tar," Dixie announced.

Jack, Caroline, and Nicole looked at him.

"All have the same three letters," Dixie said.

"Dixie," Nicole said, "you're drunk."

"And you're getting drunk," Caroline said to Jack. "It's not smart to drink with painkillers."

"It's been weeks since I've done anything smart," Jack said. "Years." He took a slug of the bourbon. "My whole life."

"I'll get you some coffee," Caroline said.

"My wife," Dixie said, "came from the last generation of women to travel with hatboxes."

"I'll get it myself," Jack said.

Jack hobbled across the room to the sideboard, which held a twelve-cup coffee urn.

"Coal chutes and straw on blocks of ice," Dixie said. "The scissor man and the junk-dealer's horse-drawn cart," sounding like Jack, when he was trying to convince Caroline he was too old for her.

"For God's sake, Jack," Nicole said, "take a towel with you."

"You're all in Technicolor," Dixie said.

"You'll ruin the rug," Nicole said.

"I live a black-and-white life," Dixie said.

Jack put a cup under the coffee spigot and depressed the handle. The cup filled. When Jack pushed the handle back upright, the coffee kept pouring.

"There's something wrong," Caroline said, getting up.

Coffee spilled over Jack's cup.

"The spigot's broken," Caroline said, trying to help Jack stop the flow. "It's burning your hand."

Caroline grabbed Jack's cup out of the way.

Nicole watched horrified as the coffee urn emptied itself onto the Kurdistan rug.

Jack said, "You people are nuts!"

He stomped from the room, slamming out the front door.

"Jack," Caroline called.

She ran to the door. Opened it.

But Jack had flagged down a car and was climbing into it.

Inside the house, Dixie was saying, "I don't think I want to be cremated after all. I want a headstone."

Caroline watched the car pull away. Heard the change in pitch as the car changed gears.

She closed the door behind her and came back into the living room.

"Now, see what you've done?" Caroline said to Dixie and Nicole. "You've driven him away."

"Did you notice the back of Jack's head?" Dixie said. "The low bulge? Above the middle part of the cerebellum? Phrenologically speaking, that indicates philoprogenitiveness. Jack will make a good father."

2

Fuck them, Jack thought as he settled in the car he'd flagged down.

"I almost hit you, standing in the middle of the street like that," the guy driving said. A wiry man in jeans and white T-shirt. The right sleeve was folded up over a pack of Camels. His short red hair stood straight up.

"What happened to your leg, man?" the driver asked.

"My girlfriend bit me," Jack said.

"Cool," the driver said.

When Jack saw the pistol angling out of the driver's belt, the driver said, "Don't worry, fella, I got a carry permit. You don't think I'd of picked you up if I was traveling light, do you?"

With his left hand the driver reached across his body and unfolded the pack of cigarettes, which he shook, held up to his lips, plugging a cigarette into his mouth.

"Want a smoke?" he asked.

"No thanks," Jack said.

The driver tossed the pack onto the dashboard. From his pocket, he took a lighter with a picture of a bathing beauty on its plastic side.

When the lighter was upside down—as it was in his hand—the bathing beauty was naked. Her flesh the color of a baby's pacifier. The driver turned the lighter right side up. A white one-piece bathing suit slid over the naked body. He lit the cigarette, slit his eyes as he inhaled.

"Don't sit on the Windex," the driver said.

Jack moved the plastic Windex bottle from behind him, where it was half tucked into the seat.

"Wiper fluid used to be ninety-nine cents a gallon," the driver said. "Now, it's five times that. Why not save a little, using Windex, until winter?"

As they passed Big Pig Bar-B-Q, smoke from the outside pit billowed across the highway into the car.

It smelled to Jack like Robert's burning body.

3

Jack climbed out of the car a few blocks away from Bix's one-story cottage. The fifty-year-old rust-colored asphalt shingles were stripped away from under the front window, revealing the tar paper beneath.

Bix's truck wasn't parked in the driveway. Two clunkers were on the lawn.

The wind dropped. The electric wires, which had been singing in the breeze, went silent.

Jack hobbled up the walk to the house, his cut pant leg flapping.

Jack opened the door. Bix never locked the house.

Bix wasn't home.

The house smelled of old bacon grease.

Jack stumbled into the living room and eased himself onto the couch.

He figured he'd just remove Caroline from his life. Bit by bit. Like shrapnel.

CHAPTER THIRTY-FOUR

1

At dawn, Jack sat bolt upright on the couch in Bix's cottage. Wide awake.

His pant leg—the previous night, he'd flopped down to sleep without getting undressed—was crusted with new blood. The couch cushion was also crusted, so thick, it flaked when Jack moved.

From outside, Jack heard a Johnny Cash and Waylon Jennings song. That must have been what woke him up.

Aching, light-headed from loss of blood, Jack eased himself up from the couch and took a few loping steps to the door of the cottage, which he opened.

Rays of green shot from the horizon into the dawn sky, like an opening fan.

In front of the shack, Jack's brother, Bix, was smashing the windshield of one of the clunkers—a battered Chevy.

The music had changed to "The Night Hank Williams Came to Town."

"County fair's next week, little brother," Bix said. "Got to get ready for the demolition derby."

"I'm too old," Jack said.

"You wasn't too old last year," Bix said, eying Jack's bloody pant leg and newly battered face.

"You got to get yourself a new hobby," Bix said, nodding at Jack's injuries.

"This year," Jack said about the demolition derby, "you ride solo."

"We ain't never missed a year since you was nineteen," Bix said.

Bix swung the crowbar backhanded and left a spiderweb crack in a side window.

"I got another crowbar," Bix said.

"I need a gun," Jack said.

"You got a gun," Bix said.

"Two guns," Jack said.

"Crowbar's better," Bix said, "for this work."

"Both untraceable," Jack said.

"You ask Mama?" Bix asked.

"I don't want to put Mama Lucky on the spot," Jack said.

"But I'm family, huh?" Bix said.

"Not the kind of spot I mean," Jack said. "I go to Mama, you find out, you go bawl her out."

"Then," Bix said, "I whop you upside the head for not coming to me."

Bix was smiling, but Jack knew how serious he was.

"You know I can get you what you want," Bix said. "Why go outside the family? You got something you want to tell me?"

"Where's the crowbar?" Jack asked.

Bix reached into his battered white Chevy truck and handed it to Jack.

Jack swung the crowbar, shattering first one then the other taillight. Despite the stab of pain in his side.

"Your condition," Bix said, "you sure you should be doing that?"

"Fuck, yes," Jack said.

2

By the time Caroline arrived, Jack and Bix had stripped most of the glass and chrome, anything that might shatter during the demolition derby, from the clunker.

"You weren't home," Caroline said. "You didn't answer your cell. I thought you might be here."

Jack was prying off trim.

"No one's going to bother you," Jack said. "Not with your uncle, your family around."

"That wasn't why I was upset you left," Caroline said.

Bix was welding the junker's doors shut. In his plastic goggles he looked like a BEM—bug-eyed monster—from a 1950s sci-fi movie, an effect heightened by the acetylene torch that seemed to shoot fire from his alien hand.

"I think we should call the cops," Caroline said.

"You trust them?" Jack said.

He circled the clunker. His leg throbbed.

"Someone should give your sister a good spanking," Jack said.

"Wouldn't she just love that!" Caroline said.

Jack gave the side trim a crack with the crowbar.

"Having fun?" Caroline asked.

Jack handed her the crowbar, which she swung with all her might at the side of the car.

"Everyone should keep a car like this in their yard," Caroline said. "There'd be fewer wars."

"Pry off the trim," Jack said.

Caroline did, working her way along the side of the car.

"Does Nicole know what happened to Robert?" Jack asked.

Caroline nodded.

"Big news in the local papers," she said. "Even over the border here in New York."

"I always said Robert was a real ball of fire," Jack said.

Caroline scowled. Not amused.

"The funeral's this afternoon," Caroline said.

The trim clattered to the stony ground.

"By the way," Caroline said, as she handed the crowbar back to Jack, "I saw someone standing outside our house last night."

Jack froze.

"Across the street," Caroline said. "I couldn't sleep. I was on my way to get a glass of water and happened to glance out the window. I'm sure he was watching the house."

Jack held the crowbar so tightly his knuckles went white.

"And all these years I've been afraid of aliens and vampires," she said.

3

"I'm not going to discuss it," Caroline said, as she and Jack crossed the grass toward Robert's funeral.

"A guy's watching your house—"

"Maybe."

"—and you think you don't need a gun?"

A dozen-and-a-half people were gathered around the grave.

"I can't kill anyone, Jack," Caroline said.

"A guy's squeezing your neck," Jack said, "you can't breathe, you know you're dying, and you tell me you wouldn't pull the trigger."

Caroline walked faster. Away from Jack.

Bix had promised to get Jack two guns. And a third for himself.

"When I'm not around," Jack had asked Bix, "keep an eye on her. When you can."

The tombstones lined up in neat rows looked like pieces on a giant Stratego board, as if someone were playing a cosmic game against—who? What?

God? Nature? Fate?

In the old cemetery to the right, all the tombstones were leaning or knocked over, as if whoever was losing had tried to end the game—against God, nature, fate—by upsetting the board.

Weatherworn skulls grinned lopsidedly from the old stones. A dancing skeleton, wearing victor's laurels, held in one boney hand the moon and in the other a smiling, spiky sun. A poker-faced Adam and Eve stood on either side of the Tree of Knowledge—or Life—staring down any passerby who might notice their effaced nudity.

Demons holding arrows of death.

Fierce angels blowing Trumpets of Doom.

Thunderbolts from stone clouds striking a stone earth.

God's wrath.

God's vengeance.

Human suffering.

Human evanescence.

Jack passed a grave decorated with a small, tattered American flag—a military flag with fringe—and a black-and-white flag in honor of missing Vietnam POWs. Along with a young man's birth and death, the tombstone was engraved with: *Hold Your Mud*.

A man in a seersucker suit and black-and-white spectator shoes caught up to Jack and asked, "Do you know where the pet cemetery is?"

Jack shook his head *no*.

The man shrugged and handed Jack a business card: *Pet bereavement: three sessions. Pet genealogies our specialty.*

"For a thousand years in Thy sight are but as yesterday when it is past," the minister droned, "and as a watch in the night . . ."

Jack took his place next to Caroline.

Under the bandages, his leg itched.

When he breathed, his ribs ached.

Across Robert's grave, Jack saw Keating. His chin seemed longer, the pouches under his eyes grayer, his cheekbones sharper. His face was crosshatched with fine lines, as if it were covered with a web of burlap.

But he stood erect, almost military in his posture, in a dark hat, dark suit, white shirt, dark bowtie, and black shoes so polished they reflected—Jack thought—the scudding clouds.

A trick of light?

Keating moved, not his head, but his eyes, and fixed his gaze on Jack's face.

"He knows," Caroline whispered, "we were with Robert when he died."

Watching Keating's raptor's eyes, Jack figured she was right.

CHAPTER THIRTY-FIVE

1

Jack caught up with Shapiro at his home on Amity Street. Shapiro had dodged calls at his office. He spotted Jack entering Judie's, where Jack had been told Shapiro was having lunch, and slipped out unseen.

Jack had to ring the front doorbell six times before Shapiro reluctantly answered.

"I'm busy," Shapiro said.

"Why did Keating Flowers get you fired?" Jack asked.

Without answering, Shapiro turned and headed along a hallway, decorated with old movie posters: Paul Muni in *I Am a Fugitive from a Chain Gang*, *Dreams of the Rarebit Fiend: Bug Vaudeville*, *Come Blow Your Horn*. . . .

On the wall next to the door at the end of the hall was a faded *New Yorker* cartoon of two modern bearded prophets, one holding a sign *Love thine enemies* and the other holding a sign *Love thy neighbor*.

The caption—one prophet saying to the other: *I'm telling you for the last time—keep the hell off this corner.*

In his cluttered study at the end of the hall, Shapiro sat at the old walnut kneehole desk. He hit play on his computer video.

Music came on. A song in German.

On the screen, over Shapiro's shoulder, Jack saw happy teenagers playing soccer, couples strolling in a park, kids romping in a kinder-garten. . . .

"Theresienstadt," Shapiro said. "The Nazi's model concentration camp,"

Shapiro said. "Where they sent the intellectuals. The artists. Like Kurt Gerron."

Shapiro explained: In the Thirties, Kurt Gerron was one of Germany's most accomplished and successful actors and directors.

Gerron played Police Chief Brown in the original stage and film versions of Bertolt Brecht and Kurt Weill's *Die Dreigroschenoper*. He was one of the stars of Josef von Sternberg's *Der blaue Engel—The Blue Angel*.

"He acted in or directed around seventy films," Shapiro said.

Unable to work in Germany after April 1, 1933, when, due to the boycott of Jewish businesses, Gerron was replaced by an Aryan director in the middle of a day's shooting, Gerron moved around Europe, each move a step down the economic and theatrical ladder. In 1942 he ended up in Amsterdam performing cabaret with one of his former leading ladies, Camilla Spira, at the Jewish Theater and, finally, as part of the *Entjudung*—the Jew-cleansing process of the Netherlands—at the transit camp Westerbork, where the camp commandant, SS-Obersturmbannfuhrer Lieutenant Colonel Albert Konrad Gemmeker, instituted a Monday-night cabaret on a stage made from a demolished synagogue to entertain the deportees who were to leave eleven o'clock Tuesday morning for the death camps in the east.

"Gemmeker opened the cabaret in honor of the forty thousandth inmate to be deported to the death camps," Shapiro said.

In all, over 104,000 Jews—along with Gypsies and Communists—were shipped out of Westerbork.

"On February 25, 1944, Gerron was shipped out in a cattle car along with Spira and her six-year-old daughter," Shapiro said. "In the cattle car, Gerron held his coat to shield the daughter when she had to use the bathroom, a single bucket in the corner."

At Theresienstadt, Gerron resumed the cabarets. As the Allies landed at Normandy and fought their way east, the Nazis had Gerron direct a propaganda film *The Fuhrer Gives the Jews a City*.

Jack nodded at a stack of printouts, CDs, art catalogs, books. . . .

Music in Terezin, 1941–1945, Theresienstadt: The Town the Nazis Gave to the Jews, I Never Saw Another Butterfly . . . Children's Drawings and Poems from Terezin Concentration Camp . . .

Books on concentration-camp memoirs, concentration-camp culture, concentration-camp humor. *Laughter in Hell.*

"Something you're working on?" Jack asked.

Shapiro gave Jack a wry sidelong look.

"You might say that," he said.

"A little out of your field," Jack said.

Silently, they watched the images from Theresienstadt.

"Sixty or so years ago," Shapiro said. "Not so long ago."

On-screen, the documentary explained that on July 23, 1944, Red Cross observers visited the camp.

The observer was so impressed by the inmates' chorus, he made the camp commandant Karl Rahm promise never to separate them—a promise Rahm kept: After the Red Cross left, Rahm sent everyone in the chorus to the gas chambers at Auschwitz together.

On-screen, hundreds of marching Nazis made up a choreographed swastika.

"Busby Berkeley, right?" Shapiro said. "It's all show biz."

The marching swastika turned like the gear of a great machine.

"I'm beginning to understand why you were fired," Jack said.

2

An ancient woman shimmered into the doorway. Shapiro's grandmother.

She still has sex appeal, Jack thought. Star power.

"I wants to be an actor lady . . . ," Shapiro's grandmother sang in a surprisingly robust, husky alto, *"be in a play up on Broadway . . . "*

She wore a wrapper with big orange flowers. When she swayed her hips, the cloth flowed. . . .

"Ms. Lucas!" Shapiro called his grandmother's nurse.

"I heard that song when I was five years old," Shapiro's grandmother was saying. "On the Boardwalk."

"Ms. Lucas," Shapiro called, "could you come and get Bubbe?"

"At Atlantic City," Shapiro's grandmother was saying.

Jack expected a large, imposing nurse to appear in the hallway behind Shapiro's grandmother. But Ms. Lucas turned out to be a sexy young woman in her early twenties, with flame-red hair and catlike eyes.

"Come on, Sadie," Ms. Lucas said to Shapiro's grandmother.

"You should have seen me when I was young," Sadie said. "I was the girl on the Carolina Cigar band."

"I saw a picture," Jack said. "In your grandson's office."

"My tits were beginning to sag," Sadie said, "but I still had the best ass in the business!"

"Dr. Shapiro has work to do," Ms. Lucas said.

"You got a pretty good caboose, yourself," Sadie said to Ms. Lucas.

"Who," Ms. Lucas said, "would've ever thought I'd consider bringing sexual harassment charges against a hundred-year-old woman?"

"Tara-ra-ra-boom-de-a!" Sadie sang, giving a grind and bump.

"We'll watch a movie," Ms. Lucas said.

Ms. Lucas started to lead Sadie out, but Sadie stopped. Turned coyly back to Jack and said in a very uncoy voice, "Watch your back, mister. They think getting old means getting simple."

"The world's a concentration camp," Shapiro said. "We try to mock up a civilization. Like Gerron's movie. For show."

3

"When I was fired," Shapiro said, "I tried to explain to everyone it was because I was going to testify about electrical pollution."

"A conspiracy, huh?" Jack said.

"Everyone said I was crazy. Said conspiracies don't exist. But sometimes conspiracies exist. Sometimes they're big. Sometimes they have awful consequences."

"You're just trying to make what happened to you bearable by making it part of something bigger?" Jack said.

"The world is filled with conspiracies," Shapiro said. *"Don't tell so-and-so we're having a party after work, just the three of us are getting together, no one else*—but conspiracy is just another tool. A compass. Let's you tell where you are in the wilderness."

Jack looked out his window at the corduroy sky.

"You think I'm paranoid?" Shapiro asked. "You think I've got a persecution complex?"

"Things just don't happen that way," Jack said.

"Then why did Flowers get me fired when I got involved in the lawsuit about electrical pollution?" Shapiro said.

"Why would Flowers care?" Jack asked.

An hour later, Caroline arrived and told Jack, "Keating is on the board of Mohawk Electric."

CHAPTER THIRTY-SIX

1

"There are no coincidences," Jack once had told Caroline.

"Try this," Jack said.

Jack was talking to Caroline from across the top of the clunker Bix had moved to Jack's shack—Jack's demolition derby car, which Jack was painting.

"Frank finds out Jean's suffering from electrical pollution. Thinks there may be money in this."

"A class-action suit against Mohawk," Caroline said.

"He finds out about Shapiro's research," Caroline said. "About why Shapiro attacked Keating. He had the docket number."

Abruptly, Jack fell silent.

"Which would explain why Frank visited Keating," Caroline said.

Jack dipped his brush into green paint and started painting lightning bolts on the car's right fender.

"To blackmail him," Caroline said.

Jack painted starbursts.

"Blackmail's easier than going to court," Caroline said.

On the car's roof, Jack started painting a night sky.

"Are we saying Keating had Frank killed?" Caroline asked.

Jack painted a star. Part of Orion's belt.

"And Jean?" Caroline said under her breath. "Jean's his own daughter."

2

Dixie drove up to Jack's shack in his '63 dark-blue Oldsmobile. As he was still coming to a stop, Nicole jumped out of the passenger side.

"Dixie guessed you'd be here," Nicole said.

She was dressed in baggy khaki shorts with oversize pockets and a man's white shirt knotted in front, exposing her tanned belly.

With a belly button that looked like a Celtic knot.

"The office called, Sweetpea," Dixie explained. "Urgent, they said."

From her pocket, Caroline pulled her cell.

"No juice?" Nicole asked.

Caroline stuck the cell back into her pocket.

"No juice," Nicole confirmed, adding, about Caroline's face, "Just look at that puss. Hey, Caroline, no juice, it's no big deal."

"I told them I'd get you the message," Dixie said.

"And I wanted to see Jack's place," Nicole said, surveying the shack. "The lap of luxury, Jack. What'cha doing?"

"It looks as if you're getting ready for the demolition derby," Dixie said, slipping out from the driver's side.

Dixie wore a three-piece white suit, white shirt, baby blue bow tie, off-white socks, white shoes, and a crushable white fedora.

"Nicole," Dixie said, "you were born and bred in this county and you don't recognize a demolition derby car when you see one?" He shook his head. "I have neglected your education. Give me a brush, Jack. It's been a long time since I've helped prepare a clunker like this."

Noticing Nicole's look, Dixie added, "When I was your age, I came close to winning a demolition derby. You driving at the county fair, Jack?"

"Day after tomorrow," Jack said.

"Friday night?" Dixie said. "I'll be there."

Dixie took a brush out of a pail of paint thinner and inhaled deeply.

"I love the smell of turpentine," Dixie said.

He studied the colors in each of the six gallon cans of paint. Daintily, he dipped his brush in black and with a few deft strokes outlined a reclining nude.

"You're such a dirty old man," Nicole said.

"She only says that," Dixie told Jack, "because last night, while we were watching a Doris Day movie on TV, I told her Bob Hope used to call her JB. For Jut Butt."

"I want a brush, too," Nicole said.

She grabbed a brush from the can of paint thinner and plunged it up to the handle in red paint.

"You're going to ruin your suit, Dixie," Caroline said.

Jack could tell she was making an effort to sound casual.

So—Jack thought—could Dixie, who shot her a glance.

3

"You're really going to drive?" Nicole said.

She flipped her brush at Jack, spattering wildflowers behind him: hollyhocks, lilies, asters.

"Is it dangerous?" Caroline asked about the demolition derby.

A mutt trotted over to check out the paint-spattered flowers, then sniffed a tree.

"He's checking his e-mail," Dixie said.

"Is it dangerous?" Caroline asked.

Another, larger dog came to check the spattered flowers. The first dog sniffed the second dog's rear.

"Now," Jack said, "he's checking the canine Facebook."

Nicole made a face and attacked the clunker with red paint, which dripped from her brush down the back of her hand and wrist.

"Is it dangerous?" Caroline asked.

Jack tilted his head and appraised Dixie.

"You've been around for a while," Jack said.

"You're not old," Dixie said, "until you have trouble pulling on your own socks."

"What have you learned from living so long?" Jack asked.

Dipping his brush, Dixie said, as if it was confidential between the two of them, excluding his nieces, "Life is simple. You go from keeping the bathroom door locked when you're a teen so you won't be caught jerking off, to keeping it unlocked when you're my age in case you have a heart attack."

Jack laughed and said, "Dixie, you're okay."

"Is it dangerous?" Caroline shouted.

Jack, Dixie, and Nicole turned to her in unison.

"Not usually," Dixie said.

"I don't want you driving," Caroline told Jack.

But Jack was staring past her shoulder.

Caroline turned just in time to see a man disappear into the trees at the top of a hill.

From Jack's face, she knew it was the man who had tried to kill him on the train.

CHAPTER THIRTY-SEVEN

1

Jack hobbled up the hill into the trees, leaving Caroline to improvise an explanation: "A neighbor Jack's having trouble with."

"What kind of trouble?" Nicole asked.

"Property rights," Caroline said.

Halfway up the slope, Jack stepped in an animal burrow. Opening up the wound in his leg. Jack felt the bandage get moist. Felt blood sliding down his leg.

Where the dirt slope was almost vertical, Jack used a row of birches as handholds, pulling himself up to the road on the crest above his shack.

Jack found footprints in the soft earth. Tire tracks where the Cowboy must have peeled out when he realized he was noticed.

Why did the Cowboy bolt?

Jack was with three witnesses.

Maybe the Cowboy wanted to keep his job simple. Not out of any humanitarian motive, but out of efficiency.

One corpse is easier to explain away than four.

After Dixie and Nicole left, Caroline told Jack, "Get me a gun."

2

"Don't forget to call your office," Jack said as he was using a screwdriver handle to tap on the cover of a paint can.

Caroline used Jack's cell phone, wandering in circles as Jack carried the paint cans into a shed beside his shack.

When Caroline handed Jack back his cell, she told him, "They said if I don't go back tomorrow, full-time, they want my resignation."

"Someone pressured them," Jack said.

"They don't want me working with you," Caroline said. "On whatever it is we're working on."

"Maybe," Jack said, "they're trying to keep you from getting killed."

3

"We're getting out of our depth," Caroline said.

"I don't think we can swim back to shore," Jack said. "Not now."

Caroline didn't answer.

"And if we get back to shore," Jack said, "nothing's going to look the same."

"So we confront Keating?" Caroline asked.

"We have no proof," Jack said.

"Then," Caroline said, "what do we do?"

"Stay alive until we get proof," Jack said.

"And if we don't get proof?" Caroline asked.

"We get revenge," Jack said.

CHAPTER THIRTY-EIGHT

1

"Meet me back here in the morning," Jack told Caroline. "Bix'll be watching out for you."

On the way to Mama Lucky's, Jack stopped in a Price Chopper to pick up a couple of jars of half-sour pickles, Mama Lucky's favorite.

Inside the supermarket, thunder rumbled over speakers in the produce department, followed by artificial rain, sprinkling the green beans, cucumbers, Brussels sprouts. . . .

Outside, as Jack crossed the parking lot, he again heard thunder, this time cracking a few miles away over the river, followed by lightning and a wind that flung the car door back on its hinges while Jack slipped behind the steering wheel.

By the time Jack got to Mama Lucky's, a downpour swept the streets with sheets of rain.

On the sidewalk, a man heading into the wind leaned over, his hand holding his cap.

Inside Mama Lucky's, a heavyset man with scabs on his shaved head was trying to strap stag antlers onto the head of a naked whore.

Mama Lucky tilted her head, offering him her cheek, not her lips, to kiss.

"You've been neglecting me, Jack Slidell," she said. "Pickles won't do the job."

"Anything you want, Mama," Jack said. "Say the word."

"You been spending your time with that girlie you brought last time,"

Mama Lucky said, unscrewing one of the pickle jars and fishing for a spear.

"Have you heard about any new talent in town?" Jack asked.

"Sport-fucking never worked for you," Mama Lucky said. "When you jerk off, you have to fall in love with your hand."

"A guy who likes razors," Jack said.

"You have a close shave?" Mama Lucky asked.

Jack dropped his pants to show Mama Lucky the bloody bandage on his thigh.

"I'll ask around," she said.

2

Unable to sleep, Caroline put her quilted robe on over the cotton panties and T-shirt in which she slept and padded downstairs to raid the refrigerator.

She was leaning over, left arm holding the door open, the glare from the refrigerator light making a pasty mask of her face, when she heard someone scuffing behind her.

She whirled around so fast, she knocked a plate of roast chicken onto the floor with a crash that made her—and Dixie, who had just come into the kitchen—both jump.

"Careful of the broken glass," Dixie said, grabbing paper towels and kneeling to scoop up the shards of glass, chicken, and jellied fat.

He was wearing an old-fashioned, ratty, maroon silk dressing gown over striped pajamas and backless leather slippers. A tuft of white hair stood up on the top of his head.

Caroline stepped out of the glass mess, also grabbed a paper towel, and ran the wad under the sink faucet.

Through the window over the sink, Caroline saw Bix standing across the street in the shadow of a large tree.

3

The next morning, at Jack's shack, Caroline said, "You're trying to make sure *I'm* safe. Is it safe for *you* to stay here?"

Ignoring her, Jack said, "We've been thinking too small."

At his laptop, Jack logged onto the Internet.

"Frank's class-action suit . . . ," he said. "Why limit the damage it could do to Mohawk? Electrical pollution's all over the country."

Jack checked the computer screen, jotted down some notes on a yellow pad, and went back to the computer keyboard.

"Keating's on the board of three other electric companies in the Northeast," Jack said. "And on the board of the North American grid."

"So," Caroline said, "we're not just talking about Keating anymore, are we?"

Jack's cell rang. He grabbed it.

"Yeah," he said.

On the other end of the line, Tremain said, "I never got fingerprints from the bowling ball your cowboy pal used."

"They couldn't lift any?" Jack asked.

"Fuck if I know what they could or couldn't do in the lab," Tremain said. "I never got the workup. Instead, I got a visit from two guys in white shirts, ties, and suits, with IDs from the Department of Agriculture. They were Feds all right, Jack, but no way these guys were from the Department of Agriculture. They wanted to know why I was asking about the prints from the bowling ball. Whatever the fuck you've gotten involved in, drop it."

Tremain hung up.

Before Jack had a chance to tell Caroline what Tremain said, his computer blinked.

The screen went black.

Jack hit some keys, thinking that his screen saver had kicked in. But Jack's screen saver was a moving star field. Not a black screen.

Nothing Jack did had any effect on the computer, which seemed as if it were being controlled over the Internet by someone unseen.

The C:/ prompt appeared on the top left corner of the screen. As Jack hit keys trying to stop it, all his files scrolled up, deleted one by one.

Any information Jack may have had on Frank or Jean or Stickman or Robert or Keating or electrical pollution was being purged.

"It doesn't matter," Caroline said. "We still know. . . ."

Which is when the electricity went out.

The computer screen on battery power cast a pale glow as the deleted files scrolled past.

CHAPTER THIRTY-NINE

1

As he drove, Jack checked cars both in front of and behind him to make sure they weren't being tailed.

Jack said, "Bix told me the job he applied for—"

"The one in the prison?" Caroline asked.

"He heard through the grapevine he got it," Jack said. "The next day, they turned him down."

Jack made a sudden, random turn up a side street.

"They're going after you," Jack said, "after Bix. . . ."

He doubled back, watching to see if any cars followed. Or if one car dropped off as another car picked him up.

"It doesn't matter," Jack said about his evasive driving. "We're not that hard to find."

Caroline looked over her shoulder out the car's back window.

"When I was a kid," Jack said, "we had a party line. You never knew who was listening in. Everybody knew everybody else's business."

Jack took a left onto County Route 9G. There were no cars either ahead of him or behind him.

"It can't just be about a class-action suit," Caroline said.

"Sure it can," Jack said. "People kill each other for fifty bucks."

2

Jack took a sharp left, almost a hairpin turn, onto Route 66. Up ahead, a woman in a sequined gown, white boa, and feathered headdress was hitchhiking, holding a sign that read: *Ghent Playhouse*.

"At this point," Jack said about the hitchhiker, "I wouldn't even trust her."

Jack drove through Chatham, East Chatham. In Massachusetts, they passed a Shaker village, which had a circular building topped by a smaller circular second floor, like a gun turret.

Jack stopped for gas at a country store. While waiting to pay, he read a flyer on the counter:

Hunters For The Hungry. Donate Venison To Food Pantries. Only Chopped Meat And Stew Cuts—Proper Labeling—Authorized Processers—Program Started In 1998—Minimum 5 Pounds. An Entire Deer Can Be Donated If It Is An Adult Doe Or Buck—Clean Kill—No Fawns—We Pay Processing—If Not Skinned Hide Becomes Property Of Processer—Special Arrangements Must Be Made For Deer Heads And Capes To Be Mounted.

Five miles down the road was an electric sign advertising: *Carpet For Less—3 Rooms Of Carpets For $119 Up To 340 Sq. Feet*.

In Mycenae, when Jack stopped at a red light, he started laughing.

Outside a *Kansas* Fried Chicken franchise, a man in a chicken suit was passing out advertisements: *Best Breasts In Town*.

Across the street, a second man in a chicken suit was also passing out advertisements—for *Kentucky* Fried Chicken.

When a man in a sports jacket stopped to take an advertisement from the second man in a chicken suit, the first man in a chicken suit shouted, "You're not going to eat this guy's roadkill, are you?"

The second man in a chicken suit shouted back, "Hey, Mac, work your own corner!"

"What?" the first man shouted, "you own the whole block?"

"Pigeons!" the second man shouted. "That's what they serve there."

The first man crossed the street.

"Get the fuck out of here," he said to the second man.

The first man in the chicken suit shoved the second man in the chicken suit.

"You want a piece of me?" the second man asked.

The man in the sports jacket, got into his car and drove away, leaving the street empty except for Jack and Caroline in their car, watching two men in chicken costumes fighting.

"That's it," Jack said. "That's it—everything anyone needs to know about what we are. What human beings are."

Jack laughed so hard he wept.

The light had turned green and red and green again.

"I'm scared," Caroline said, her voice small.

Catching his breath, Jack hit the gas.

"We can't drive around in circles all afternoon," Caroline said.

Jack stopped the car and kissed Caroline. Her lips were chapped. Her hair smelled of strawberry shampoo. And the rank sweat of fear.

"I want to go home," she said.

3

Carrying an old, discolored straw boater with an equally ancient *All The Way With Adlai* campaign button pinned to the hat's frayed ribbon, Dixie sauntered out onto the terrace.

"I think we have time for a sail," he said to Jack.

"I don't think so, Dixie," Caroline said. "Look at the weather."

The clouds were boiling over the Catskills. Far off, a dog barked. A cat stopped stalking through the grass and laid its ears back.

From a house down the street, through an open window, the sound clear even from so far away, Jack heard a TV newscaster saying, "Flooding's going to be serious if these winds continue. Storm surge expected to be five to eight feet. Wind gusts up to one hundred twenty miles per hour. . . ."

Caroline went into the house to prepare the salad. Dixie touched Jack's elbow.

"I woke up last night," Dixie said. "At two in the morning. I heard someone driving an all-terrain vehicle through the fields. The noise rattled the windows."

The wind was stronger.

"Some young man—or young woman—I assume they're young—out there alone, racing under the sky," Dixie said. "What makes someone do that? Drive at night? All alone."

The clouds were blacker. They swallowed the sun. A gust of rain spattered against Jack's face.

Abruptly, Dixie asked, "How did you cut your leg, Jack?"

More black clouds rolled in from the Catskills.

"My brother—Caroline and Nicole's father—and their mother died before I did," Dixie said. "Caroline and Nicole are what I have. I'm not afraid of death, not for me. But for them. And before they have children."

"I thought Caroline couldn't have kids," Jack said.

"She told you that?" Dixie said. "She's convinced herself. The doctors took a lot. She wants to believe they took everything."

Dixie looked through the kitchen window at Caroline chopping a green pepper.

Dixie waited for Jack to say something. Jack had nothing to say. The rain rattled on the water as if the river were sheet metal.

CHAPTER FORTY

1

Thunder and lightning came almost simultaneously over the river, which smelled like soured milk. Drenched, Jack and Dixie retreated to the kitchen, which was a pool of light in the surrounding darkness.

"You're bleeding," Caroline said.

Jack's pants leg was stained with washed-out blood. He'd barked his leg on the kitchen doorjamb.

Upstairs, Caroline, who had changed into dry clothes, washed Jack's wound and wrapped it with gauze. Jack sat on the edge of the tub. She crouched at his feet. Jack looked lovingly at her pale scalp, which showed through her damp hair.

Someone knocked on the bathroom door.

Jack, naked, stood—painfully—and wrapped a bath towel around his waist.

Caroline opened the door, revealing Nicole, who held out an armful of dry old clothes.

"I raided the dress-up trunk," Nicole said. "Blue-and-white striped slacks, a white silk shirt . . . very retro. If you want socks, I can rustle up a pair of white gym socks or a pair of argyles. I don't think we have any shoes that will fit you."

Caroline took the slacks and shirt.

"We don't keep underwear in the dress-up trunk," Nicole said. "Dixie's got some cotton boxers, but I figured you'd rather go without."

"Clever girl," Jack said.

"Dinner in ten," Nicole said.

They sat around the near end of the dining room table, the breakfront and Caroline's great-great-uncle looming over them. They each had a bright-red, steaming-hot pound-and-a-half lobster. Caroline drank Heineken from a bottle. Nicole drank homemade lemonade. Jack bourbon neat. Dixie sipped a tall reddish drink on cracked ice.

"J&B," Dixie said, "vermouth, cherry juice. . . . My own concoction."

"It's Dixie's hobby," Caroline said, "inventing cocktails."

Caroline wore a white robe with a pattern of tiny blue flowers. She had rolled up the voluminous sleeves so they wouldn't drag in the lobster or melted butter.

As she ate, her eyes were wide. Her hair, which she had brushed forward, framed her face. Her left nostril quivered. Her cheeks were flushed.

"Don't stare, Jack," Nicole said. "No matter how smitten you are, it's not polite. Look, Caroline, he's blushing."

2

After dinner, the four of them sat, Jack drinking bourbon; Caroline, beer, her third; Nicole, chamomile tea; and Dixie, coffee. Listening to Brahms' "In Stiller Nachte." And reading: Jack, the Albany *Times Union*; Caroline, the *New York Times*; Nicole, *New York*; and Dixie, a Thorne Smith novel.

"*Night Life of the Gods*," Dixie said, holding up the old, faded, buff-covered book. "A novel about a scientist who invents a ray that turns people into statues and a sexy lady leprechaun who can turn statues into people. She brings the Olympian gods to life, and they have a delightful time, but realize—the scientist and the leprechaun—they there is no place for them in this disenchanted, solemn world. At the end, when they turn the gods back into statues, they embrace and turn themselves into statues, too. Every year, I reread it, Jack. If you want, you can borrow it. Thorne Smith was the Cole Porter of American novelists."

"No thanks, Dixie," Jack said.

"You can stay the night," Dixie said.

"You can't go home," Caroline emphatically told Jack.

"The guest room's at the top of the stairs," Nicole said. "Caroline can get you a towel and washcloth and anything else you need." She smirked at Jack and said, "If you get bored with Ms. Appropriate, Jack, my biological clock just went off daylight saving time."

"Tomorrow, the fair starts," Dixie said.

"And you drive in the demolition derby," Caroline said, unhappily.

3

Caroline led Jack up the stairs and steered him into her bedroom.

The rain had almost stopped.

Caroline's room had four large windows, two on each exterior wall. The curtains were dark blue and held back with blue sashes. The wallpaper was a lighter blue with pink-and-white blossoms. The wood trim—around the windows, the molding, the baseboards—was semigloss, eggshell.

A large framed reprint of a post-World War I French train ad dominated one wall. Smaller, framed photographs of Dixie and Nicole were scattered on the other walls. Pressed behind an antique oval glass was a large fern.

Instead of a closet—it was an old house—there was a large wardrobe with chipped veneer and, on one door, a clouded mirror. Between the two windows facing the river was a white-painted dressing table with another mirror. A quilted chair. A carved three-shelf cherry-wood bookcase filled with new novels and college editions of the classics. On the top shelf of the bookcase was an iPod in a docking station and two stacks of unsorted photographs. Between the other two windows was a small easy chair upholstered in a blue flowered pattern that matched the wallpaper. The polished, honey-colored wide-board floor was covered with small, old Oriental rugs, one with a repeating pre-Nazi, Sanskrit swastika pattern.

A double bed with a canopy the same material as the curtains stood in the middle of the room, the mattress so high you needed a two-step wooden stair to climb in. The quilt was light blue. The sheets and pillow cases were white. On one side of the bed was a side table with a parchment shaded lamp, an amber-colored plastic pill bottle, Zoloft, a tiny wooden sheep, and a hardback copy of a Stuart Woods mystery.

She closed the half-open drawer, which held safety pins, elastic bands, a purple scrunchy, coins, Band-Aids, a dozen loose blue Bicycle playing cards, and a small pink vibrator.

Caroline did not turn on the overhead light, but, starting with the bedside light, made a circuit of the room, turning on lamps with low-wattage bulbs, which gave the room a cozy glow.

Jack and Caroline took turns using the bathroom in the hall, Caroline first. When Jack returned to the bedroom, Caroline was already in bed, naked from the waist up, the sheet pulled up right below her breasts. Her nipples were pale.

Jack stripped and slid between the sheets, which smelled fresh and felt ironed. Caroline's skin smelled of soap. Her hair held a not-unpleasant trace of melted butter.

Caroline lay on her back, staring at the ceiling. Jack lay on his left side, staring at Caroline.

Caroline was silent.

"While you were in the bathroom," Jack said, "I took a quick walk around the house."

Caroline did not answer.

"As far as I can tell," Jack said, "no one's out there who shouldn't be."

Caroline stared at the ceiling.

"Sometime during the night," Jack said, "I'll check again."

Rain spattered against the windows.

"Caroline?" Jack asked.

She turned her head toward Jack and said, "I was praying. I pray every night. For Dixie, my mother, my father, Nicole, Robert—"

"Robert?" Jack asked.

"—you," Caroline said.

"Keating?" Jack asked.

Caroline nodded.

"The guy trying to kill me?" Jack asked.

Caroline nodded.

"That's promiscuous," Jack said.

"Every night," Caroline said, "the list gets longer."

"Where do you draw the line?" Jack asked.

"I don't," Caroline said.

"I never would have taken you for a believer," Jack said.

"Don't you believe in God?" Caroline asked.

"I'm not saying *no*," Jack said.

"But?" Caroline asked.

"But the world is filled with horror," Jack said.

Caroline pushed down the sheet.

"Are you ready for some happy-face sex?" she asked. A little too brightly.

She hooked her finger under the crotch of her panties and pulled the cloth aside for him.

CHAPTER FORTY-ONE

1

Much later, in the dark, Caroline told Jack, "My mother would have liked you. She would have given you a hard time, she gave everyone a hard time, but she would have liked you.

"She was old pioneer stock," Caroline said. "She used to tell us— Nicole and me—the secret of life is to be the gunfighter who's not afraid to die. Maybe she said *killer*. The killer who's not afraid to die."

2

Even later, Caroline asked Jack, "What about your mother and father?"

"My mother ran off when Bix and I were little," Jack said.

"And your father?" Caroline asked.

"Worked at the auto seat–cover factory," Jack said. "On Front Street. That old building across from the train station. He stood at the assembly line doing six separate actions. Over and over. Eight hours a day. Every day. Five days a week. His whole life."

"Now, it's some kind of experimental theater," Caroline said, "the old seat-cover factory."

Outside the wind howled.

"What happened to your dad?"

"Old age."

"How old was he?" Caroline asked.

"When he died?" Jack said. "Sixty-two. Old age comes sooner to the poor."

3

Caroline couldn't sleep. She slipped out of bed without waking Jack, who was softly snoring and slightly drooling from the corner of his mouth.

At the end of the dark hall, Caroline looked through the window and saw Bix in the shadow of the large tree across the street.

No. Bix was taller, broader.

In the shadows, this guy smoothed back his hair and fixed a cowboy hat on his head.

Caroline ran back into her bedroom, considered waking Jack, and then decided she'd rather prove she was as tough as he was. *The killer who's not afraid to die.*

She pulled on jeans and a top and, barefoot, scuffed on sneakers.

From a desk drawer, she took the gun Jack had given her. Solid in her hand. She loaded it as Jack had taught her, made sure the safety was on, and slipped it into her waistband.

She hurried down the stairs and through the kitchen into the mud room, where she grabbed a heavy black Mag-Lite.

Quietly, she opened the kitchen door, the screen door, and edged into the backyard.

The rain was steady. Cold. The wind was loud in the trees.

She crept from one backyard to another. At the end of the block, she slipped across the street and through more backyards until she was next to a garage opposite Dixie's house.

Ahead of her, the man in the cowboy hat stood so close to the tree trunk, he was almost invisible. Rain dripped off his hat brim.

Caroline pulled the gun from her waistband, clicked off the safety, held the gun in two hands—as Jack had demonstrated—crouched, raised the gun, aimed, and was about to squeeze the trigger.

From behind, someone grabbed her in a hug, forcing the gun down.

"You can't kill him," the man who held her whispered in her ear. Bix.

"We just *wait*?" Caroline angrily whispered. "Until he kills Jack?"

Ahead of them, the Cowboy turned his head towards them—as Jack, bare-chested, barefoot, just in slacks, burst out of Dixie's front door.

The Cowboy dodged sideways and ran diagonally into the street and then down the middle of the street.

Jack ran after him.

Bix and Caroline ran after Jack.

The rain semiblinded Jack.

Jack smelled wood smoke.

Jack dove, hooking the Cowboy's right leg. The Cowboy spun, freed himself, and kicked Jack in the face. Jack bulled forward, his shoulder against the Cowboy's thigh, and slammed the Cowboy against a tree.

The Cowboy pulled his gun and pressed it against the back of Jack's neck—as Jack pulled his gun and jammed it into the Cowboy's crotch.

Bix plowed into both of them.

The Cowboy tumbled over Jack's body, staggered, and ran up someone's driveway.

Caroline was on his heels. When she got to the end of the driveway, a closed two-door garage, she couldn't see the Cowboy in the yard.

He stepped out from a bush behind her and, grabbing her around the neck, pressed the gun into her head.

She swung her gun around and fired. She didn't hear the shot. She heard the ringing silence after the shot.

She missed, but the Cowboy released her, stepped back, and fired.

She heard that gunshot. And felt something ruffle her hair. The side of her head felt moist. Something trickled down her cheek.

Jack was there—she didn't recall him arriving—touching her head.

"You got creased," he said.

She was dizzy. Suddenly sleepy.

"You'll be okay," Jack said.

"No one wants the cops," Bix said—and melted into the shadows.

Grabbing Caroline's arm, Jack ran her through backyards, across a field, and waited for two patrol cars to pass.

"I woke up," Jack said, "you were gone. Your gun was gone."

They crossed the road and sneaked through more backyards.

When they reached Dixie's house, Jack gave Caroline his gun and said, "When you get inside, put alcohol on the wound. Go!"

Jack vanished around the side of the house.

Afraid someone might see her entering the house, might figure out she had something to do with the ruckus out front, Caroline scrambled up the trellis to the back porch roof, across the roof, and through her bedroom window.

Like Peter Pan. Like Dracula.

She had become the alien creeping into her room she had always feared.

As Caroline stepped though the window she saw a stranger in the mirror. Herself. Unrecognizable. Drying blood striped one cheek. But that wasn't what made her look different to herself. Stepping close to the mirror, she examined her face.

Maybe the difference she saw was in her eyes.

The secret of life is to be the killer who's not afraid to die.

She'd been not just ready but eager to shoot the Cowboy. The same way, when she was a teenager, once she'd decided, she had been not just ready but eager to lose her virginity.

She wished Bix hadn't stopped her.

Grabbing her cell phone, she took a photo of her face and sent it to Jack—with a text, *Where R U?*

No answer.

She crept out of her bedroom down the hall, into the screened sleeping porch above the front porch.

The trees and bushes, the street, the telephone pole, the people were all flashing red and blue in the rotating patrol-car lights.

Jack, still shirtless and barefoot, came out the front door of the house as if he'd just been awakened and was checking to see what the ruckus was about.

Some uniformed cops were pointing across the street at where the Cowboy had been standing.

A volunteer rescue-squad truck with a red light on its roof and a Chevy with a revolving blue light on its dashboard pulled up.

Jack was talking to a thin man in a suit, a detective, Caroline figured. The detective shrugged.

Jack turned back to the house and walked over to Dixie—in his maroon bathrobe—and Nicole—in her white terrycloth robe—who had just hurried onto the front porch.

Caroline crept back along the hall—red and blue lights reflecting off the ceiling—to her bedroom, where she took off her blouse and slipped out of her jeans and sent Jack cell photos of herself.

She took and sent him a picture of her breasts. Sent a second, a picture of her cunt, spreading her lips—the labia majora, the labia minora. Her own private constellations. The Big and Little Dipper.

Her cell phone pinged.

Jack texted back, *Wanted to make sure Bix got away.*

Her phone pinged again—a response to the photograph of her cunt.

The universe in a grain of sand, Jack texted.

Her phone pinged again. *As above so below.*

Her phone pinged again. *Lie down.*

Naked, she did.

Jack opened her bedroom door. He crossed the room and knelt between her legs.

She smelled like rain water. And tasted like the sweet syrup Jack used to suck from wax straws when he was a kid.

From the hallway, Nicole called, "Caroline . . . ?"

Caroline's breathing was hard, loud, throaty.

"Are you okay?" Nicole asked, close to the door.

Jack felt Caroline's solar plexus pump in and out with her breathing.

Nicole knocked.

Jack buried his face deeper between Caroline's thighs. Caroline gasped.

"You don't sound so good," Nicole said, opening the door. She stood for a moment trying to understand what she was seeing, then quickly backed out, saying, "My bad," and softly closed the door behind her.

After they made love, as they were curled in each other's arms, Caroline's head against Jack's chest, she said, "The universe in a grain of sand."

Jack's sweat smelled smoky. Pleasantly acrid.

"He's my favorite poet," she said. "Blake. . . ."

She could hear Jack's heart beating. She lifted her head slightly and pushed back her hair, so she could hear Jack's heart louder.

"When I'm old and married," she said, "I want to be like Blake and his wife, sitting together naked in our garden, surrounded by angels."

"In the sixties," Jack said, "early seventies, there was a rock group, The Fugs, I used to hear in the East Village. They sang a song from Blake. . . ."

Softly, Jack sang, "Sunflower, weary of time . . ."

"In London," Caroline said, "at the church—I think St. James's Church—where Blake was baptized, the base of the baptismal font is made up of a carved Adam and Eve and serpent, like a Blake print. I think when Blake was a baby and they sprinkled water on him, it must have been so cold, he opened his eyes and saw, *saw* the carved base, and Adam and Eve and the serpent were imprinted on his imagination."

"The head of the Fugs," Jack said, "Ed Sanders—he had a bookstore, the Peace Eye Bookstore, I hung out at. I used to wander through Tompkins Square Park, high on acid. Knowing most of the people I passed were high on acid, too. A lot of trust. No one worried about getting ripped off. Getting strung out. Getting old. . . ."

Jack kissed the top of Caroline's head.

"Why worry?" Jack said. "It didn't matter. Nothing mattered. We all thought the world was coming to an end. . . . Which meant, I guess, no consequences. Or our little consequences were swallowed up in Big

Consequences! The Bomb. The Age of Aquarius. The end of reality. If you took enough acid, the whole world, everything, was going to change the day after tomorrow."

"When Dixie's gone," Caroline said, "you'll protect us. You'll protect me."

"From what?" Jack asked.

"The day after tomorrow," Caroline said.

CHAPTER FORTY-TWO

1

Fat drops plopped around Jack and Caroline as they hurried toward the county fair.

"I feel like I've been let out of school," Caroline said.

"I figured you needed a break," Jack said, "and Bix is right. The fair is the last place the Cowboy—or whoever—is likely to be. Too many people. Too little privacy."

"Bix really wants you to be in the demolition derby," Caroline said.

"I haven't missed one since my first, when I was nineteen," Jack said. "Anyway, no one'll be crazy enough to try a hit here."

Caroline was silent.

"What?" Jack asked.

"A crowd like this," Caroline said, "is where I'd make my move."

"You're not a killer, Five Spot," Jack said, adding when he saw her expression, "I'll keep my eyes open."

Dixie and Nicole lagged behind them.

Wind rattled the chain-link fence enclosing the field filled with the clunkers painted and numbered for the demolition derby.

From a radio in the Boy Scout encampment, Jack heard a report of the approaching storm: *Sixty thousand homes without power . . . dumping torrential rains . . . heading northeast at twelve miles per hour . . .*

Before lunch, Bix had made two trips to bring his car and Jack's to the fair.

"You be back here by four, Jackie," Bix said.

A red cloth sign tied to a wooden fence said: *Budweiser Welcomes You.*

Next to it was another sign: *Seventh-Day Adventist Church at Kinderhook—Sabbath Services—Saturday—Salvation Is Free—No Strings Attached*. More signs: *4-H Archery; Olde Chatman Kettle Corn; Verizon Wireless Zone; Fresh Cold Cider Here; Face Painting; Chair Massage—10 Min = $10*. . . . Yellow diamond-shaped gag traffic signs warned: *Cattle Xing, Donkey Xing, Tractor Xing, Llama Xing, Pussycat Xing, Marines Xing, Snow Mobile Xing*. . . .

The midway was crowded. People wore Cowboy hats, baseball caps, held newspapers over their heads, used plastic garbage bags as makeshift ponchos, ignored the rain. . . .

But no Cowboy, Jack thought.

A burly man with red hair on his arms wore a blue shirt with cut-off sleeves. His daughter? Girlfriend? Wife?—it was hard to tell which—wore a T-shirt that said *Jeter 2*. An older man wearing a bright-orange slicker and a large Canon camera bellied up to the *Free engraving while-u-wait tent: Baby bracelets—anklets—Dog tags*. A woman with fat arms wearing a lime green top and white pants examined the ABATE of New York motorcyclists display: *Dedicated to the Freedom of the Road*. An elderly biker with a graying ponytail wore a shirt with a cartoon of a Hells Angel on a Harley and the motto *Ya Hated Us—Now Ya Wannabe Us*.

Down the way was another biker stand: *The National Coalition of Motorcyclists. NCOM. Region VIII*. A sign proclaimed: *A UNITED VOICE FOR ALL BIKERS* with a map of the United States overlaid with two shaking hands. A biker with a beer belly was handing out business cards.

Next to that was a tent with American flag bunting and a black POW-MIA flag, which whipped in the wind so hard it sounded like gun shots.

Jack scanned faces: No Cowboy.

State troopers strolled by in twos—as did county sheriffs, local police, and fair security. Guys and gals wore matching camo pants. Towering above the crowd were kids on fathers' shoulders, faces smeared with ice cream and red dye from the candied apples.

At the Columbia County Sportsmen's Federation booth, a stuffed fox with an old man's narrow, withered face gazed across the path at a four-foot-tall, fanged, cross-eyed, and goofily grinning stuffed bear. A chimney sweep—Dr. Soot-n-Cinders—advertised a free exorcism for sick houses with every job. Everyone passing was reflected in the lenses of a hundred sunglasses arrayed on a long table.

The air smelled of frying sausage and onions, deep-fried dough, spun sugar candy, mud, and manure. Under a glass window, ruby heat lamps glowed over pizzas. A tall woman with perfect features shot out her lower jaw to catch the sauerkraut dripping from her hot dog roll. A seven-year-old boy gnawed on a turkey drumstick almost as large as his fist and forearm. A jarhead in a muscle shirt wore spaghetti sauce like war paint.

Two men in kilts, sporrans, with mud-spattered knee socks played bagpipes and paraded through the crowd, followed by three more men in kilts, one carrying crossed swords, one carrying a bottle of scotch on a silver platter, and the third carrying a large tray with what looked like two damp, overstuffed maroon socks: Haggis.

"Have you ever tried it?" Caroline asked Jack. "You know how you sometimes bite your tongue and taste the blood? That's what haggis tastes like."

A blue kids' plastic wading pool empty of water was weighted down by a cinder block. The wind snapped banners decorating the US Army recruiting stand. Behind one food stand were a dozen fifty-pound bags of potatoes. Two sheared sheep lay in their pen dressed in white robes and white hoods with nose holes, eye holes, and ear holes. They looked like bovid Ku Klux Klan members. The insides of their ears were pink.

Rustic chairs and gliders, whirlpool hot tubs, leather vests, vacuum cleaners, satellite dishes, strings of colored beads, teddy bears, and signed baseballs were ranged along the path for sale. So was the farm machinery, forklifts, big Cats, and small John Deeres.

"You're jumpy," Jack told Caroline.

"I keep seeing cowboy hats," Caroline said.

"You get that at a county fair," Jack said.

People tried to pop balloons with darts, shoot water into bull's-eyes, and toss rings around knives. They threw pennies into goldfish bowls, shot BBs at targets, and played Whack-A-Mole. There were rocket-ship rides, Tilt-A-Whirls, a haunted house, a carousel, bumper cars. A zoo designed like Noah's Ark with real animals that looked like worn-out stuffed toys.

Looking at all the rides, all the colored girders, Dixie murmured, "It's a Jules Verne world."

All around the fair were scarecrows—farmer scarecrows, marrying scarecrows, sleeping scarecrows, even an alien scarecrow with almond eyes and a red bandana. A busty angel with a pouty porn-star's face hovered over the entrance to one of the exhibit buildings.

In one pen display chickens strutted, their crests like elaborate hats. Ducks quacked around a mud puddle dimpled by rain. Flop-eared rabbits glared red-eyed at the passersby. A nine-year-old boy led a cow through the throng toward the *Salute to Agriculture Tent and Dairy Birthing Center.*

A Culligan water purification salesman competed for attention with the woman behind the apiary booth. A man in a gold-colored jacket from the Pro-Life Booth—which displayed gallon jars with what looked like real fetuses—argued with a woman from the Pro-Choice Booth across the way.

"You're against slavery, aren't you," the pro-life man said. "It's a moral issue."

"But not a legislative one," the pro-choice woman said.

"I've known you since I was a kid," the man said. "You baby sat me."

"What's that got to do with anything?" the woman said. "And I think your display—those fetuses—is obscene."

"You're like those people who eat meat," the man said, "but don't want to know where meat comes from!"

"You're comparing fetuses to meat!" the woman said. "I'll tell you what, that's all I need to know, to know you're so wrong."

"When I was nine years old," the man said, "I had such a crush on you."

"Get over it," the woman said.

"I did," the man said. "Long ago."

As they argued, step-by-step they approached each other, leaving their displays behind.

"So," the man said, "on your break, we'll go to Perozzi's stand and get some dinner. . . ."

"Let's go to the Legion tent," the woman said. "They got platters."

Next to them was a stand that sold bumper stickers—*Rehab is for Quitters*—and T-shirts—*This is your brain* with a Yankees logo; *This is your brain on drugs* with a Red Sox logo. *Get famous get $. I may not be Mr. Right, but I'll fuck you 'til he comes along.*

At a display of different kinds of apples from upstate New York, Nicole polished a Cortland against her shirt and handed it to Caroline, who took a bite and offered it to Jack.

"No, thanks, Eve," Jack said to Caroline.

"Superstitious?" Nicole asked, grabbing another apple and polishing it before taking a bite. "If she's Eve, that makes me the serpent."

"Nicole," Jack said, "sometimes you can be a real pain in the ass."

"So," Nicole said, a fleck of apple sticking to her lower lip, "if Caroline is tossed out of Eden, you'll stay happy and comfortable inside? What a gentleman."

Jack grabbed the apple from Caroline, took a bite, and made a face.

"Too tart?" Nicole asked with a smirk.

2

To get away from Nicole, Caroline pulled Jack over to the haunted house. A car emerged from the exit, snapped around the turn, and stopped in front of them. They climbed in, pulled the safety bar down. With a jerk, the car started along the track and entered the urine-smelling tunnel. Caroline leaned her head on Jack's shoulder—and jerked up when a skeleton fell toward them.

Laughing, she snuggled back against Jack, squeezing shut her eyes.

"You're missing the ghosts," Jack said.

"Are there any vampires?" Caroline asked.

"Just one," Jack said. "And a Frankenstein monster. And a werewolf."

"I can hear it howling," Caroline said.

A moon on a wire rattled toward them in a collision course. Their car made a ninety-degree turn just before the crash.

"Tell me when it's over," Caroline said.

The car stopped at the entrance to the mirror maze.

"You can open your eyes," Jack said.

Caroline did.

"Why did you want to go on the ride if it scared you so much?" Jack asked.

"I like being scared," Caroline said. "Like a horror movie. When it's over, I feel safer."

They got out of the car, which continued on its way toward the exit, and entered the mirror maze. They were alone, the only people in the maze. Within a few minutes they were separated by glass panels, confused by the multiplying images, unsure which Jack or Caroline they should turn to, talk to, which were the real bodies and which were the reflections.

"Why did you say you were hollowed out?" Jack asked. "Dixie said—"

"Have you ever made a jack-o'-lantern?" Caroline said. "Cut off the top of the pumpkin, reach in, and rake out all the seeds and membranes and damp strings? That's what they did to me."

Jack turned from one Caroline to another.

"So Dixie's wrong?" Jack asked.

Caroline tried to decide which of three Jacks was the real one.

"No," she said.

Jack walked toward what he thought was the real Caroline and slammed into a wall of glass.

"But they took so much," she said.

Jack backed up. His nose hurt. His eyes watered.

"It'll be a miracle if I ever have kids," Caroline said, turning in a circle, surrounded by Jacks.

Jack felt his way along a wall of glass until he found a space.

"Why did you say you were empty?" Jack asked.

He went through the space—into a cul-de-sac.

"It's easier to accept that," Caroline said.

She put her palms on a glass wall.

"No hopes," she said. "Fewer complications."

On the other side of the glass wall, Jack put his palms up to hers—and realized that he was facing a reflection of a reflection.

3

Dixie was orating on the progress of civilization to a young man handing out Distributionist literature—*The Mississippi Delta and the Nile Delta, all those fertile triangles giving birth to commerce and civilization—those seductive, luxurious, lush, damp crotches where water meets land*—when he looked up and noticed something was wrong.

Jack, Caroline, and Nicole sat three abreast in the Whip. Their car was rotating on the end of a mechanical arm that was revolving around the center engine.

Like an old model of the solar system, Dixie thought.

Loudspeakers blared the *bop-de-bop-de-bop-bop-bop* of a Bo Diddley song, covered by Sha Na Na, older but still energetic, which was finishing up its show on the grandstand.

Loud enough for Dixie to feel it inside his body.

On the Whip, braced against the speed of the ride, Jack's mouth was turned down, a mask of tragedy. Caroline's mouth was turned up, a mask of comedy. Nicole's face looked as if it were breaking up into pieces.

Nicole opened her mouth. Wide.

Like Munch's *The Scream*, Dixie absently thought at the same time he knew Nicole was in trouble.

And she vomited. A great, multicolored plume of puke that arced out right in the path of the couple sitting in the next car.

An inexorable collision.

The faces of the young man and woman who were about to splash into the plume of puke shuttled rapidly through the five stages of grief: denial, anger, bargaining, depression, and acceptance.

Just as the collision happened.

Pressed back against the car by the speed of the ride, the couple couldn't wipe their faces.

Again, Nicole vomited.

Again, the plume of puke arced into the path of the couple in the on-coming car.

When Nicole vomited a third time, Dixie—up until them horrified and helpless—began to laugh.

Uncontrollably.

He doubled over, grabbed his chest, which hurt, he was laughing so hard, and for a moment thought he was going to lose his balance.

The vomit-covered couple, teenagers on a date, got off the ride. Eyes wide. Stunned.

"I'm so sorry," Dixie stammered though his laughter. "My niece. So very sorry . . ."

Jack and Caroline supported Nicole between them. Her chin was covered with drying vomit.

"I'll take her home," Dixie said. "Jack, I'll have to miss the demolition derby."

CHAPTER FORTY-THREE

1

"Gentlemen," the voice over the loud speaker said, "start your engines."

Jack had been sitting on the roof of his junker—Number 45—smoking a cigar, his legs, crossed at the ankles, dangling in the hole where the car's windshield had been. They had done a good job of stripping off all the glass and chrome, anything that might be jarred loose and under impact become a projectile.

"This year, Jackie," Bix—Car Number 46—said, "I'm gonna cream you."

"You do that, Pops," said a nineteen-year-old girl in bleached jeans and a sequined Bugs Bunny top—Car Number 52—who was slipping through her windshield hole into her driver's seat.

Jack tamped out the tip of his cigar, tucked it into the left flap pocket of his brown leather jacket, and slipped behind his wheel.

Jack heard a metal clamp clang against a flag pole. Then, chaos.

All around him engines were revving. Clouds of exhaust billowed into the air and hung over the junkers like cartoon dialogue balloons.

Jack and Bix were in the first heat. Four cylinders.

Usually, there were three or four four-cylinder heats, but this year the price of scrap metal was so high there were fewer clunkers available.

One by one, as the announcer called their numbers, cars nudged forward from the field where they had been parked, through the gate and into the football field–size arena, where, following the flagmen's instructions, they lined up, fifty cars to the left, fifty cars to the right, rear

bumpers facing rear bumpers, across the no-man's land that would become the center of combat.

The trick was to accelerate in reverse, crashing your rear end into everyone else's front, in order to disable their engines.

Out of one hundred cars, the last car running would win.

Some drivers circled on the outside, waiting for the rest of the cars in
the tight knot in the center to eliminate each other.

Jack's strategy had always been to stay in the center, where cars had
less room to maneuver. It was so crowded, no one could get up any
speed. Which benefited drivers who were skillful at targeting other cars'
weaknesses.

This car was vulnerable in the front right. If you tapped that car just
so, you could cripple its cooling system. . . .

Flagmen on the field stopped all action if a car's engine blew up or if
a car caught fire and they prevented—or tried to prevent—any car from
plowing into a car's side. Especially the driver's side. The cars were not
reinforced.

If you hit someone broadside, you could kill him.

Jack, his right arm over the back of his seat, turned to get a good look
through the empty back window frame and started to back up fast, aiming at a red Chevy coming up, four o'clock, on his right when, out of the
corner of his eye, he saw the Cowboy in a blue-and-rust Pontiac heading
straight toward his driver's-side door—clearly intending to crush him.

2

Jack slammed his car into drive and hit the accelerator. His wheels spun
in the mud, whined, caught, and he shot ahead through a gap between
two other cars.

The Cowboy missed Jack's door, bashed into his rear left quarter
panel, and spun Jack around ninety degrees. Just in time for Bix to reverse into Jack's front.

Jack saw Bix's grinning face, looking across his front seat back. He smelled the haze of gasoline that was settling over the field.

Bix lurched forward. Just far enough to give him room to back up again, hard, into Jack's engine.

Jack's wheels couldn't get traction. He was stuck in place.

As Bix again slammed into him in the front, another car crashed into his back.

And the Cowboy, having slewed around 360 degrees, came at Jack from nine o'clock, driving forward, gunning straight at Jack's side door.

Jack's wheels caught. And his car jerked back a few feet—just far enough to keep Jack from being crushed when the Cowboy hit Jack's left front bumper instead of Jack's left front door.

Jack jockeyed forward and back, forward and back, bashing into Bix's car and the car behind him, trying to make enough room to turn his clunker to the right, to get away from the Cowboy's car, which was again circling the crush, ready to make another run at Jack's front left door.

Over the grinding of gears and the ripping of metal, Jack heard the flag-men's whistles, saw two of them running toward him, waving red flags.

Jack shot out in the space that opened up between two cars that were backing away from each other.

He caught Bix's attention and pointed at the Cowboy's car.

Bix's eyes looked blank, then puzzled, finally comprehending—as the Cowboy's car was coming a third time at Jack broadside.

A bashed-up Ford slammed into Jack's rear left, swinging him into a perfect side-on target for the Cowboy.

Hand over hand, Jack turned his steering wheel as he popped the gear shift into drive.

The Cowboy was leaning forward over his steering wheel. His face was composed, revealing neither glee nor anger nor sorrow nor satis-faction.

Jack's wheels spun.

The Cowboy seemed—in that frozen moment—to be sucking on a back tooth.

Jack's wheels kept spinning.

The Cowboy braced himself for the collision.

Jack considered diving away from the driver's side, trying to scramble out the passenger's window—but two cars were about to collide on his right. One was scraping his car, rocking it.

The Cowboy's car seemed huge—like the moon in the haunted house ride.

Jack smelled his spinning tires burning.

He, too, braced himself for the collision—when Bix's car slammed into the side of the Cowboy's car, spinning it ten degrees off target.

Jack's tires caught. Jack's car leapt forward.

Flagmen were all around them, calling a temporary stop. Because the Cowboy had been illegally aiming at Jack's driver's door. Because Bix had illegally hit the Cowboy's side. Because Jack's engine exploded, sending flames thirty feet into the air.

Jack popped his seat belt and scrambled through the front windshield frame, his face and hands scorched by the flames.

He dropped to the ground as a fire engine was already hosing his car's engine, and ran toward the Cowboy's car, which was also burning.

But the car was empty.

The Cowboy was gone.

3

"Must of stolen some poor sap's car," Bix said.

"Or bought it," Jack said.

They were walking off the field. Beside them, a tow truck was dragging Jack's clunker into the parking lot. Another tow truck was pulling the Cowboy's clunker. One of the field men was driving Bix's car, which was bucking and rearing like a bronco, past them.

"Demolition derby," Bix said. "Accidents happen all the time. If you were killed, nobody would of thought nothing."

Jack reached into the flap pocket of his jacket, took out his cigar, and lit it with a Zippo lighter.

"A truly cool guy would have relit his cigar in the flames from the engine," Caroline said.

She had come up behind them. From the stands where she'd watched the heat.

"That was exciting," she said. "For a while, it looked like you were really in trouble."

"He was," Bix told Caroline.

"The guy who kept trying to broadside me," Jack said, "was the Cowboy."

Caroline said, "Let's find the son of a bitch!"

CHAPTER FORTY-FOUR

1

Jack and Caroline put their cell phones on speed dial to each other's number. Bix didn't have a cell phone that worked, but he said, "Don't worry, Jackie. If I spot the Cowboy, you'll know because of the racket."

They split up at a stall filled with a hundred bright-orange rubber ducks with beady black eyes floating in a metal tub.

Jack headed past the Ferris wheel and started searching the cow barns. The ammonia smell of the manure tickled Jack's nose. The cows, their rumps facing the aisles, their depleted udders swinging like empty bagpipe bags, chewed and chewed. They switched their tails to brush away flies. Kids, some as young as eight or nine, cared for the animals. A few kids lay asleep or reading or, eyes closed, listening to iPods on cots beside the stalls.

No Cowboy.

In the goat barn, Jack walked along an aisle of wicked-looking animals with black bandit face markings. As Jack passed, one of the goats, a huge hairy brute, stood up on its hind legs, propped its forelegs on the slats of the pen gate and, staring at Jack, bleated accusingly.

Jack worked his way through the sheep barn, past a pile of baled hay taller than he was, some green, some older and tan, past the display of farm equipment, huge machines painted in bright nursery colors as if farming were a child's game, past the small theater where a swing band, all women over sixty, was singing "Boogie Woogie Bugle Boy," past the American Legion tent, past the 4-H Building, past the demonstration of antique tools, past the bookbinding exhibit, past the modular house display, and along an aisle of booths selling Harley-Davidson kerchiefs, unicorn tapestries, plastic Star Wars laser swords, and water filters.

No Cowboy.

The Cowboy had probably left the fair as soon as he bolted from the demolition derby, Jack figured. Although, Jack second-guessed himself, maybe Caroline was right. Maybe he hung around, figuring what better place to nail Jack than in such a crowd.

Jack walked through the schoolhouse, his attention snagged on the student art work: self-portraits, watercolors of farms and malls, collages of kids hanging around the renovated outdoor movie theater, a ceramic of suckling pigs in a row, a metal sculpture of a horse hit by lightning, its mouth opened in a scream.

Such talent, Jack thought; where did it all go when the kids graduated and started flipping burgers or working as sales associates at big-box stores?

Past the kiddie rides: the goose boats, the carousel—its horses with wild eyes and frenzied painted faces—the moon walk, the tiny rockets.

At one game, where kids were diving under the multicolored foam balls as if snorkeling, the woman with sunken eyes who ran the ride stopped Jack and said, "You ever sleep on foam balls, Chief? Come back after the fair's over."

Jack ducked into the men's bathroom, a knocked-together wooden building painted dark green outside and cream inside. One wall held six booths with warped plywood doors. The facing wall held a metal urinal trough the length of the room.

A man standing at the near end of the urinal held his cock with one hand and his cell phone with the other. While he peed, he said into the phone, "No. No, of course, I love you. . . . Of course, I would. . . . That's what I'm talking about. . . ."

A dozen or so men were lined up to the right of the cell phone lover, some eyes closed, some humming to themselves, some staring blank faced at the wall, one whistling, another talking to himself—or rather to his penis: "Come on, Skipper. You can do it. You've done it before."

Jack stood at the trough right inside the door and unzipped.

He started to pee. A strong, forked, almost dark-orange, musty-smelling stream. *I must be dehydrated,* Jack thought.

The man who had been encouraging his cock was finishing. "I knew you'd do it, Boss," he said. "The Little Engine That Could."

The cell phone lover also finished and wrapped up his call at the same time, "Got to go, Babe. Yeah, love you, too."

As Jack urinated, out of the corner of his right eye, he caught a flicker, something familiar, the Cowboy, who was standing at the far end of the trough and who, at the same moment, noticed Jack.

Neither could stop peeing. Both struggled to finish—a race to see who would be the first to empty his bladder.

Across the dozen or so bodies—some men leaving, others taking their place in line—Jack and the Cowboy stared at each other. Still peeing.

The Cowboy was the first to smile at the absurdity of the situation.

Jack smiled back.

The Cowboy shrugged at Jack.

Ruefully, Jack nodded.

The Cowboy shook his cock, tucked it away, and zipped up. As he strode past, he clapped Jack on the back.

Jack squeezed out the last stream of urine, stuffed his cock inside his pants, and headed out after the Cowboy.

On the other side of *Settembrini's House of Horror,* Jack spotted the Cowboy. Jack started around the horror house.

The Cowboy tried to blend into a crowd, a dozen people of various ages who all had the same piggy faces. A family.

Jack started to run. He vaulted over a raised black electric cable and ducked under a fence.

The Cowboy was gone.

Jack stood on the midway looking around.

The sky went green. Thunder cracked. The almost instantaneous lightning flash lit up the fair, which for a moment looked frozen like a black-and-white postcard. The heavens opened. Rain slammed down.

People ran for cover. Or ignored the rain. Or turned their faces up to the rain.

Jack held up his wrist to show the guy who ran the ride that he had bought an all-day, all-ride plastic bracelet. While waiting to get on his gondola, Jack called Caroline.

"I'm going on the Big Wheel," Jack said. "I'll see if I can spot the Cowboy from up there."

There was another crack of thunder and a flash of lightning as Jack settled into his seat and felt himself being lifted backward, up away from the fairgrounds. Below, he could see a few of the rides, mostly for children, were being shut down.

Jack scanned the fairgrounds for the Cowboy.

Impossible, Jack thought—just as he spotted the Cowboy in another gondola just over the crest of the turning wheel.

The Cowboy must have seen Jack get on and followed.

A third crack of thunder made the Ferris wheel shudder. Lightning illuminated the Catskill range across the river and the legendary outline of the sleeping Rip Van Winkle; a giant Rip Van Winkle, hundreds of miles long, his forehead and shoulder and hip towering crags, like an angel fallen to the Earth.

The guy running the ride was trying to get people off. Someone said, "They should have closed the fair down when they got the weather report."

Jack felt the fourth crack—right above them—in his chest and belly.

Lightning forked out of the sky and hit something on the ground below and to the right of Jack, who caught a flash out of the corner of his eye. All over the fair, lights went out. Jack smelled burned metal.

The main generator was blazing, casting the surrounding fair booths—selling the fried dough, roast beef sandwiches, fresh lemonade, blooming onions—in a hellish glow.

The Ferris wheel stopped.

2

Sliding sideways, Jack squeezed himself from under the safety bar, stood and grabbed a metal strut, which was cold and wet. He stepped out of his gondola and, clutching one wire support after another, edged up and across the Ferris wheel in the direction he figured the Cowboy to be.

He felt as if he were climbing a huge, industrial spiderweb, the spider a mechanical horror waiting at the center with furnaces for eyes and a coal-fed maw.

Another clap of thunder was instantly followed by a flash of lightning.

Jack saw the Cowboy thirty feet away, climbing out of his gondola, making his way toward Jack.

The ground sixty or so feet below looked far away. The people, small, insignificant.

No one looked up. No one knew Jack and the Cowboy were edging toward each other in the stinging rain, their feet unsteady on the slick struts, coming closer and closer, hand over hand—until they faced each other across a two foot gap.

With one hand, the Cowboy let go of a cable and punched Jack in the face.

Jack staggered back. His left foot slid off the cross beam on which he was balanced. His left hand slipped from a cable. Jack fell backward, suspended by his right hand and right foot.

Thunder, lightning.

The Ferris wheel shuddered.

In the sudden glare, the Cowboy, arms outstretched, gripping cables, swung up his legs and with two feet kicked Jack in the chest.

Jack fell. Dropping three feet and landing on his back on top of a gondola.

"What the fuck!" Jack heard someone in the gondola below him say.

Jack scrambled to his feet, rain blinding him, as the Cowboy landed, crouched, on the gondola canopy.

Scrabbling crabwise, Jack knocked into the Cowboy's left calf with his right shoulder.

The Cowboy's feet slipped out from under him. Holding on to a cable with just one hand, the other waving free as if he were doing a Highland fling, his legs dancing in air, the Cowboy dangled over the sixty foot drop.

Jack scrambled up. Supporting himself with one hand clutching a cable, Jack hammered with his free fist on the Cowboy's knuckles until the Cowboy let go and dropped a few feet to the canopy of the gondola below.

Faces—like paste masks dripping, streaked with paint—gazed at Jack and the Cowboy. The couple in the gondola across the wheel from them. Three teenaged girls, agog, in the gondola above the couple. In the gondola below, a mother covered her six-year-old son's eyes while her husband shouted something lost in the sound of the storm, a humming and hissing that could have been the racket of the Ferris wheel's engine.

Jack jumped, unsteadily, down beside the Cowboy, who lashed out at him.

Jack ducked and head butted the Cowboy in the lower back.

The Cowboy went down. Jack drove his right knee into the muscle of the Cowboy's left arm.

The Cowboy twisted one way, the other.

Jack punched the Cowboy in the face, felt something give.

Thunder and lightning.

In the flash, Jack saw the Cowboy grinning as blood spurted from his broken nose.

Jack hammered on the Cowboy's windpipe as if he were pounding on a table at a drunken dinner.

Again, he felt something give.

Jack heaved the Cowboy over the side of the gondola canopy. The Cowboy fell, bouncing and ricocheting from one strut to another, from one gondola to another, a human pinball in an indifferent pinball machine. The Cowboy landed, his back broken on the lever that made the machine go. The Cowboy was dead.

3

The squad car's lights flashed garish red and blue on the faces of the men and women and children, eyes hollow, mouths agape, skull-like, pressing forward to watch as the cops tried to handcuff Jack with old-fashioned metal restraints.

"Son of a bitch's wrists are too big," said a young officer Jack didn't recognize. "Jesus, this guy's massive."

"You got the plastic doohickeys?" said the other young cop, equally unfamiliar to Jack.

"You got plastic?" the first young cop shouted to a third young cop, sounding like a checkout clerk at the Price Chopper.

The rain was letting up. The fair's generator gave a great gasp and started running. Lights snapped on.

The faces lost their hollow-eyed, gaping-mouth, skull-like look and once again became merely human.

The Cowboy's body, in a zip-up bag, leftover meat, was dumped into the back of a van, which cranked up its siren as it crept through the watching crowd.

The first cop was binding Jack's wrists behind his back, too tight, with zip ties, when Jack spotted Caroline in the crowd—shocked, the power of the emotions draining her cheeks of color, the only skull-like face left.

CHAPTER FORTY-FIVE

1

Kipp, the Pakistani from the haunted motel, sat up on the metal cot when Jack was shoved into the jail cell.

"I know you're not coming to see me," Kipp said. "They took your belt and shoelaces."

He had a yellow bruise below one eye.

Unconsciously, Jack touched his own face.

The cell reeked of disinfectant.

"What's the charge?" Kipp asked. "Drunk and disorderly?"

"Murder," Jack said.

"No shit," Kipp said. "You do it?"

"Couple of hundred witnesses watched," Jack said.

"The guy deserve it?" Kipp asked.

"He was trying to kill me," Jack said.

"Self-defense," Kipp said.

From another part of the jail came a radio call: *10-33—toll collector requires assistance.*

Through the doorway leading to the bull pen, Jack saw a woman—a girl? She couldn't have been more than sixteen, dressed in a wig the color of cotton candy, a tight metallic-blue skirt made out of what looked like fish scales, and a gauzy, translucent halter that revealed her nipples.

"I was dancing," the girl whined. "I'm a ballet dancer."

She twirled.

"What'ch'you looking at?" the girl asked a male cop.

Another call came over the radio: *10-34—defective sprinkler system.*

"Can you believe the shit we have to deal with?" a cop, unseen in the hallway, said.

"You sure that's what it means?" the female cop asked.

"How long you been on the job, Provenzano?" the unseen cop said.

"She got hooks," a second unseen cop said. "Didn't have to study the Patrol Manual to get her job."

"The house mouse puts in his two cents," the female cop said.

"They should stick you back on DV," the second unseen cop said.

"You want to see domestic violence?" the female cop said. "Come here, Mouse. After all, compliance says we're one happy family."

"If you was my daughter," the second unseen cop said, "I'd take you across my knee."

"As if," the female cop said. "Like all old guys, you're just searching for TLGF. The Last Great Fuck."

"Which ain't you, babe," the second unseen cop said.

"Amen," the female cop said.

"Last Thursday," the second unseen cop said, "at Mitch's poker game, Paris Hilton here keeps spreading her knees and giving us all a peek at her *kapak*, we lower our cards while we're looking, she sees what we're holding."

The female cop's laugh was low, lovely.

"If you wasn't half a fag," the female cop said, "I would've taken more than your money."

"Excuse me," the girl in the cotton-candy wig said. "Cell me already. My feet hurt."

"What happened to you?" Jack asked Kipp.

"You don't read the newspapers?" Kipp asked.

"Not lately," Jack said.

"Yeah," Kipp said. "Killing. Being killed. It's a time-consuming hobby. Any of this got to do with Hussein? His dead girlfriend?"

"Somewhat," Jack said.

He sat on the cot across the room from Kipp. The mattress was so thin Jack felt the metal strips supporting it. From somewhere in the building, someone was singing "Ghost Riders in the Sky."

"What did I miss in the papers?" Jack asked.

"Motel burned down," Kipp said.

"Electrical fire?" Jack asked.

"More like cotton balls smeared with Vaseline," Kipp said. "Who the fuck knows? My take: Anything but an accident."

"Anyone hurt?" Jack asked.

"Some bad burns," Kipp said, "but nobody killed. We're all in our skivvies, standing around, don't know what to do, watching the fire burn everything we own when the red-white-and-blues show up—"

"Red-white-and-blues?" Jack asked.

"Immigration," Kipp said.

"Convenient," Jack said.

"Ain't it?" Kipp said. "With three big, yellow school buses. They load everyone on board. Everyone's illegal, right? Even if they're not. I got a green card. One of the feebs pushes me toward the bus. I say, *You pushed the wrong guy*. He says, *Join the party, Osama* and pushes me again harder. I take a swing. Deck him. He starts to cry—imagine that—big, bad government man, sitting on his ass in the motel parking lot, fire burning behind him, big, black billows of nasty-smelling smoke rolling around him, just his head showing above the smoke like it's a balloon, floating there, his body covered in this black—wasn't even smoke. It was, like, oily. You could feel it on your skin. Taste it. Then, the smoke kind of settles, you know, around our ankles. I'm thinking *What kind of fire is this?*"

"They used an accelerant," Jack said.

"Whatever," Kipp said. "The red-white-and-blue sitting, bawling, the smoke just drifts down his back. Looked like Batman. Like he was wearing a big, black, glossy cape. The Dark Knight defending the homeland from us aliens! You see that movie? A real psycho protecting real Americans. You go to any movie today, the go-to guys for villains—that'd be me. My brothers. My cousins. Maybe a slinky Asian chick to keep you watching when you get bored with the explosions and the blood."

"That's when they arrested you?" Jack asked.

"You bet'cha," Kipp said. "Real gentle, too."

"Resisting?" Jack guessed. "Assaulting an police officer?"

"For starters," Kipp said. "Dipshit charges compared to murder, but I bet you're out of here before me."

"So I guess you won't be enrolling in a prelaw course at Columbia Community," Jack said.

"You want to tell me about Hussein and his girlfriend and what you been up to?" Kipp asked.

"No," Jack said.

A guard unlocked the cell door.

"Slidell," the guard said.

"Norman," Jack said, recognizing him. "Where you been keeping yourself?"

"The wife decided I was spending too much time at Mama's," the guard said. "So I bought a flat-screen TV and watch junk all night. Wife says, *You don't get AIDS from a porn movie.* She watches with me. Likes to talk about the guys' equipment. *Trying to make me feel inadequate,* I ask her. *No, hon,* she says. *I'm satisfied. But it's like looking at travel ads. Sometimes you want to dream about a place you never been.* What the fuck you step into this time, Jack? Playing tag on the Ferris wheel with some guy who can't keep his balance. . . ."

"That's what they're saying?" Jack asked. "He fell?"

"That's the story, Morning Glory," the guard said. "Sciortino's waiting to drive you home."

"Knew you'd be out of here before me," Kipp called after Jack, who called back over his shoulder, "I'll see what I can do."

"You do that," Kipp said. "Surprise me with justice."

Sciortino handed Jack a nine-by-twelve manila envelope containing his effects: watch, wallet, change, belt, shoelaces. . . .

"You're letting me slide?" Jack asked. "How'd you arrange that?"

"I don't catch your drift, Jack," Sciortino said.

"A man's dead," Jack said.

"A guy stupid enough to climb out of his seat in the Ferris wheel slips and falls," Sciortino shrugged. "What business is that of yours?"

"Uh-huh," Jack said. "Someone called from DC?"

"Why, Jack," Sciortino said. "Whatever do you mean?"

"You ID the Cowboy?" Jack said.

"Who?" Sciortino said, this time authentically puzzled.

"That's what I've been calling him," Jack said. "My dance partner. The one who forgot he couldn't fly."

"You mean Rumpelstiltskin," Sciotino said.

"I can find my way home on my own," Jack said.

"You leave a trail of bread crumbs?" Sciortino asked. "This is where I look around to see who's listening and lower my voice. We used to play hide-and-seek, Jack. Now, you're playing it with some ghost. I knew you were out of your league on this one. But, man, I didn't know how far. We send the dead man's prints in. Whatever else we can to get a fix on this mook. We get back an official *No such person exists.* And some black suits come to collect the body. Sorry, what body? Remember that song? *I Ain't Got No Body*? You live a charmed life, my friend. You can't kill a man that never was."

"What are you going to do with all those witnesses who saw me fighting with him?" Jack asked.

"Stay close, Jack," Sciortino said. "In a week, two, you and me, we have a big *mange*, okay?"

2

As Jack left the police station, he turned on his cell phone, glancing at it as he came down the front steps.

Caroline and Dixie were waiting outside the jail.

The cell's screen lit up and, in the dark, cast a blue light on the underside of Jack's chin.

Like the yellow reflection a buttercup casts on a summer day, Caroline thought, looking at Jack's battered face.

Every day, Caroline thought, *another scar.*

"No messages," Jack said. "Time was, if my phone was turned off for three, four hours, I'd have thirty messages."

"They wouldn't let us in," Caroline said.

"They said you'd be right out," Dixie said.

"They first said you weren't there," Caroline said. "I said I knew you were there. I saw them take you."

"Where's Bix?" Jack asked.

"He had to go to work," Caroline said. "He said to tell you he's okay. He said if you weren't out by the time his shift was over, he'd reach out to some people he knows."

"I used to be better connected than Bix," Jack said. "Before people stopped taking my calls."

Jack held Caroline a bit longer than he meant to.

"What did you go after that man for?" Dixie asked.

Jack glanced at Caroline, who gave a slight shake of her head.

"He was after me," Jack said.

"He lured Jack into attacking him," Caroline explained. "That way he could seem innocent."

"That way," Jack said, "he could get close enough to me to kill me."

"But," Dixie said, "why would he want to kill you?"

"Dixie," Jack said, "I'm still trying to figure that out."

Dixie gave Jack a steady look.

Uncomfortable with his half lie, Jack said, "I got some ideas."

"Watching you scramble on the big wheel," Dixie said, "I always said you had pep! If you need any help . . ."

"What I need," Jack said, "is a ride home—"

"I'll draw you a bath," Caroline said, "and see what I can do about your new cuts."

"My home," Jack said. "By way of a motel. Or where a motel used to be."

All that was left of the motel where Kipp and his family and friends had lived was rubble. Jack got out of the car, followed by Caroline and Dixie. The site smelled of damp ashes—*tasted* of damp ashes—melted plastic, and scorched wires.

"Poor ghost'll have nowhere to roller skate," Jack said.

The rain had temporarily stopped. Above, clouds rolled like breakers.

On the other side of the road, the wind moaned out of the woods and stirred rubbish in the ruins of the motel. In the night sky, Mars burned, a reddish pinprick, to the upper right of an orange moon. Close to Earth.

"You got a prayer, Dixie?" Jack said.

"For the dead?" Dixie asked.

"For the living," Jack said.

"Be kind," Dixie said.

3

Jack's cell phone rang. He answered as he, Caroline, and Dixie returned to the car.

After talking for a bit, he pocketed the phone and told Caroline, "Mama Lucky got lucky. One of her gals knows the Cowboy."

Mama Lucky's hooker—Sunny Diefenbach aka Tiffany No Last Name aka Kalifornia Kutie—saw the Cowboy five times in the past couple of weeks, which meant he would have been around when Frank and Jean were killed.

The next morning, Jack and Caroline drove, according to Mama Lucky's directions, north of Mycenae.

The previous night's storm had uprooted trees, split trunks, revealing wood as white as flesh. Jack steered around broken branches on the roads. The neon sign of Barney's Grill lay, shattered, a quarter of a mile away from the restaurant.

Jack headed up Route 203 through Valatie, north toward Albany. On one hill, every tree had blown over. Like a great game of pick-up sticks. The road curved around the hill. Jack passed a Hannaford's Supermarket; fewer than a dozen cars were parked in the vast lot. At a car dealership, two men were putting plywood over cracked showroom windows. The food shack—Hotte Dawgs—was doing a booming business.

At the edge of the woods in which Sunny and her boyfriend, Tu, lived, Jack parked on the grass. On foot, he and Caroline followed a path through the trees until they came to a clearing, where they found a miniature cathedral, thirty feet tall, built out of flattened soda and beer cans, stolen railroad ties, a wrought-iron gate, six different kinds of shingles, planks scavenged from a dozen or more sites, used bedsprings, all sorts of junk.

In the intermittent sunlight, the cathedral glinted, its tin cans looking like tiles.

Carved monkeys and toads, imps with old women's faces, a camel, snakes, and gnomes decorated the door frame—demons that couldn't enter.

The wind shook the treetops and spun a few early fallen leaves in spirals.

Two mutts bounded, barking, towards them.

Caroline bicycled back.

"It's okay," Jack said. "They're wagging their tails on the right; they're friendly."

Caroline stopped backing up, but didn't move forward.

"If their tails lean left," Jack said, "that's when you got to worry."

The irregularly shaped door opened. Sunny stepped out as if she were making an entrance onto a stage.

She knew she was sexy, knew she had an effect on men, who tended to like her, and on women, who didn't.

"Mama Lucky said to expect you," Sunny said, reaching down and scratching first one dog, then the other, behind the ears. Quieting them.

She stood aside so Jack and Caroline could enter the soda-can cathedral.

"We found the place empty," Sunny said, "and moved in."

Sunny had freckled apple cheeks, which made her look like a cheerful chipmunk. Her eyes were green—not hazel, but true green—and the iris looked like the cross section of a kiwifruit. Her black hair, cut short in an ebony helmet, made her—Jack thought—into a warrior goddess, Athena.

But the black hair had blond roots.

Jack thought, *A beauty-parlor Athena.*

Sunny's mouth was wide. Her teeth, square, like Chiclets.

Athena—Olympian or beauty-parlor—was not the image that came to Caroline, who thought Sunny looked like a goth Betty Boop—all innocence and piercings. Gold rings in her eyebrow, nose, her lip, her tongue, a row of studs along her right ear.

Sunny wore a white sports bra, not the cleanest, damp in spots.

"I was jogging," she said. She tilted up each bra cup and plucked off nipple guards. "So it don't chafe," she added.

The pajama pants she had run in were decorated with Tinkerbells. Each Tink in a skimpy green outfit barely covering her pixie ass.

Sunny put her weight on her left leg, raised her right hip, going up on her right toe, and plucked at the seat, which was caught in her ass crease.

It was obvious she wasn't wearing any panties.

Sunny kicked off her running shoes and peeled off her thick white socks. Her feet were dirty. With chipped black toenail polish.

"Aurora Love is my porn-movie name," Sunny said. "I was a background player in the orgy scene in *The Curious Case of Benjamin Buttocks* and *I Like to Watchmen*."

The floor was crawling with millipedes, the dead ones curled like toenail clippings. They crunched underfoot.

"This is nothing," Sunny said. "You should see them in spring."

Her boyfriend, Tu, dapped fists with Jack, then Caroline. "What'sup."

Tu was at least twenty years older than Sunny. His face was weathered, flushed. On his chin, his soul patch was not centered, too far to the left. His right eye was milky.

"Quite a home you've got," Caroline said, gazing around at the miniature cathedral.

"We were looking for a spot to plant weed," Tu said, "and found it."

"Figured whoever built it must have of left," Sunny said. "In a hurry."

Jack noticed a 1960s-era Smith Corona manual typewriter with a yellowing piece of paper in the carriage. Nothing had been typed on it.

When Jack rolled up the page, the paper crumbled.

Tu said, "We found a half-empty cup of coffee—"

"Tea," Sunny corrected.

"—on the table," Tu said. "We figured we'd keep the place up for whoever it was. Good citizens that we are."

Tu laughed gently.

"That was last spring," Sunny said.

"April," Tu said.

Tu was also barefoot. When Jack first saw him, he thought Tu was wearing a multicolored knit sweater tucked into boxers with a rocketship pattern.

But the sweater was tattoos—hence his name; not the French familiar for *you*—which covered every inch of skin from his wrists to his neck to his waist. Vines and flowers spiraled along his arms. Leaves and stalks and roots. Petals and stamens. Spathe and spadix. Spike and raceme and panicle. Spur and corolla.

"Lady's slipper and butter-and-eggs," Tu said, pointing the flowers out. "Nodding pogonia and false dragonhead. Grape hyacinth and Jacob's ladder. It's my way of showing respect for Gaia."

Every inch of his body was covered. It looked as if Tu were made out of plants.

Like the Green Man in English folklore, Caroline thought.

To himself, Jack sang a snatch of the Groucho Marx song, "Lydia, the Tattooed Lady."

Tu offered no last name.

Sunny said, "His *mother name* is Jacob Ten Brock."

The single large room was bathed in red and blue, green and gold light from the stained glass windows, which displayed not Christian scenes, but Celtic, Greek, Roman, and Norse mythology.

Ogmios, the Celtic Hercules, bald, old, dressed in a lion's skin. Hermes, naked, with winged helmet and heels, and Dionysus, his erect cock as large as Ogmios' club. Prometheus and Loki, both bound and punished. Thor, the Thunderer, his hammer raised, filaments radiating from his body—halo? aura? sound waves?—like Sunny's irises.

Two ceiling-to-floor bookcases flanked a fireplace large enough for a child to stand in.

Jack glanced at the titles.

A brown six-volume set of Shaw's plays, *Don Quixote*, Sigrid Undset, half a shelf of the pocket-size hardback edition of the Yale Shakespeare, Chaucer, Spencer, Milton, the complete Dickens, Robert Louis Stevenson, half a dozen books by John Cowper Powys, *Rob Roy*, Trollope, *The Letters of Horace Walpole*, a faded-green set of the eleventh edition of *The Encyclopedia Britannica*.

Very few contemporary novels. Mailer's *The Deer Park*, a couple of Updike, *Burr*, *Portnoy*, half a dozen Auchincloss. Nothing recent.

Some oddities. *The Encyclopedia of Erotic Literature*. Pierce Egan on boxing.

On one shelf was a stack of *Playboys*. Jack opened a copy at random: "The Girls of Germany," Bill Iverson on "A Short History of Shaves and Haircuts . . ."

On another shelf, yellowing copies of *The New York Review of Books*: Gore Vidal, Jack Richardson, Nicholas Von Hoffman . . .

Life, February 27, 1970: "Hollywood puts its past up for sale. . . ."

Adventure Comic, March 1968: "Battle for the Championship of the Universe. . . ."

Military Life, December 1965: "People without a Past. . . ."

The books and magazines gave off a musty smell. The spines of the books were speckled with mold. The inside pages so covered with mildew they looked marbled.

Jack pulled out a copy of Dante's *Inferno* with Dore's illustrations. "Paolo and Francesca." The boards were drilled through with wormholes. The pages, mouse-gnawed.

Jack slipped Dante back on the shelf.

It didn't look as if Sunny or Tu had touched the books since they had moved in.

There were only a few pictures on the wall: A faded photograph of Blaze Starr; a Baskin print of Ahab; a copy of a Reginald Marsh Coney Island painting; a Thomas Hart Benton torn from a magazine; an Edward Hopper—a woman sitting in late afternoon sun at a window; a Norman Rockwell—a man in a short brown jacket standing up at a town meeting. Mostly American artists.

A cabinet held—on top—an old stereo; underneath, a couple of hundred LPs.

No CDs.

Without thinking, Jack lifted the turntable arm and felt for dust on the needle—as he used to with his own stereo years ago.

Noticing Jack, Tu said, "The needle was bad. The minute I tried to do a DJ thing, scratching, see, it snapped right off."

An art deco freestanding bar held a couple of single malt Scotches, an almost full bottle of B&B, a vintage port—nothing Sunny or Tu drank, Jack thought.

It seemed as if Sunny and Tu were squatting in a house still occupied by its temporarily absent owner.

Although maybe whoever left the Scotch was not the original owner, wasn't the man who built the place. Maybe whoever left the Scotch was also a squatter, who in turn had replaced an even earlier squatter.

Maybe the man who built the place, the original maker, had never lived there. Had only created this world in the woods and then lost interest and left.

"When we got to go somewhere," Sunny was telling Caroline, "we hitch."

"To the supermarket, to the laundromat," Tu added, bouncing from one conversation to another. "Cars cost."

The kerosene lamps, the only illumination, had been in the place when Sunny and Tu had arrived.

"Sometimes," Sunny said, "the mantles catch fire, and we got to get a new one at the Agway."

There was no plumbing; Sunny and Tu used an outhouse out back.

"A two-seater," Sunny said. "It's more sociable that way."

"Flush toilets," Tu said, "if they hadn't been so expensive back when, we would've had two- and three-seaters inside, and everybody would get along better, sharing a shit."

Jack noticed a white, powdery footprint, large, Tu's foot, tracked in after Tu had stepped in the lime they used in the outhouse.

Proudly, if paradoxically, Sunny said, "Tu put in the generator—"

"Gas powered," Tu said

—which ran the new flat-screen HDTV across the room, next to the ladder leading to a sleeping loft.

An iPod in its battery-powered Logitec docking station and speaker system stood on a side table.

It was playing "Newfoundland, Celtic rock," Tu explained. "Great Big Sea."

It surprised Jack how few traces Sunny and Tu left in the place: some clothes, a sketch pad—opened to a design for a ring; Tu's, it turned out, not Sunny's—a paperback novel about the Rapture . . .

"Hon," Sunny told Tu, "you got another call from Mickey D's."

They shared Sunny's cell phone, which she charged at the whorehouse.

"They think I'm hot to flip burgers," Tu said, adding sarcastically, "My age? They gotta think I'm eighteen."

Caroline started to ask a question, but Jack signaled her to keep silent.

Sunny and Tu knew why they were there. Jack didn't want to spook them.

Let them get to it in their own way.

Sunny had started making French toast with a hole in the middle, which she filled with scrambled eggs, scallions, and cheese.

She asked Jack and Caroline, "You want a Papajoe?" Which is what she called the dish.

Caroline said, "No."

Jack shook his head.

Later Caroline told Jack, "It smelled so good, but on their budget I didn't want to eat any of their food."

"The money's crap," Tu said, still talking about the McDonald's. "If I was young enough, who the fuck knows what I'd do? You desperate enough, who the fuck knows what anyone'd do?"

"Tu knows a guy who kept his mother's corpse in the freezer for the social security checks," Sunny said, putting a plate in front of Tu, who sat at the big round oak table.

"I used to steal bikes," Tu said between forkfuls of French toast and egg. "Jerks spend big buck on Kryptonite locks and don't realize you can open them with the back of a Bic pen."

"Tu wants me to get out of Mama Lucky's," Sunny said.

"You know how boring that job's got to be," Tu said. "Trying to make conversation with perfect strangers."

"Wants me to go back to working in the nail salon," Sunny said. "But those chemical smells, I used to get these bad headaches. . . ."

Sunny took her plate and sat down opposite Tu.

"Big deal," Tu said. "I sell drugs. When I was digging graves for the county, I look into the office and see my boss, Powerhouse Welty, smoking reefer. And he's making real money. Sitting tipped back in his chair. Doesn't get his hands dirty. I wanted to go in kick the chair legs out, son of a bitch."

The iPod shuffled to what sounded like massage music: flute, bells, trickling water. . . .

"It's not like when I was a kid," Tu continued, "shoveling with a spade for three-something an hour. Now, they use a backhoe and get paid big money. I can't get that job. I'm out of work. After child support—my ex is on my case every week—I'd only make eighty-six dollars a week. How you going to live on eighty-six a week with a sixteen-year-old son who can eat a whole turkey at one sitting? My ex is on oxygen. *You* try making it on eighty-six dollars a week."

"Some jobs," Sunny said, "you got to pass the pee test."

"Or worse," Tu said.

"They don't give you any respect," Sunny said.

"And those tests," Tu said, "you take Advil or Nuprin or B12 and you get a false positive on tests for marijuana. NyQuil, Contac, Sudafed, Dimetapp—you get false positive for amphetamines. You eat a poppy-seed bagel, you get a false positive for opium."

"He's an expert," Sunny said.

"I got to be," Tu said, "or they'll nab my ass."

"Do you know," Sunny said, "even someone who works in a popcorn plant, mixing the flavors that make popcorn taste good, can get a kind of disease? At least, at Mama's you know what to do to stay healthy. And Mama takes care of us."

Again, the iPod shuffled: A woman sang a cappella, a song that was not familiar to Jack, haunting. The hair on the back of Jack's neck prickled.

Sunny sang along, hitting a high note.

Proudly, Tu said, "Sunny could be a professional singer."

"I took lessons," Sunny said. "When I was a kid."

"On the high C," Tu said, "sometimes she'll go sharp, just to show she can go even higher."

"Tu thinks I should be on TV," Sunny said.

They both look expectantly at Jack, then at Caroline.

They weren't anticipating Jack or Caroline's opinion on Sunny's possible show biz career.

Jack said, "How much?"

All that talk about money—Jack got the point.

Tu looked at Sunny.

"Two—" he studied Jack, who had inadvertently leaned forward, "—five hundred."

Jack counted out the money on the table.

Tu—egg smeared on the corner of his mouth—recounted it and nodded at Sunny who said, "The guy with the cowboy hat, big guy, decent manicure, broken knuckles—"

Jack hadn't noticed the broken knuckles.

"—played the banjo," Sunny continued.

Jack hadn't known about the banjo either.

"—tried to teach me how to play this Japanese, Chinese game with black and white stones," Sunny continued. "I saw him maybe three, four times. Tried to see me out-call. Wanted to deal direct. Said that way Mama wouldn't get her sixty percent."

"Course," Tu said, "she told him *no.*"

Tu knew Jack was a friend of Mama Lucky. He wasn't going to get Sunny in trouble.

"Wanted to meet before he left town," Sunny said, "before whatever business he was up here for was done."

"You know his name?" Jack asked.

Sunny shook her head *no*.

"I guess he was some kind private cop," she said. " 'Cause the other number he gave me, not his cell, was at the college, security, up at the Sewall Observatory."

CHAPTER FORTY-SIX

1

The setting sun bathed the dome of the Sewall Observatory in rose. The telescope's shutter was closed.

From this distance, across the river, the structure looked to Jack as if he could hold it in the palm of his hand.

The wind was still strong enough to make the tops of the trees on the hillside lean left. When Jack turned off the highway, the car was buffeted so hard he had to grip the steering wheel to keep from being knocked off the road.

They crossed a humpback bridge, a metal rainbow that had lost its magic and was now merely made of girders.

As they started up the approach to the complex of observatory buildings, Jack was unprepared for—up close—the sheer size of the dome, which in the rapidly fading light was purple. Huge above them.

The dome slid up the car windshield. Out of sight. Jack leaned forward, craned his neck, and peered through the glass to look up at the observatory on the top of the hill.

Caroline was half leaning out the passenger window to keep the dome in view.

A door to a metal-and-glass office building next to the dome was unlocked. When Jack and Caroline entered, a young man, a graduate student in a blue polo shirt, jeans, and black high-top Keds, who was passing with an armful of files, asked if he could help them.

Jack showed him a slip of paper with the telephone number he had gotten from Sunny.

"Do you know the office with this extension?" Jack asked.

"The last three numbers," the student said. "Two-oh-seven. Second floor. All the way back."

"Whose office is that?" Caroline asked.

"For floaters," the student said. "Whoever happens to be in town. You here for the seminar?"

"Who's been using it this week?" Caroline pressed.

"You mean the Cowboy?" the student asked.

"You call him the Cowboy?" Jack asked, amused.

"You wear a hat like that here," the student, "you're asking for it. Nice enough guy, though. Quiet. Keeps to himself."

"He works for the observatory?" Jack asked.

"He must if he's here," the student said and continued on his way.

"Well," Caroline said, "getting *in* was easy."

"It's a university facility," Jack said, shrugging, also surprised at how easy it had been to get in.

Caroline nodded and said, "I guess." As if trying to convince herself, she added, "It's not like it's a nuclear reactor. What's the worst-case scenario? Someone comes in and copies your star map?"

They climbed the stairs to the second floor and headed down the hall.

2

Room 207 showed no signs of use. The desk held a computer monitor, but it wasn't attached to a keyboard or a CPU. A telephone was unplugged. The desk chair was rolled across the room, next to a wall with a blank white board. There was no second chair for visitors.

On a long side table were three large paper clips, a pad of yellow Post-its, an empty—washed—ceramic coffee cup with the observatory logo: a cartoon of a scientist in a white coat peering with one bugeye through a telescope, which looked like a gun barrel.

There were no windows.

"When he was a boy, I made sure Robert made his bed every morning," Keating said. "Robert said the maid could do it."

Keating stood in the doorway, dressed in a light blue cardigan, a white shirt, suspenders, chinos, loafers.

"I showed him how to make hospital corners," Keating continued. "Showed him how to do it well. The morning he died, he still took pride in how good he was at making his bed."

"How did you know we were here?" Jack asked.

"Surely," Keating said, "you know the building is monitored?"

"You got here fast," Caroline said.

"You have to learn to be less self-centered, Caroline," Keating said. "I wasn't here because of you. There's a seminar I was interested in, one I'm missing, it's true, because of you. I suppose we can chalk this up to a happy coincidence."

Keating paused.

"At least," Keating said, "I hope it will turn out to be happy."

"Why did you hire someone to kill me?" Jack said.

Keating ignored Jack's question and asked one of his own:

"Why did you visit the motel that burned down?"

"You've been tracking us?" Caroline said.

"Based on cell phone data," Keating said, "peoples' daily roaming habits mimic movements of carnivores looking for prey."

"That doesn't sound like we should be less self-centered," Caroline said. "It sounds like we *should* be paranoid."

"Things are rarely what they seem," Keating said. "The Duchess of Windsor worked for Allied Intelligence. Her job was to seduce Edward, who was pro-Nazi, so he would have to abdicate and the British government could go forward with an unambiguous anti-Nazi policy. Errol Flynn was spying for the Nazis, while Cary Grant was working for the OSS. Have you been to East Brunswick? To the copper mines? Where they kept Tories during the War of Independence. Like Guantanamo. But successful nations forget their sins."

"Everyone finds his own conspiracy," Jack said, thinking of Shapiro.

"There are no conspiracies," Keating said. "Just like-minded people trying to get something done. And some things are better done in secret."

"Why, Mr. Flowers," Caroline asked, "are you a spy?"

"I wouldn't go into the business today," Keating said. "Now, it's all private contractors who spend most of their time investigating each other."

"Electrical pollution is a secret," Jack said. He didn't frame it as a question. "National security."

"The strength of the people," Keating said, "is that they survive the stupidity and incompetence of their leaders."

"Even when they're kept in the dark," Caroline said.

"The greatest nation in the history of history," Keating said, "the shining city on the hill turns out to be a shopping mall, its flickering lights running on emergency power. We all know it's a rigged game."

"And Frank threatened to blow the whistle," Jack said.

"As people become aware, they feel cheated," Keating said. "That's why most people prefer not to know."

"You don't believe they have a right to know?" Caroline asked.

"In Micronesia," Keating said, "testicular ablation—crushing of a testicle—was once common practice. A practice no one questioned because of the authority of the community."

"Of the community *leaders*," Caroline said.

"When people begin to question their leaders," Keating said, "the community suffers. Unfortunately, we're going through such a period. Today, everything's change and conflict."

"And it's your job to make sure the American people don't find out that the electrical toys they depend on are poisoning them?" Jack said.

"Because," Caroline said, "we'd end up marching backward two centuries."

"The American people," Keating said. "You make them sound like some monolithic creature. Some great beast like—You've seen the vegetable man."

"*Stan the Vegetable Man*," Caroline said.

"That's the one," Keating said. "Zucchini legs, a tomato head. An American Leviathan. An agrarian colossus appropriate for a society that finds its mythic roots as an agrarian Eden."

"*You* make the American people sound like something alien," Jack said.

"As alien to me as any bugeye monster," Keating said. "My world is dead, Mr. Slidell."

"Mr. Slidell," Jack said. "Jack no more?"

"It's been a delightful game," Keating said, "but any game that goes on too long is a bore."

"Tell me about your dead world, Mr. Flowers," Jack said. "I think I missed the funeral."

"It died half a century ago," Keating said. "When we bombed Hiroshima and Nagasaki, we also destroyed our country as surely as if we'd unleashed thousands of atom bombs in a global holocaust. We destroyed the Old Republic. My world." He nodded at Caroline. "Her world."

"Not my world," Caroline said.

"Oh, yes," Keating said. "Your world ended so completely before you were born, you don't even know what you're missing."

"Class warfare, huh?" Jack asked.

"I would think you might understand all about class warfare, Mr. Slidell," Keating said. "After all, your side won."

"Too bad I missed out when they distributed the spoils," Jack said.

Keating shook his head.

"What a terrible century," he said, "full of horror and fast food. Fast food and reality TV."

"At least we have some sort of reality," Caroline said.

"Some sort, yes," Keating said. Almost to himself. "Caroline, go back to work. Mr. Slidell find something to do. Get your law license back. I'm sure there's a way. You seem to like each other. Get married. Settle down. You don't need to cause problems for yourselves."

"The guy you sent to kill me is dead," Jack said.

"You keep making assumptions," Keating said.

"You're saying he wasn't working for you?" Caroline said.

"It's complicated," Keating said. "And it doesn't matter anymore."

"Because—" Jack started.

"Because," Keating said, "as far as you're concerned, he never existed."

"I was attacked by a ghost?" Jack said.

"If you want," Keating said.

"Frank's dead," Jack said. "Jean's dead."

"You can't change anything," Keating said.

"Jean was your daughter," Caroline said.

"*We* can't change anything," Keating said.

"Robert's dead," Jack said.

"Civilization," Keating said, "happens when we give up revenge."

"And let the state handle it," Jack said. "Whatever *it* is."

Keating nodded.

"Who hired the Cowboy? Caroline asked.

Keating was silent.

Caroline got very still.

"The state *was* handling it," Caroline said.

3

"I'd rather you left," Keating said. "But—"

Keating sighed.

"Okay," Keating said, "Frank realized Jean was suffering from something more than drugs. He thought a class-action suit against Mohawk Electric might make him rich and famous. But he ran into problems."

"You scared off witnesses," Jack said. "Like Shapiro."

"What he really wanted," Keating said, "was to make it all-inclusive. National. Global. All electric companies."

"That's why you got rid of him?" Caroline asked.

"He was a diligent researcher," Keating said. "Too good. He was looking for anything that would help him in his suit. Including anything in my life he might use to prevail upon me to cooperate."

"Frank wasn't a blackmailer," Jack said.

"Not only a blackmailer. " Keating said. "A magnificent blackmailer. The Napoleon of blackmailers. Or so he believed. He began to think a shakedown might be more profitable than a lawsuit. Of course, that way he'd get rich but forgo fame."

"How many people have you killed?" Jack asked. "Had killed?"

"Frank stumbled on something much bigger, much more sensitive than electrical pollution," Keating said.

Keating held the door open.

Jack and Caroline glanced at each other—*in for a penny, in for a pound*—and went through the door into the hall, waited for Keating to take the lead, and followed him down the hall, down the stairs, down a second set of stairs, below ground.

Keating led Jack and Caroline into a tunnel.

The walls, ceiling, and floors were white. Shoulder height were kids' crayoned pictures from some school visit to the observatory. Amber-Lynn. Amanda-Lynn. Carol-Lynn. Tashi. Cyndi. Porn star names. Raphael. Toshi. Henree.

Above them, the white neon tubes buzzed. Red, blue, and green stripes ran along the floor, as in a hospital.

First the red stripe branched off. Then, the blue.

Keating kept them on the green stripe.

A corner of the molding was water stained.

"It's amazing what science can do," Keating said. "At the University of Pittsburgh and Carnegie-Mellon, macaque monkeys with electrodes in their brains have learned to control a robotic arm with their thoughts."

At an elevator door, Keating pressed a button, which lit up.

"When I was a young man and the world was new," Keating said. "Or when it seemed new to me, we read *Idylls of the King* in school. King Arthur and his Round Table."

The door opened. They entered the elevator, which was white top, bottom, and sides.

The enclosure smelled like old sweat socks.

"That Christmas," Keating said, "Becky Foster gave me a toy knight on a charger. I still have it."

The elevator rose.

Caroline felt her stomach drop.

"The seminar I'm missing," Keating said, "the seminar you're causing me to miss, is on an interesting topic. FOPEN. A foliage penetration devise developed by Lockheed Martin, which allows unmanned planes to see targets. Or, rather, the child of that project—TRACER."

"Why are you telling us that?" Jack asked.

"To show I trust you?" Keating said. "No. It's not that big a secret. Neither is this: On Norway's Spitsbergen Island in the Arctic Circle, the Svalbard Global Seed Vault is storing seeds from all over the planet. Eventually, two billion two hundred and twenty-five million seeds. At minus-eighteen degrees Celsius. The seeds can last two hundred years even if the power were lost. Some seeds could last longer. Sorghum seeds could last twenty thousand years."

"Why?" Caroline asked.

Keating didn't answer.

The elevator door opened.

They entered a circular room, filled with banks of electronics. A dozen people, some in white coats, others in street clothes moved purposely to and fro.

The floor of the laboratory was reddish brown, like a desert. The lighting was bright, but not glaring. Above them was a catwalk. Above the catwalk was the dome, criss-crossed with girders. Vast. Like a cathedral.

Cradled in a giant horseshoe was the telescope as large around and as tall as a silo.

"This two hundred inch is one of four telescopes we have on site," Keating said. "It has a single borosilicate mirror. We also have a sixty inch. A forty-eight inch. And an eighteen inch. I wish I could take requests and show you something in the heavens you've always wanted to see. But we have our nightly schedules. Our rituals."

Jack felt something. Not exactly a vibration. Not exactly a sound.

"A forty-kilometer-wide object looped past Neptune and is headed back to the Oort Cloud, a source of long-period comets," Keating said. "A twenty-two thousand five hundred year elongated orbit will take it back to a region two-hundred-forty billion kilometers from sun. It was first spotted in two-thousand six."

The telescope started moving. Raising its eye higher—as the shutter of the dome began to open, revealing the night sky, spangled with stars.

"One of the largest members of the asteroid family is Baptistina," Keating said. "Twenty-five miles across. Among two thousand smaller objects from the same family."

The whole dome began moving, swinging around in a circle as the telescope came to a rest at about a forty-five degree angle.

Like a carnival ride, Caroline thought.

"One hundred and sixty million years ago, give or take twenty million years," Keating said—like a senator talking about the economy, comfortable with inconceivably large numbers—"an asteroid, maybe a hundred ten miles across, collided with another large planetary body, producing a very large chunk of space rock—Baptistina—and some smaller bodies, one of which may have landed in the Yucatán Peninsula in southern Mexico. Another may have hit the moon and caused a crater we can see named after Tycho Brahe, the sixteenth century Danish astronomer. The object that hit the Yucatán—there's discussion on what exactly it was and where it came from—may have caused the Cretaceous-Tertiary extinction event sixty-five million years ago. Which resulted in the death of the dinosaurs and many other species."

"What's this got to do with Frank?" Jack asked.

"Then, there's Apophis," Keating said. "We were a little concerned about it. At first, it looked as if there were a two point seven probability it would hit Earth in two thousand twenty-nine. Now, we're not quite so worried. We like to keep track of things like that. We—and some other people. The Southwest Research Institute in Boulder. And other places around the globe."

Caroline, who had been staring at the night sky, looked at Keating.

"It's beautiful," she said.

"We think of the orbits of the heavenly objects as if they were God's clockwork," Keating said. "But it's pretty chaotic up there. As chaotic as weather."

Keating went to a computer and typed. A video screen came up.

"The last time someone showed me a video on a computer," Jack said, thinking of Shapiro, "it showed a holocaust."

"Oh, yes?" Keating said.

Keating hit enter.

On the monitor, Jack and Caroline saw an animation of a giant asteroid approaching the Earth. Casting a shadow across continents. Across seas. Hitting—its impact blasting outward in concentric circles. The firestorm pulsing out in concentric circles. Until the whole planet was on fire. Burning until the Earth was nothing but a cinder. Dead rock.

"There are three kinds of near-Earth asteroids," Keating said. "*Amors*, which approach Earth from outside its orbit. *Apollos*, which cross Earth's orbit, and *Atens*, which approach Earth from within its orbit."

Keating gestured to Jack and Caroline to get inside a cage on a mechanical arm, which lifted them thirty feet in the air, halfway up the telescope.

"There's no privacy," Keating said. "Not in the offices. Not in the hallways. Up here, we can talk."

They could see bolts the size of a baby's fist.

"If an asteroid did hit the Earth," Keating said, "if we did end, I wonder, will everything end with us? Was Bishop Berkeley right? Without the observer there is nothing to observe?"

"If we aren't around to perceive?" Caroline said. "It's the end of the world?"

"It's," Keating said, "the end of reality."

"What if God is the observer?" Jack asked.

"If there is a God," Keating said, "or a God who perceives. Or a God who cares."

"You think God's just a blind watchmaker?" Caroline asked.

"If we're lucky," Keating said.

"No," Caroline said emphatically. "If we are lucky, there's a God who holds us in his hand and—"

"No hymns, please," Keating said.

"God is not a crutch," Caroline said.

"You think God, if there is a God, needs an audience to exist?" Keating asked

"God's not that crippled," Jack said, "and neither are we."

"No," Keating said, "we're not! That's the point. What if the Anthropic principle is right? That the universe was made just so we could exist. We were the whole reason the universe came into being."

"And if we're gone?" Caroline said.

"It all goes," Keating said. "The pyramids and Mozart and Yankee Stadium—"

"Stalin and Mao and Hitler and what's left of a three-year-old who stepped on a cluster bomb," Jack said, thinking of Shapiro.

"Everything that makes us human," Caroline said. "The good and the bad."

Below them, the scientists and tech support looked miniature. As they moved, they made patterns that they were unaware of but that Jack could see.

That Jack could impose on them.

"But, even without the asteroid, it will all end eventually," Keating said. "The sun will go out. The solar system will fall apart. The galaxy. The universe."

"And then what?" Jack asked.

"The Mad Hatter's tea party," Keating said.

Keating turned to face Jack.

"Something's coming," Keating said.

Jack was watching a man in a beige sweater and jeans who was entering the dome, drop a file folder.

"Coming?" Jack asked absently.

Far below, papers fluttered to the floor.

"What do you mean?" Jack asked.

The man who had dropped the folder bent over to pick up the papers.

When Keating didn't answer, Jack turned to look at Keating—and at Caroline who blinked rapidly.

"Something's coming?" Caroline said.

Jack saw the image from the video of a vast shadow moving across the face of the Earth.

"How big?" Jack asked.

"Big," Keating said.

"When?" Caroline asked.

"Soon," Keating said.

"How soon?" Caroline asked. "How much time do we have? Is the government going to send up missiles? Blow it up?" To Jack she said, "I've got to tell Dixie. Nicole."

Caroline interrupted herself. She stood, her mouth open.

"Now," Keating said, "you understand?"

Looking at Caroline's face, Jack got it, too.

"Frank found out," he said.

"While checking you out," Caroline said, "about the electrical pollution."

"And he tried to blackmail you about *this*," Jack said. "Not about electrical pollution. About—what's coming. He tried to blackmail the government."

"What would happen if news of this leaked out?" Keating asked. "Panic. Death and destruction. The end of civilization."

"Which will come from the asteroid anyway," Jack said.

"But in the meantime," Keating said. "All the suffering."

"Your contempt for *The People*," Jack said, "is not as great as you claimed."

"I have no contempt for individuals," Keating said. To Caroline, Keating said, "You know you can't tell anyone. *Ever*. That's what Frank couldn't understand."

Caroline studied Keating's face.

"You're suffering," she said.

"Now that you know," Keating said, "you will, too. Every time you hear a happy father talk about seeing his son grow up to play baseball. Every time you hear a couple plan on having kids."

For the first time since they had entered the dome, Keating looked up. At the heavens.

"Unless you can understand that the asteroid isn't tragic," Keating said. "When the end is coming and everybody is still worrying about getting and spending, status and territory, it's comic. Or unless you can accept consciousness is just a machine fueled by glucose. Or that realities are like matrushka dolls, one within the other forever—from microcosm to macrocosm. I want to feel that. But I can't. I only see the loss . . ."

"What if you're wrong," Caroline said. "What if the meteor, asteroid, or whatever deviates by a hair up there and, hundreds of thousands of miles later, misses us?"

"That's a possibility," Keating said.

They were silent.

"Old men have apocalyptic dreams," Keating said. "They think the world's going to end with them. Usually, they're wrong."

Another silence.

"And in the meantime?" Keating said.

"You killed your own daughter?" Jack said.

When Keating answered, he was hoarse: "One or two people die so hundreds of millions won't suffer. So for some uncertain time they will have Bach, Yankee Stadium, and each other."

"What do you do about us?" Jack asked.

"What we chose to do before," Keating said, "wasn't my decision."

"And now?" Caroline asked.

"Oh," Keating said, "as far as I'm concerned you have free will to choose what you will do. If you tell, it leads to chaos; if you cover it up, cover up Frank's death, Jean's death . . . even Robert's death—"

"All the other deaths," Caroline said.

"—there's no justice," Keating said.

"How many deaths will it take?" Jack asked.

"To protect the world from itself?" Keating asked.

"Don't people have a right to know?" Jack asked. "A right to choose how to react to the news? Just like you do?"

"And, now," Keating said, "just like you do."

He looked from Jack to Caroline.

"No one should have to suffer," he said. "And they'll suffer if they know."

"Eventually, whatever we choose," Jack said, "things are going to end."

"Then," Keating said, "what do you care?"

"Because," Jack said, "Frank was my friend."

"Robert and Jean were my children," Keating said.

"You're going to let us go?" Caroline said.

"On August 25, AD 79, Mount Vesuvius exploded," Keating said. "There was a rain of burning lava, which buried people and made them immortal. Our sacrifice—the asteroid—will leave no trace of us behind. Not immortality, just extinction."

A second time, Caroline asked, "You're going to let us go?"

"I always thought King Lear doesn't go mad at the end of the play, but is crazy at the beginning," Keating said. "All that hoopla about his daughters performing. And, during the play, he gets sane. In the storm on the heath, he is quiet, not shouting, not raging. He finally understands, *Man is just a poor forked creature,* negotiating with God like Abraham over how many to save in Sodom. Increasingly sane. Until, by the end of the play, he has no illusions left. Just *never, never, never, never, never.* If this thing comes, there will be no saving remnant."

A third time: "You're going to let us go?"

This time, Keating nodded.

"Frank was damage control because he found out about what's coming," Keating said. "You were damage control because you found out about Frank. I can't have you killed here. Now. Too many witnesses. Most of the people who work here don't know what's going to happen. They're all working on their projects. And, once you leave . . ."

Keating shrugged.

"After you, what damage control will be necessary?" Keating asked. "Your brother, Mr. Slidell? How much does your uncle know, Caroline? Your sister? What would they do to find out what happened to you. And the whore? Her boyfriend? How many others?"

For the first time, Keating seemed old. Defeated.

"Do you think I loved my daughter less than my son?" Keating asked. "I didn't want Jean to get hurt. That was a mistake. There have been too many mistakes. Only your friend Frank was supposed to be dealt with. Only because he refused to cooperate."

"And Stickman?" Jack asked.

Keating gave Jack a blank look.

"Jean's Pakistani friend," Jack said.

"Oh, yes," Keating said.

He was silent.

"Did he also refuse to cooperate?" Jack asked.

"Things take on a life of their own," Keating said. "I'm not a monster. I didn't want anything to happen to you."

"Because," Caroline said, "you thought we'd cooperate?"

"I told them you would not be as foolish as Frank," Keating said.

"They'll be watching us?" Caroline said. "Listening to us? At work? On the street? At home? In bed?"

Keating nodded.

"You'll be living as I grew up," he said. "In a small town in which everyone knew everyone else's business."

"And," Jack said, "what happens if you think we're going to tell?"

"It's an insecure world," Keating said.

Outside, the sky was clear. There was no wind.

"Remember Dixie's story about the night life of the gods?" Jack said. "About the scientist and the leprechaun who wondered if there was a place for them in this world?"

Jack saw a flicker in the sky.

"A shooting star," Jack said. "I'm not as comfortable seeing it as I would have been yesterday. Make a wish."

Instead of making a wish, Caroline said, "I missed my period."

The world stopped.

And started again.

Jack kissed her.

And kissed her again.

"So what do we do?" Caroline asked.

About Keating. About the asteroid. About Frank's death. And Jean's. And Robert's. And all the others'.

About their baby.

Jack didn't want to live in a disenchanted world.

He wanted to believe in UFOs and Peter Pan and vampires and ghosts in motels. And in asteroids that hang above us on a thread, just as there is always something hanging over us. Life can always end in a moment. And in the meantime—

Hand in hand, Jack and Caroline faced the future, which like any other future could be the beginning of the end.

They had to give their lives meaning by what they chose to do.

Above them, along with the asteroid, was a heaven, glorious with stars.

"What can we do?" Caroline asked again.

Quoting Dixie, Jack said, "Be kind."

David Black is an award-winning journalist, novelist, screenwriter, and producer. His novel *Like Father* was named a notable book of the year by *The New York Times* and listed as one of the seven best novels of the year by *The Washington Post*. *The King of Fifth Avenue* was named a notable book of the year by *The New York Times*, *New York* magazine, and the Associated Press.

Mr. Black received the Edgar Allan Poe Special Award from the Mystery Writers of America for Best Fact Crime Book for *Murder at the Met*. His second Edgar Allan Poe Award nomination was for "Happily Ever After," an episode of *Law & Order*. His third Edgar Allan Poe Award nomination was for "Carrier," also an episode of *Law & Order*.

He won a Writers Guild of America Award for *The Confession*. He was also nominated for a Writers Guild of America Award for an episode of *Hill Street Blues*. He received an American Bar Association Certificate of Merit for "Nullification," a controversial episode of *Law & Order* about militia groups, which the *Los Angeles Times* called an example of "the new Golden Age of television."

Among his other awards, he has received a National Endowment of the Arts grant in fiction, *Playboy*'s Best Article of the Year Award, *Best Essays of the Year 1986* Honorable Mention, *Forward*'s Book of the Year Special Mention, and an *Atlantic Monthly* "First" award for fiction. He has received a Pulitzer Prize nomination for *The Plague Years*, a book based on a two-part series that he wrote for *Rolling Stone* that won a National Magazine Award in Reporting and the National Association of Science Writers Award.

Researching articles, David Black has risked his life a number of times, including being put under house arrest by Baby Doc's secret police in Haiti, infiltrating totalitarian therapy cults, being abandoned on a desert island, and exposing a white slave organization in the East Village.

Among the television shows he has produced and written are the Sidney Lumet series *100 Centre Street,* which was listed as one of the ten best shows of the year, the Richard Dreyfuss series *The Education of Max Bickford, Monk, CSI: Miami,* the new *Kojak, Hill Street Blues, EZ Streets, Miami Vice, Law & Order: Criminal Intent, Law & Order: Trial by Jury,* the original *Law & Order,* which received an Emmy nomination for Best Dramatic Show and a *Golden Globe* nomination, and *Cop Shop,* an innovative PBS series filmed in one-take, three-camera real time, which won a Prism Award in 2005. He has been nominated for the PGA Golden Laurel Award.

His TV movie *Legacy of Lies,* a drama about three generations of Jewish gangsters and cops in Chicago, which starred Eli Wallach, won the Writers Foundation of America Gold Medal for Excellence in Writing. It also received an ACE Award for Martin Landau for Best Actor.

His feature *The Confession,* starring Alec Baldwin, Ben Kingsley, and Amy Irving, was praised in *New York* by John Leonard and in *The Hollywood Reporter,* among other places, and was described in *Metroland* as "an almost miraculous act of storytelling."

He has published nine books and more than 150 articles in magazines, including *The Atlantic, The New York Times Magazine, Harper's,* and *Rolling Stone.* His novel *An Impossible Life* has been praised by, .among others, Nobel Prize–winning author Czeslaw Milosz, Erica Jong, Bruce Jay Friedman, and Leslie Epstein, who called it the best writing about Jewish gangsters since Isaac Babel. *Contemporary Authors* describes Black as "a versatile, multimedia writer who has distinguished himself in both fiction and nonfiction."

He has taught writing at Mt. Holyoke, NYU, Columbia, Yale, where he is a Fellow at Pierson College, and Harvard, where he is a scholar-in-residence at Kirkland House. He is a former board member of the Mystery Writers of America and a member of the Century Association, the Williams Club, the Columbia University Club, PEN, the Writers Guild, the Explorers Club, the Players, and the National Arts Club.